...y, mas-
... a sus-
... novel
...ls a full
story that's equal parts romance, family drama, and
sheer terror."   *—Publishers Weekly*

Praise for *The Perfect Family*

"[An] exciting thriller."   —The Best Reviews

"Gritty and gripping psychological suspense is rap-
idly becoming Cassidy's hallmark. *The Perfect Family* is creepy and frightening—but really intense, fun
reading."   *—Romantic Times*

Promise Him Anything

"Exciting romantic suspense . . . a terrific tale."
                             —Midwest Book Reviews

"Ms. Cassidy grabs you from the first page. . . . I
highly recommend this read to any fan of the romantic suspense genre. You won't be sorry."
                               —Romance Designs

"Impressive."   *—Romantic Times*

"Edge-of-the-seat suspense . . . a dynamic read."
                               —The Plot Queens

WITHOUT A SOUND

Carla Cassidy

A SIGNET ECLIPSE BOOK

SIGNET ECLIPSE
Published by New American Library, a division of
Penguin Group (USA) Inc., 375 Hudson Street,
New York, New York 10014, USA
Penguin Group (Canada), 90 Eglinton Avenue East, Suite 700, Toronto,
Ontario M4P 2Y3, Canada (a division of Pearson Penguin Canada Inc.)
Penguin Books Ltd., 80 Strand, London WC2R 0RL, England
Penguin Ireland, 25 St. Stephen's Green, Dublin 2,
Ireland (a division of Penguin Books Ltd.)
Penguin Group (Australia), 250 Camberwell Road, Camberwell, Victoria 3124,
Australia (a division of Pearson Australia Group Pty. Ltd.)
Penguin Books India Pvt. Ltd., 11 Community Centre, Panchsheel Park,
New Delhi - 110 017, India
Penguin Group (NZ), cnr Airborne and Rosedale Roads, Albany,
Auckland 1310, New Zealand (a division of Pearson New Zealand Ltd.)
Penguin Books (South Africa) (Pty.) Ltd., 24 Sturdee Avenue,
Rosebank, Johannesburg 2196, South Africa

Penguin Books Ltd., Registered Offices:
80 Strand, London WC2R 0RL, England

First published by Signet Eclipse, an imprint of New American Library,
a division of Penguin Group (USA) Inc.

First Printing, December 2006
10 9 8 7 6 5 4 3 2 1

Prologue

She was supposed to be in school, but eight-year-old Molly Ridge had awakened with a sore throat that morning and her mom had kept her home.

Two slices of French toast and a glass of milk had somewhat eased the sore throat, and now Molly ran down the hallway in the house as her mother counted from the kitchen.

". . . three . . . four . . . You'd better find a good place to hide, my little lollipop, because when I find you I'm going to eat you up! Five . . ."

Molly stifled a giggle with her hand as she careened into her mother's bedroom. The closet? No, her mom would find her there for sure. Behind the curtains? Her feet would stick out and besides, the curtains were kind of see-through with the late morning sun shining in.

"Six . . ."

Excitement ripped through her as her mother's counting continued. When she reached ten she'd come looking for Molly. She looked around the room and finally slid beneath the bed, ignoring the dust on the wood floor and the pinch of the metal springs against her back.

"Seven . . ."

Beneath the bottom of the bright yellow dust ruffle she could see the bedroom doorway and she held her breath as she waited for her mother to come to find her.

"Eight . . ."

A loud knock on the front door interrupted her mom's counting. Molly sighed, hoping whoever was at the door would go away fast.

"Hi! What's up?" Her mother's voice drifted down the hallway from the living room. "Wait! Oh my God. What . . . what are you doing?"

A scream pierced the air.

Molly froze, her heart pounding frantically. A crash resounded, followed by the sound of glass breaking. A bang. More screams.

Something was wrong.

Something awful was happening.

In horror Molly watched as her mother appeared in the bedroom doorway. Bright red splashed her white blouse and she staggered across the room and fell to the floor next to the bed.

"Mommy?" Molly whispered.

Monica Ridge turned her head and saw her daughter beneath the bed. "Shush, Lollipop. Don't move. Don't make a sound." The words were slurred and barely audible. Molly stuffed a fist in her mouth as she heard footsteps coming down the hallway and her mother tried to get up.

"No. Please," Molly heard her mother say as Molly squeezed her eyes tightly closed.

More noise.

Scary noise. She opened her eyes once. A flash of blue. A knife slashed downward. She quickly squeezed her eyes closed again.

Then silence.

She had no idea how long she remained, eyes tightly closed, listening to the silence. When Molly opened her eyes once again she saw her mother lying on her back nearby.

Blood. It was everywhere. On her mommy, on the floor, on the walls.

Mommy? She wasn't moving but her eyes were wide open and staring at the ceiling. Her hand was stretched out toward where Molly hid and Molly wanted to reach out and grab her mommy's hand and tell her to get up and to stop staring like that.

Molly screamed inside her head as she shoved her fist harder against her mouth.

Shush. Don't move. Don't make a sound.
Shush. Don't move. Don't make a sound.

Chapter 1

Two uniformed cops delivered the news of death to Haley Lambert just after eight in the evening on a Friday. She'd just changed into her pajamas and plopped in front of her computer to answer her e-mails. A slice of cold pizza sat on a plate beside her and a chilled beer awaited her attention.

It was an ordinary Friday night. Pajamas, cold pizza and beer had become the norm since she'd broken up with her latest boyfriend three months before. Tim had been a great guy, a terrific boyfriend.

Unfortunately she'd discovered that he wasn't just a great boyfriend to her, but to two other women as well. At least she'd learned his snake-in-the-grass qualities before she'd slept with him. She'd never been a good judge of character, as her sister had often reminded her.

It was an ordinary Friday night until she answered her doorbell. One look at the officers' face and she knew they weren't at her apartment to collect for a charity or invite her to the policemen's ball.

"Haley Lambert?" The officer who spoke had a baby face, round and pleasant-looking, but it was the expression in his eyes that caused a sense of terrible dread to sweep through Haley.

"Yes, I'm Haley Lambert."

"Ms. Lambert, I'm Officer Sinclair and this is my partner, Officer Banks. Could we come in?" It was the older one who spoke, his eyes holding the same expression as his partner's did: deep sympathy, coupled with the dread of somebody bearing bad news.

Haley wanted to slam her door in their faces, refuse to allow them entry. She had the crazy thought that if she didn't let them come into her apartment, then nothing bad had happened.

But of course she didn't slam the door. Heart crashing against her ribs, she allowed the two officers inside. "Please, tell me what's happened. Why are you here?"

Officer Sinclair frowned. "Is there a Mr. Lambert? Or perhaps a friend or a neighbor who could be here with you?"

She knew then that the news they carried wasn't just bad. It was devastating. She had never felt as alone as she did at this moment, knowing there was no friend, no neighbor whose presence could get her through whatever was about to occur.

She shook her head. "Just tell me why you're here."

"You're the next of kin of Monica Ridge?" Officer Banks asked.

Oh God, not Monica. Why would two cops be at her apartment in Las Vegas to talk about a woman who lived in a suburb of Kansas City, Missouri?

"Monica is my sister. Has something happened? Has there been an accident? Is she all right? Is she in the hospital?" The questions spilled out of her as her stomach twisted into a knot of anxiety.

"I'm sorry to inform you that your sister has been murdered," Officer Sinclair said gently.

Haley felt the words like a physical punch to her stomach, the punch so severe it took her breath away and she stumbled backward and down on the sofa.

Dead? Monica? Murdered? It wasn't possible. There had to be some sort of mistake. Haley's brain refused to wrap around the concept of her sister being dead.

Numb. She'd never felt so numb and so cold. Monica gone? How was that possible? Of the two sisters Monica was the one who never took chances, who always did everything right.

Officer Banks sat next to her, his plump baby face and blue eyes radiating deep sorrow. He took her hand in his and she allowed the touch even though his warm fingers wrapped around hers did nothing to reassure her. "Your sister was murdered sometime this morning in her home by an intruder."

Haley stared at him for a long, horrified moment. She'd heard the words, but they didn't make sense. Not possible, she thought in some irrational part of her brain. Murders happened to strangers that she read about in the newspapers. People she knew didn't get murdered, especially not people like Monica.

Her brain worked to process it all. Somebody had entered Monica's house and had killed her? Oh God, how had it happened? How in the hell had something like that happened? Who was responsible? "Do they know who did it? Do they have somebody in custody?"

"We don't have any of that information," Officer Sinclair said.

"What about Molly?" Haley released Officer Banks's hand and shot up from the sofa at thoughts of her niece. "Is Molly okay?" Surely Molly had been in school on a Friday morning in early May.

"We don't have any information other than what we've given you," Officer Sinclair replied. "Are you sure there isn't somebody we can call for you? Somebody who could come over and be with you?"

"No." Haley gazed around her small apartment in a daze, as if the answers to a million questions resided in the cheap furnishings and dusty surfaces.

Monica was dead. Where was Molly? Monica was dead. Monica was dead. She focused back on the two officers. "I've got to get out of here. I've got to get to Kansas City." She needed to find out exactly what had happened to her sister.

Grief would have to wait. There would be time for that later. Right now there was an eight-year-old little girl who had just lost her mommy and whose only other relative in the world was her Aunt Haley.

SHE WASN'T SUPPOSED TO BE HOME!
WHY WAS SHE THERE?
WHAT DID SHE SEE?
WHAT DID MOLLY SEE?
SHE WASN'T SUPPOSED TO BE HOME!

Chapter 2

Later she might think about the fact that it had taken her less than ten hours to quit her job and pack up her life and be on a plane carrying her to the city of her childhood.

Later Haley might find it somehow sad that thirty-two years of living fit so neatly in two fake leather giveaway suitcases from Harrah's Casino. As it was, feelings were something she refused to indulge.

The numbness that had filled her when the police told her about her sister had lingered throughout the long night and remained with her even now. She clung to it, knowing that when it was gone her grief would be too much to bear.

As the pilot announced their descent toward the Kansas City International Airport, Haley stared out the window to the patchwork of fields below.

After the police had left her apartment the night before, she'd contacted the authorities in Kansas City and had finally connected with Owen Tolliver, the lead detective on the case.

He'd been reticent to talk to her about the crime

over the phone but had let her know that the Division of Family Services had taken Molly to a foster home until relatives could be found.

Haley tugged on a strand of her long blond hair and fought against the sheer panic that threatened to overwhelm her. She'd managed so far to keep her grief at bay, but the terror kept rising up, trying to take possession of her.

What was she going to do? What was she going to do about Molly? It had been two years since she'd seen the little girl. At best she'd always been a long-distance aunt, a birthday and Christmas present in the mail, a voice on the phone.

According to Monica, Haley didn't know how to take care of herself. How was she supposed to help Molly? How was she supposed to know what was best for a little girl whose mother had just been murdered?

The plane touched down and within minutes she stood at the luggage carousel waiting for her worldly possessions to spit out of the conveyor and onto the belt.

Exhaustion weighed heavily on her shoulders. She was beyond exhausted. Sleep had been impossible the night before. She'd contacted her boss at the lounge where she worked as a bartender and quit her job; she'd packed and contacted her landlord to let him know she was leaving.

Getting out of her apartment hadn't been a problem. Haley always rented on a month-to-month basis because she never knew when the wanderlust might hit and she'd want to pack up and leave.

But the night before she hadn't given herself a minute to think, for she feared the dark path her thoughts might take. She just wanted Detective Owen Tolliver to give her some answers, to somehow make sense of all of this.

It was almost eleven when she pulled her rental car into the Pleasant Hill patrol station where Detective Tolliver had said he'd be available to meet with her the moment she arrived in town.

This wasn't her first visit to the Pleasant Hill patrol station. When she'd been fourteen years old she and a couple of her friends had been guests in the official brick building for several hours when they had all been caught shoplifting. Not one of Haley's prouder moments.

The parents of the other girls had arrived within thirty minutes and arranged for their release. Haley had spent three long hours waiting for her mother to come, three hours of agony because she wasn't at all sure her mother would come to get her out.

It smelled the same as she remembered from that time so long ago, a combination of burned coffee, sour body odors and fast food. "I'm here to see Detective Owen Tolliver," she told the man behind the counter that separated the officers from the general public. "I'm Haley Lambert."

"I'll see if he's available," the officer said. "Just have a seat." He pointed to a row of plastic chairs that ran along one wall.

She sat and once again reached up to tug on a strand of her shoulder-length hair. In minutes she'd find out all the details of Monica's murder.

Murder. Jesus, it still felt so unreal. Somebody had willfully taken her sister's life. Murder. The very word filled her with a shuddering horror.

She leaned her head back against the wall as a

trembling began in the very pit of her stomach. A home intruder: what did that mean? Had armed men broken through the front door in an attempt to rob the place and encountered Monica?

It had to have been a random act of violence. Monica wasn't the type of woman to have enemies. She was kind and good and everyone who ever met her adored her.

What she hoped was that somehow this was all a terrible mistake, some sort of horrifying computer glitch or a ridiculously bad clerical error. It hadn't been Monica's house that had been broken into, and when her sister heard about all this they would laugh together.

Oh God, she wanted to laugh with her sister. She wanted to see Monica's eyes lit with humor, hear the laugh that had always been more giggle than guffaw.

"Ms. Lambert?"

Her eyes sprang open to see a tall, balding man with the kindest blue eyes she'd ever seen. "I'm Detective Owen Tolliver. Why don't we go someplace where we can talk privately?" He carried with him a file folder.

She nodded and stood, slightly unsteady on her feet as the trembling moved outward to possess her limbs. Get it together, Haley, she admonished herself. You can fall apart later, but not now.

Detective Tolliver led her down a long tiled hallway. He said nothing as they walked, but she could see weariness in his gait and in the slight slump of his shoulders.

She could identify. Her eyes felt gritty from lack of sleep and if it hadn't been for Molly she would have simply crawled into bed and pulled the covers up over her head.

He took her into a small room that held only a table and two chairs. He motioned her into one of the chairs. She sat and looked at him expectantly.

"Can I get you something to drink, Ms. Lambert? Perhaps a soda or a cup of coffee?"

"No, thanks, and please, call me Haley." Thankfully her trembling had stopped and all she felt was a need to get this whole thing over with.

He drew a hand down his face, lines of strain radiating outward from his eyes, then sat in the chair opposite her and slapped the file folder onto the table.

"I'm hoping you're going to tell me this is all a mistake," she said. "I'm hoping you'll tell me that the woman who was murdered wasn't my sister."

"I wish I could tell you that," he replied. "But your sister was positively identified by the neighbors. There's no mistake."

There's no mistake.

There's no mistake.

The words reverberated in her brain like the beat of an irritating drum in a parade. "From the beginning. I want to know everything." Her voice was little more than a strained whisper.

He nodded and opened the folder. "We received a call yesterday afternoon from a post office employee who indicated there might be a problem at your sister's home. He had a package to deliver there, and when he went to the front door it was open and he could see that something was wrong. There was blood on the walls of the entryway."

He paused and looked at her, as if assessing how

much to tell her, how much she could handle. "I want it all," she said, her voice stronger. Dammit, she owed Monica that. "I need to know it all."

Once again he gave a curt nod. "I caught the call along with my partner, Frank Marcelli, who, by the way, lives next door to your sister. We went to the address and immediately realized we had a crime scene on our hands." He kept his voice brisk, businesslike, as he reviewed the notes in the file.

She had the feeling he didn't need to read the notes, but preferred looking at the paper instead of looking at her as he told her the horrifying details of her sister's death.

"Because of the blood splatter we saw on the walls, we decided to go inside and investigate. We found your sister in what appeared to be the master bedroom. She'd been stabbed."

Again a stir of emotion wobbled in her stomach, like a halfhearted top at the end of its spin. Stabbed. Her sister had been stabbed. "Was it a robbery?"

He looked up at her then. "We don't believe so. There was no forced entry and nothing appeared to have been taken from the scene."

"Then who did this? Do you have any suspects? What's being done to catch my sister's killer?"

The detective frowned, a deep furrow cutting across his broad forehead. "You have to understand, we're only at the very beginning of this investigation. We've had less than twenty-four hours on the case."

The case. That's what her sister had become. A pile of papers in a file folder with a case number like a candle on top. The emotion spun a little tighter, pressing against her chest and making it difficult for her to draw breath.

Detective Tolliver closed the file and leaned back in the chair, his gaze sympathetic. "I know this is difficult, Haley, and I know you've just arrived in town and haven't had time to process things, but we could use your help. We need to know everything we can learn about your sister's life. We need names of her friends, perhaps people who had problems with her."

"Nobody had problems with Monica," she protested. "She is . . ." She stopped herself and closed her eyes against the stabbing pain as she realized "is" was no longer a working word where her sister was concerned. She began again. "Monica was a wonderful person. She didn't have an enemy in the world."

"She had one," Tolliver replied. His blue eyes took on a hint of steel. "Somebody didn't like your sister. Our guess right now is that this was a rage killing."

"What do you mean?"

He looked distinctly uncomfortable. "It was overkill. She wasn't stabbed just once. She was stabbed multiple times with the force of somebody very angry. We believe she knew the person who attacked her. In interviews with neighbors they told us that she was vigilant about keeping her door locked all the time. But she opened the door and allowed her killer in."

"Didn't any of the neighbors see anything? Didn't they hear anything?"

"Right now all we have is Molly."

Haley sat back in the chair and stared at him. "What do you mean, all you have is Molly?"

He looked at her in surprise. "Nobody told you?" He grimaced. "When the crime scene unit began their work in the bedroom they found Molly under the bed, mere inches from where your sister lay dead."

The spin of emotion that had been churning inside her threatened to explode out of control. For a moment she couldn't breathe. Tears blurred her vision as grief clawed up the back of her throat. She struggled against it, swallowing hard several times before attempting to speak.

Owen Tolliver got up and went to the water dispenser to get Haley a glass of water. At fifty-six years old, he had been doing this long enough to know when somebody was on the verge of losing it.

He got the paper cup of water, set it in front of her, then returned to his chair. Haley Lambert was pretty and looked a lot like her sister. She had the same long blond hair framing an oval face and rich green eyes that at the moment held a hint of shock.

Owen recognized the close resemblance between the sisters not by viewing the body of Monica Ridge but rather by seeing a photo of the deceased on her fireplace mantel. In death, Monica had been nearly unrecognizable.

Nothing in Owen's thirty years of police work had prepared him for the little girl under the bed. She'd been like a feral kitten when they'd finally pulled her out, biting and kicking with eyes wide in terror. But the worst part of all was that as Molly fought them she didn't make a sound. That unnatural silence had been deafening.

Haley picked up the water with hands that trembled slightly and took a long sip. When she placed the cup back on the table she appeared to have regained some control.

"Why was she at home? Why wasn't she in school?" Her green eyes searched his face as if somehow he could fix things. But nobody and nothing was going to fix the tragedy that had just begun in her life.

"We talked to the officials at Molly's school and apparently your sister called her in sick yesterday." Owen once again leaned back in his chair, weary beyond words.

"Look, I'll be honest with you. We've been working on this since the moment we discovered your sister and right now we have nothing solid. What we do have is a little girl who we think might have witnessed the murder, but we haven't been able to get her to tell us anything. In fact, we weren't able to get her to say a single word."

"Oh my God." She reached for the water cup once again.

"It's obvious she's traumatized and frightened. I'm hoping that now that you're here you can get her to talk to you, tell you what happened in that house yesterday morning."

"Of course, I'll do whatever I can." She took another sip of the water, then gazed at him with haunted eyes. "I don't know what happens next. I'm assuming I can't go to the house?"

"It won't be released for another day or two," he replied. "I recommend you plan on staying with friends or in a motel room for a couple of days. Whatever you decide, I need to know where you'll be."

He hesitated a moment, wondering how much information she could handle in this first meeting. "When we release the house to you, you might want to consider hiring a service to come in and take care of things."

"Take care of things?"

"There was a lot of blood. I can give you the name of a service that does that kind of thing."

She nodded once. "When can I see Molly?"

"Now." He shoved away from the table and stood. "I made arrangements with the foster parents for us to go over there as soon as you got into town. I'll drive you."

As they left the station and walked out into the early afternoon sunshine, Owen realized there were two things he hadn't told Haley Lambert.

The first was that her sister's murder was one of the worst he'd ever seen. The second was that Monica Ridge had been stabbed not once, not twice, but twenty-seven times.

Somebody had really wanted her dead.

Chapter 3

Pleasant Hill, Missouri, had once been a small farming community thirty miles north of Kansas City. But in the last twenty years Kansas City had widened its boundaries and now knocked on Pleasant Hill's front door. The end result was that the small town now felt more like a suburb of the bigger city than an entity in and of itself.

Farmland had been sold and subdivided into lots for high-end housing and condo developments. New banks, fast-food drive-ins and restaurants had appeared as the small town had grown.

Haley stared out at the passing scenery as Detective Tolliver drove her to the foster home where Molly had been taken the day before.

By the time Haley was fifteen years old she'd been consumed with the need to get out of this small town, away from the provincial people with their square box thinking, and experience real life.

She'd wanted pink hair and a guitar. She'd wanted freedom from rules and judgments. God, she'd been young. By all rights she should be the one who was dead. She was the one who had taken all the risks and flown through life without a net.

Monica had been the sister who had done everything right. She'd gone to college, gotten a degree, met a wonderful man and gotten married. Monica had lived her life by the rules.

Haley sensed Tolliver glancing at her and turned her head to meet his gaze. "She always locked her doors. She never went out alone after dark. She never invited men to her house. She didn't even date."

It suddenly seemed vitally important that he know these things, that he understood what kind of woman her sister had been. "She was a devoted mother. She could have worked anywhere. She had a degree in business, but she chose to work part-time in sales so she could be home for Molly."

"Molly's father, where's he in this picture?" Tolliver asked as he made a right-hand turn down a tree-lined street.

"Dead. He died in a car accident coming home from his office when Molly was a year old." She sighed. "I'd say the husband-did-it angle is a dead end, no pun intended."

"How sure are you about the dating thing?"

Haley frowned thoughtfully. "Fairly sure. Monica always said there would be time enough for dating when Molly was older. She didn't want to confuse Molly by introducing her to men who might never have an important role in their lives."

"But you aren't positive that she wasn't dating?" He pulled the car against the curb in front of a neat ranch house painted beige with forest green shutters. He shut off the engine and turned to face her once again.

"All I can tell you is she never mentioned it to me." Haley stared at the house, the terror that she'd managed to stuff deep inside awakening again. She turned her attention to Tolliver. "We spoke to each other at least two or three times a week. We talked about what was going on in our lives. I can't imagine that if she had a man in hers she would have kept that a secret from me."

She looked back at the house. Molly was inside there with strangers. Molly, who had been under the bed when they'd found her. Oh God, what had she seen? What had she heard? Did she even understand that her mommy was gone forever or was she waiting for Monica to come and get her and take her home? Was she waiting for her world to be set right again?

"The Robertses are good people. They've fostered a lot of children over the years."

She turned her head to look at the detective once again. "You have children, Detective?"

"Two boys, both grown." His eyes filled with a kindness that was nearly her undoing. "I know this is difficult, Haley, but we need to know what Molly saw. Anything she can tell us will help in the investigation. According to the Robertses she hasn't spoken a word since the caseworker dropped her off yesterday afternoon. She's a frightened little girl and she needs you. We need you too. We need you to break through her silence for us."

Haley didn't want the detective depending on her. She didn't want anyone depending on her. She squeezed her eyes tightly closed against a mist of tears.

"You can't fall apart on me now, Haley," Tolliver said gently. "That little girl in there needs you."

He was right. Her grief would have to wait. She had to be strong. For Monica. She had to be strong for Molly. "Let's do it," she said and opened her car door.

Selma Roberts, a woman who appeared to be in her late fifties or early sixties, opened the door. Her gray hair was short, emphasizing warm brown eyes and a smile that instantly put Haley somewhat at ease.

The air inside the house smelled vaguely of cinnamon and a lemon-based furniture polish. Selma led them into the living room where the sofa and chair were threadbare but looked comfortable, and a wall unit of shelves held an array of children's books, puzzles and games.

Every space on the walls was covered with pictures of children of all ages and sizes. "These are our kids," Selma said to Haley. "Thirty-four of them over the past twenty years. They all came through our front door frightened and alone, but usually within a couple of hours we'd have them laughing and feeling more comfortable. Not your little Molly."

"She still hasn't said anything?" Tolliver asked.

Selma shook her head. "Not a peep. But I know her muteness is nothing physical. I know she can talk if she wanted to."

"How do you know that?" Haley asked curiously.

"She must have had a nightmare because she

screamed in the middle of the night." Selma offered Haley a halfhearted smile. "Poor little thing. I'm sure she'll feel much better seeing you. Why don't I just go get her, and Detective, I have coffee and freshly baked cinnamon coffee cake in the kitchen."

"Sounds good," he agreed. "If you need me, I'll be in the kitchen," he said to Haley, then left the room.

Selma disappeared down a hallway and Haley was left in the room alone. She stepped closer to the photos on one wall. So many children, some dark skinned, some coffee colored, and some pale and blond, but they all had one thing in common: they all wore brilliant smiles.

Haley reached for a strand of her hair and tugged with nervous tension. Molly wouldn't be smiling. Would she even remember her aunt Haley? It had been over two years since Haley had been in Pleasant Hill for a brief Christmas visit.

She and Monica had fought for almost the entire time Haley had been in town. Monica had wanted Haley to quit her job in Las Vegas and move back to Pleasant Hill. "You're all the family I have," Monica had said. "I'd really like to have you here in town with me and Molly."

How Haley now wished she had done as her sister had wanted. They would have had the last two years to fight and make up, borrow each other's clothes and share each other's lives.

"Here's your girl," Selma said.

Haley turned from the pictures to see her niece standing rigidly in the doorway. A million impressions flashed through Haley's mind. Two years ago

Molly had been a chubby, round-faced imp who giggled incessantly.

A slender, more grown-up little girl stared at the floor. Her long, pale hair had been neatly braided and with one hand she tugged at the braid. She was clad in a pair of jeans and a pink T-shirt that read PRINCESS LOLLIPOP across the chest. Haley had sent her the shirt for her last birthday.

"I'll just leave you two alone to have a little chat," Selma said. As the plump woman headed for the kitchen Haley fought the impulse to beg her to come back.

It was ridiculous to be afraid. Hell, Haley had faced more than one drunken lech in the lounge where she worked. She'd gone toe-to-toe with a boyfriend who had erupted in a jealous rage and thought she'd take his crap. Surely she could handle one frightened eight-year-old.

"Molly?" She walked over to the child and dropped to one knee in front of her. "Molly, honey. You remember me? Aunt Haley? It's going to be all right. We're going to be all right."

Molly dropped her hand from her hair and slowly raised her head to look at Haley. Her long-lashed dark green eyes met Haley's and there was such torment in their depths that it broke something inside Haley.

As she pulled Molly into her arms her grief finally tore free. She hugged Molly tight as a deep wrenching sob ripped through her. What were they going to do without Monica? Oh God, what were they going to do?

She allowed herself only that single sob, then swallowed the rest, wanting to be strong for Molly, who trembled in her arms like a frightened little bird and cried without making a sound.

Haley held her for several minutes, then released her and stood. She took Molly's hand in hers and led her to the sofa where they sat side by side.

Molly held tight to Haley's hand, as if it were a lifeline through the nightmare she'd plunged into. Haley wanted to tell her not to hold too tight, not to depend on her too much.

For a long moment she said nothing. She simply sat next to her niece, who smelled of bubblegum-flavored toothpaste and stared at Haley expectantly.

"It's been a long time since we've seen each other," Haley said. "Do you remember me?" Molly nodded. "I just want you to know that everything is going to be okay." Haley forced cheerfulness into her voice. "You're going to be just fine."

Molly stared at Haley as if she were a creature from some half-forgotten planet. Haley plunged forward, wanting to get the ugliness out of the way as quickly as possible, aware of Tolliver waiting in the next room.

"Molly, honey, can you tell me what happened at your house? Can you tell me who hurt your mommy?"

Molly's grip tightened on Haley's hand and she shook her head vehemently, eyes widened in terror. "Okay, okay, you don't have to talk about it right now," Haley quickly said. Even though she knew Detective Tolliver needed whatever was in Molly's head, whatever horror lingered in her thoughts, she wasn't about to push the little girl. Maybe she could get her to talk about something else.

"I know things are scary right now. Are they nice

to you here?" Molly hesitated a moment, then nodded her head, and Haley continued. "You need to stay here a couple more days, until I figure things out, okay?"

Molly searched her face, as if trying to decide if she could trust Haley or not. A frown etched across her little forehead and she grudgingly nodded once again.

"Is there anything you need?" Haley wished Molly would just say one word. It was unnatural for a child to be so quiet. She'd half hoped her question would provoke a cry from Molly for her mommy, but instead she shook her head as tears filled her eyes.

Once again Haley gathered her into her arms and hugged her tight. Haley had never done anything right in her life but as she held her sister's child, she swore that somehow, someway she would do right for Molly.

It was after five when Haley and Tolliver left the Roberts home and headed back to the police station. "No matter what I said, no matter what I asked, she never made a sound." Haley frowned wearily.

"Seat belt," Tolliver said and slowed the car until she had it fastened. "Maybe we just need to give her a little time," he said, although she could tell the idea didn't sit well with him. If Molly had information that would lead to the killer, then Haley knew he wanted it sooner rather than later.

And she wanted it sooner rather than later. She wanted the animal who had killed Monica behind bars. "Where does the investigation go from here?"

"We do some more talking to neighbors and friends, we find out as much as we can about your sister and her life. We found an address book at her house. We're checking through the names and numbers. We hope that somebody knows something or heard something or saw something that might give us a lead to follow."

He pressed his lips together, as if he was afraid he'd said too much. But he hadn't told her anything other than the fact that they didn't know squat.

"What about forensic stuff? You know, hairs and fibers and all that CSI crap I see on television?"

He cast her a wry look. "Real life rarely works as neatly and quickly as television." He sighed. "Whoever killed your sister had the foresight to wipe the scene clean. We found no foot- or fingerprints, no hairs that weren't consistent with your sister or niece. Of course, we're still in the process of analyzing everything. It takes time to get lab reports back."

He pulled into the police station parking lot, cut the engine, then turned to look at her. "What are your plans? Needless to say we'd prefer you not take Molly out of the city until she talks to us."

"You don't have to worry about that. Yesterday I was living in a furnished dump in Las Vegas and working in a lounge as a bartender. Today I am jobless and homeless and the legal custodian of an eight-year-old girl who might have seen her mother murdered and isn't talking."

She heard the rising hysteria in her voice, heard it and recognized it but was incapable of stopping it. "I've never had a long-term relationship. Hell, I've never even had a pet. And now I have a fragile little girl who's expecting me to fix things for her."

She opened the car door and started to get out, but was half strangled by the seat belt she'd neglected to unfasten. Fingers fumbling with the latch, she gazed at him almost accusingly. "I couldn't even remember to put on my seat belt. How am I supposed to handle all this?"

By the time she finally managed to get out of the car, Tolliver was at her side. She stared up at him, an irrational anger swelled tight inside her. "You find who did this. You get whoever killed my sister." She punched him in the chest with her finger.

Tolliver's face seemed to melt as the grief that she'd managed to keep at bay suddenly crashed through her. She would have fallen if he hadn't grabbed her by the upper arms. She collapsed into him, leaning against his broad chest as sobs ripped through her.

He didn't say a word, didn't attempt to pull away or stop her outburst, but rather placed a hand on her back and patted her, like a parent consoling an upset child.

Haley couldn't remember the last time she'd cried. She thought it might have been when she'd been fourteen and had found a stray dog. The dog, a little poodle mix with fur matted and filled with brambles, had joyously jumped into her arms as if finding salvation.

Haley had taken him home and begged her mother to let her keep him. "Absolutely not," Ann Lambert had replied. "I can't even get you to clean your room. You certainly aren't responsible enough to take care of a dog." She had called animal control.

As the animal control officer had taken the dog from Haley's arms, the little creature had looked up at her with winsome eyes and licked the underside of her chin.

She'd cried for two days.

She didn't cry that long now. After several minutes she pulled herself together well enough to step back from the detective.

"I'm sorry." She swiped at her cheeks, embarrassed by her break of control.

"Don't apologize," he replied. "I'd say you had that coming."

For a moment they stood facing each other as an awkward silence descended. "You know I intend to do everything I can to find out who's responsible," he finally said. "We're making this our number one priority at the moment."

At the moment.

She nodded, but she also knew that it would only take another murder, another victim, to shove this investigation out of the limelight and down the priority list.

She knew from watching television and reading crime books that the first forty-eight hours were critical in solving a crime. But over half of that time had passed and they had nothing.

"So, what are your plans from here?" Detective Tolliver asked. "Where will I be able to get hold of you?"

"Is Lazy Ray's still out on Highway 169?" she asked. He nodded. "Then you can reach me there. And at the moment the only plan I have is to head to the nearest bar and get rip-roaring drunk."

Chapter 4

She didn't get rip-roaring drunk, although she did check into Lazy Ray's, a motel that had stood on the edge of town for as long as she could remember.

She'd only been in the room long enough to unpack when the walls began to close in on her and she felt the need to go out.

Somewhere.

Anywhere. She just needed to get out.

Although her intention had been to do exactly what she'd told Detective Tolliver, to find the nearest bar and drink herself into oblivion, she didn't.

Instead she found herself back in her rental car and driving aimlessly down the streets of the small town. The light of dusk was kind, painting the houses and lawns she passed with a soft golden hue.

The downtown of Pleasant Hill consisted of two blocks of Main Street. When Haley had last wandered the sidewalks many of the storefronts had been boarded up or filled with struggling businesses. Now chic boutiques had opened, along with coffee shops and cell phone places. Pleasant Hill had finally come into the twenty-first century.

She didn't realize she had a destination in mind until she turned left at the corner of Oak and Maple. It was only then that she realized she was heading home.

Maple Drive was a dead end that culminated in a cul-de-sac, and at the exact center of that cul-de-sac was the house where Haley had grown up, the house Monica had taken over after their mother died five years ago.

Monica had told Haley at the time of their mother's death that they should sell the house and split the proceeds. The house was paid for and would probably bring a tidy sum that could be divided equally. But Haley hadn't wanted that and instead had insisted Monica take the house and live in it.

It had been a perfect place for Monica to raise Molly without having to worry about paying rent. The three-bedroom ranch had a terrific wooded backyard complete with a tree house the girls' father had built when Haley was ten and Monica was twelve.

He'd finished the tree house on a Tuesday and had died in his sleep from a heart attack on the following Friday.

After that, Haley had never gone up to the tree house again. She'd tried once, months after her dad's death, but the minute she'd grabbed on to the sides of the wooden ladder she'd been overwhelmed with a sense of vertigo and had suffered the first panic attack of her life. Unfortunately it hadn't been the last panic attack she'd had, although thankfully they were few and far between.

She tightened her fingers around the steering wheel as she approached the cul-de-sac.

The yellow crime-scene tape fluttered in the faint evening breeze. It looked obscene stretched across the cheerful, bright-red painted front door.

A patrol car sat in the driveway, and as Haley pulled to the curb in front of the house a blond officer got out and eyed her suspiciously. She shut off her car engine and got out of the car, but made no approach toward the house.

"Can I help you?" The officer walked down the driveway toward her. As he came closer she saw that he looked very young and very officious. He was stiff-shouldered and led with his prominent chin. "If you're with the paper, we aren't giving any statements." He rested a hand on the butt of his gun.

"No, I'm not a reporter. I'm . . . this is my house. It was my sister who was murdered."

His chin lowered a notch. "I'm sorry, ma'am. But I can't let you go inside. Nobody is allowed in." He dropped his hand from his gun. "Frankly, you wouldn't want to go in there right now anyway. It's a pretty big mess."

His words were like a new punch to her stomach. *A pretty big mess.* A mess because somebody had stabbed her sister over and over again.

"I just needed to come by." She didn't want to go inside. She didn't want to see Monica's blood splashed on the walls and floor.

In fact, when the house was released she'd contact the service that Tolliver had mentioned. Imagine, a group of people whose work was cleaning up death.

She'd had a regular customer at the bar in Las Vegas, an old woman named Maddie who was crazy as a loon. She came in about three times a week and ordered a gin and tonic, and while she nursed the drink she talked about little people who lived in her attic and wicked electromagnetic currents taking over her mind.

Haley had asked her boss about Maddie and he'd told her that a couple of years before, Maddie's husband had committed suicide in their living room by blowing his brains out with a gun. Maddie had found him when she'd come home from the grocery store.

The authorities had come, his death had been ruled a suicide and his body had been taken away. Maddie had been left alone in the house with his blood and brain matter splattered all over the room. She'd spent two days scrubbing the walls and when she'd finally cleaned it all up, according to urban legend, during those two days Maddie had gone quite mad.

Haley had no desire to see the remains of her sister leaked into the carpeting, splattering the walls. That wasn't the way she wanted to remember Monica.

The officer murmured another platitude, then walked back to his patrol car and got inside. Haley leaned against the front of the rental car, reluctant to go back to the solitude of her motel room.

Her mother would roll over in her grave if she knew Haley was the only one left to raise her grandchild. Ann Lambert would have thought Molly better left to be raised by wolves than by Haley. Haley's biggest fear was that her mother was right.

She knew nothing about kids and specifically

nothing about Molly. She didn't know what she liked to eat, how she spent her time or when she went to bed at night. She had no clue about anything important to her niece.

What she'd told Tolliver was true. She'd never been responsible for anyone but herself. She didn't even have houseplants.

With a heavy sigh she slid back behind the steering wheel, unsure what she'd hoped to gain by coming here.

As she drove around the cul-de-sac to leave, she realized she didn't know Monica's neighbors. There had been a time years ago when Haley was growing up that she knew everyone in the circle drive. But most of those people had either died or moved away and new families had moved into the neat ranch houses.

The infrequent times that Haley had returned to see her sister, her visits had been too brief for socializing with the others in the immediate neighborhood.

Lights were on in several of the homes as if to ward off the approach of night. Families would be sitting down to evening meals. Haley's stomach rumbled and she realized she hadn't eaten anything since the day before.

It somehow seemed obscene to even think about food with Monica dead. But she had to eat. There were so many things to take care of, so many things to do. She had to eat and she needed to sleep.

She had to figure out what to do with Molly, needed to make some sort of plans for the future. She'd always been a seat-of-the-pants kind of person, ruled by impulse and unafraid of consequence.

But now she didn't have just herself to think about. Every move she made would affect another little person.

Maybe after eating she wouldn't feel so overwhelmed. Maybe after a good night's sleep she wouldn't feel so terrified by what lay ahead.

"What's she like?" Frank Marcelli bit into his cheeseburger deluxe and reached for a French fry from the box in front of him.

Owen Tolliver frowned thoughtfully. He and his partner sat in the break room of the police station, eating yet another fast-food dinner.

He could remember each and every murder case he'd ever worked on by what he and Frank ate during the investigation. The rape and murder of nineteen-year-old Sasha Wilkins had been Pizza Hut. The beating death of eighty-two-year-old Velma Burke had been Chinese. And Monica Ridge was Big Bill's Burgers.

"She's scared and grieving." Owen dug through the papers on the table and pulled one out. "Haley Lambert, thirty-two years old. Never been married. No criminal record. Lives in Las Vegas and works as a bartender at Joey's Lounge on the strip. She's been in Vegas several years working a variety of jobs. Before that she lived in Chicago, Atlantic City, and Reno for a while."

Owen put down the sheet of paper and leaned back in his chair. "She's pretty. Blond hair, good figure, looks a lot like her sister. She also seems overwhelmed by everything."

"Is she going to be any help with Molly?"

"I hope so," Tolliver said fervently. "It's starting

to look like Molly is our only hope for cracking the case."

Marcelli shoved his half-eaten burger aside, his brown eyes darkening as he raked a hand through his hair. "I still can't believe it. Monica was a terrific woman, a great mother. I wish I knew something that would explain this." He broke off, a deep frown cutting across his forehead.

Frank seemed to be taking this case harder than any other they'd worked on together, but Tolliver understood his partner's torment. Monica Ridge had been his next-door neighbor. Marcelli's two children had often played with Molly Ridge. Tolliver had suggested to Frank that maybe he shouldn't work the case, but Frank had been adamant.

"I woke up this morning before dawn in a cold sweat, Tolly," Frank now said. "I kept thinking, why Monica's place? Why not mine? Why not the house on the other side? I had to get up and check on my kids, make sure they were okay." His eyes flashed. "I had to make sure they weren't hiding beneath their beds in terror."

Tolliver could certainly understand Frank's fears. Death had come knocking right next door. It was only natural that when something like that happened a person would fear that death might come knocking on his or her own door.

"I still say this was personal. This wasn't some random act. Whoever stabbed Monica Ridge did it viciously with tremendous force. I'm telling you, somebody hated that woman."

Frank ran a hand across his lower face where a five-o'clock shadow darkened his handsome square jaw. "I just can't imagine it. She was a nice lady. All she seemed to be interested in was raising Molly and living a quiet life."

"Even nice ladies with quiet lives have secrets," Tolliver said. "She was your neighbor, but who knew what was going on in her life that might have led a killer to her doorstep."

"At least she wasn't raped," Frank said, his gaze focused on the cheeseburger in front of him.

"But she was," Tolliver countered. "The only different was the perp used his knife instead of his dick and stabbed her in the chest instead of sexually assaulting her. Same rage, same violation, just different tools."

Tolliver took a sip from his soda, then continued. "What I don't understand is that the murder itself has all the markings of a rage killing, but the cleanup at the scene tells me that the killer was very organized, very methodical, which is not characteristic of a rage killer."

"It would be nice if tomorrow Haley could get Molly to tell us what she saw." Frank looked up and once again his dark eyes flashed with emotion. "I can't believe that poor kid was hiding under the bed when it all went down."

"What worries me is that the kid was so traumatized it might be months before she can talk about what she heard or what she saw." Tolliver shoved the last of his burger aside, his appetite gone as he thought of Molly Ridge.

What horrors had she seen take place in that bedroom? Had she seen the face of her mother's killer? Had she heard the killer's voice? What clues might rest inside that little mind, and how could they unlock them and use them to their benefit?

Tolliver sighed. "If she doesn't get Molly to talk in the next day or two, I'll check with Grey Banes. He can put Haley in touch with a therapist who might be able to break through Molly's silence."

"Too bad Grey isn't taking patients anymore. Kids were his specialty. Maybe you should get Grey to talk to Haley as soon as possible. I got to tell you, Tolly. This one is giving me nightmares."

Tolliver didn't reply. Even a town the size of Pleasant Hill saw more than its share of violent crime. Over his career, which had spanned thirty years, there had been only two cases that had haunted Tolliver's sleep.

The first had been the kidnapping of sixteen-year-old Abigail Tanner from a bus stop just outside her house. Initially it had been thought that the pretty teenager had run away, although her mother had insisted that wasn't the case. Victoria Tanner had been adamant that her daughter wasn't a runaway kind of kid, that there had been no fights, no drama to even believe that she might have bolted from home.

Abigail's body was found three days later, raped and strangled and thrown into a drainage ditch. They'd never caught the perp.

Victoria Tanner had haunted the station for weeks, needing an arrest, desperate for a specific face, a specific name to curse to hell. And then one day she just stopped coming.

After two days of trying to call her, with a horrible sense of dread pounding through his head, Tolliver had finally driven to her house to check on her.

He'd found her in the bathtub, slit wrists no longer bleeding and a suicide note on the counter.

The second case that he'd never really let go of had been less complicated, although no less tragic. A young man had broken into a home and encountered eighty-four-year-old Margaret Mason. In a panic, the kid had shoved Margaret backward. She'd fallen and hit her head on the edge of the coffee table and had died instantly.

It hadn't been Margaret's death that haunted Tolliver, but rather it had been the dignity and quiet resignation of her husband, Sam. Sam was wheelchair-bound and had been unable to help his wife. All he'd managed to do was crawl out of his chair and wrap his arms around her as he waited for the police to arrive.

The perp, a neighborhood teenager, had been caught and when questioned had broken down and sobbed a confession. He hadn't meant to hurt anyone, but that didn't keep him from going to prison.

Two cases in thirty years. Two cases out of hundreds that had grabbed hold of him and never quite let him go. What he feared the most was that this would be the third.

Chapter 5

She was running. Her breaths came in sharp pants as a stitch in her side shot pain through her stomach. She was running as fast as she could, her legs pumping frantically as fear crashed through her. Lungs burned. Muscles cramped. Run.

She couldn't turn her head, refused to look behind her, afraid of what she'd see, afraid of what chased her. All she knew was that if she was caught, her life would be over.

Run, Haley, run!

Haley awakened with a sharp gasp, heart pounding as she shot straight up in the bed. Her gaze darted wildly around the semidark room as she struggled to get her legs free from a tangle of blankets.

Faint light spilled from the bathroom, illuminating cheap furniture and orienting her to her surroundings as the remnants of the dream fell away.

Lazy Ray's. She was in a room in Lazy Ray's Motel and her sister was dead. Haley fell back against the pillow and waited for her breathing to return to normal.

It wasn't the first time she'd had that particular dream, although no matter how often she had it, it always disturbed her. And no matter how frequently she had the nightmare, she never managed to get the courage to look behind her and see what she was running from.

She was glad she hadn't gone to the bar last night and tied one on. It was depressing enough to wake up in this room with its scarred furniture and worn shag carpeting. It would have been worse to wake up with a raging hangover.

Glancing at the clock next to the bed she saw that it was almost seven. She'd like to go back to sleep, escape from all the questions she knew the day would bring.

But even as she squeezed her eyes tightly closed in an effort to find sleep once again, she knew she wouldn't. Instead she pulled herself from the blankets and padded into the bathroom for a long, hot shower.

The shower was neither long nor hot. Hot water apparently was a precious commodity at Lazy Ray's. She took a short, tepid shower, then dressed in a pair of jeans and a navy T-shirt that advertised Joey's Lounge.

She promised herself she wouldn't think about anything until after she'd had her breakfast, but the minute she sat down in a booth at the local Denny's, questions flew through her head.

Where were they going to live? Haley couldn't very well pack Molly up and take her back to Las Vegas with her. Monica would rise from the dead to kill Haley if she did that. In death Monica had gotten her wish: it looked like Haley had come home to stay.

"What can I get you, honey?" The waitress wore a name tag proclaiming her to be Betty and a smile that indicated she just might be one of the few people in America who actually liked what she did for a living.

"Grand Slam with bacon," Haley replied. She handed the menu to Betty. "And coffee . . . lots of coffee."

"Got ya covered." Betty poured her the hot brew, then left a silver carafe on the table.

As Haley waited for her breakfast and sipped the coffee that was too strong, she struggled to figure out what needed to be done.

The one thing she had done right over the years was save a little money. She had enough in a savings account to pay living expenses for several months without worrying about getting a job.

She needed to contact Monica's lawyer and see what Monica's finances had been at the time of her death. If there was a life insurance policy she was certain her sister would want the funds to be used for Molly's future.

The most logical thing to do would be to move into the house where Monica and Molly had lived. The house was paid for and only required the yearly taxes to be paid. But would Molly want to return to the house where her mother had died? Where her mother had been murdered?

Maybe the best thing to do would be to sell the house. What was the going rate for a house where a woman was murdered? Would anyone even want to buy it?

Of course they would. There were strange people in the world, people who got off on owning a place where a murder had occurred, people who would bid on macabre items owned by a killer. Sick.

She needed to make arrangements to get Molly out of foster care, but she couldn't very well bring Molly to stay at Lazy Ray's. Should she check into renting an apartment or a house?

"Here you are, sweetheart, one Grand Slam with bacon." Betty set the plate before Haley. "Anything else I can do for you?"

Find me a place to live. Give me parenting lessons. Raise my sister from the dead. "No, thanks, I'm fine," Haley replied and watched as Betty flitted to the next table.

It wouldn't have been so difficult if the stakes weren't so high. It wasn't like she'd suddenly gained custody of a plant that just had to be watered occasionally.

She needed to talk to Tolliver. She needed to find out when the house would be released to her, how soon she could get that cleaning service in. More importantly, she needed to know when she could bury her sister.

Bury her sister. The very idea brought with it a grief that knew no boundaries and a simmering rage at the unfairness of it all.

It was Sunday morning. She wouldn't be able to accomplish much of anything today. Maybe she should pick up a Sunday paper and look through the classifieds for someplace to live.

If Monica were here, she'd be dressing for church. Haley knew her sister and her niece attended services at the First Methodist Church every

Sunday. Church attendant, PTA mom, community servant: Monica had done it all and had done it all very well.

Haley had been known to take the Lord's name in vain; she'd attended AA meetings and had occasionally done community service by buying a customer a drink. Oh yeah, Molly was screwed.

After picking at her breakfast, she left the restaurant and headed back to the police station. It was a gorgeous spring day, the kind she never saw in Las Vegas.

Rebirth was everywhere, shoving up from the ground in clumps of brightly colored petunias and zinnias. New grass covered lawns, so green its beauty almost ached inside her. It didn't seem fair that there would be such beauty when her sister was dead.

Maybe death was easier to handle in the autumn, when the leaves were dying and falling from the trees and everything looked a little barren rather than so full of life as it did now.

It was only a few minutes after nine but Owen Tolliver looked as if he'd worked through the night. A coffee stain decorated the front of his rumpled white shirt and his gray slacks were wrinkled from hours of sitting.

He didn't look particularly happy to see her but greeted her with a tired grimace that she assumed was supposed to resemble a smile.

He led her back to a small interview room and gestured her into a chair at the table, then sat across from her. "What can I do for you this morning, Haley?" he asked.

Fix my world. Let me go back to my uncomplicated life in Las Vegas. Tell me this has all been a horrible nightmare and when I wake up Monica will still be alive. That's what she wanted to say, but didn't.

"I was wondering when I can bury my sister." The words were like shards of glass as they ripped from someplace deep inside her. She cleared her throat and continued. "And I'd like to know how soon the house will be released to me and if I can get the name of that cleaning service you mentioned."

"I'll check, but I think we'll probably be done with the house by tomorrow." His gaze shifted from her to the wall just behind her. "You can make arrangements for your sister anytime. Have you spoken to Selma Roberts this morning? Is there any change with Molly?"

Haley shook her head. "I called a little while ago. No change. She hasn't said a word."

"There's somebody I'd like you to speak to. He's a psychologist who consults with the police department. I saw him here earlier and I'm going to see if he's still around." Tolliver stood. "His name is Grey Banes, Dr. Greyson Banes. I'll send him in and I'll get the number to that cleaning service for you."

He left her alone in the room and Haley once again fought the impulse to run, to escape all of this. Molly would probably be better off in foster care than with her.

According to Monica, Haley's lifestyle had always been one of dysfunction. Haley had joked with her sister that stability was a place she didn't mind visiting, but she wouldn't want to live there.

A surge of anger welled up inside her: anger at the person who had stolen Monica's life, anger at

Monica for opening her damn front door and allowing death to come inside.

She slammed a hand down on the table, a momentary vent of the rage, then gasped and twirled around in the chair as the door to the room flew open.

"Hi. Dr. Greyson Banes." The tall man walked over to the table and held out a hand.

She gave his hand a perfunctory shake and at some place in the back of her mind registered the fact that Dr. Greyson Banes was a hottie.

His black hair held just the right touch of silver at the temples to make him look sexy rather than old. He wore a pair of reading glasses that he pulled off and set on the table. Dark lashes flirted around deep blue eyes, eyes that were filled with sharp intelligence.

"Detective Tolliver asked me to come in to speak with you," he said.

She tried not to notice that the man not only possessed attractive facial features but also boasted broad shoulders. His slim hips and long legs looked specifically made for the jeans he wore. The man was definitely a hunk, but she gazed at him warily.

"Ms. Lambert? Are you all right?"

She flushed, realizing she'd been staring. "Tell me, Dr. Banes, does Detective Tolliver think I need my head to be examined?"

He flashed her a quick smile that exposed dimples as he sat at the table across from her. "Not at all, Ms. Lambert. And everyone around here calls me Dr. Grey."

"You can call me Haley," she replied as she noticed he had no wedding ring in sight. Not that she cared. Not that it mattered.

"Tolliver wanted me to come in and talk to you about Molly. I saw her briefly just after she was discovered under the bed. By the way, I'm sorry about your sister."

The words would have sounded like an empty platitude coming from anyone else, but for some reason as she gazed into his deep blue eyes, she believed he meant it. It was so much easier to focus on how attractive he was than to think about the reason she was here in the police station.

"Thank you. Then I guess you know that Molly isn't talking."

He nodded. "I couldn't get her to speak to me yesterday and Tolliver says that situation hasn't changed." He had the kind of direct, piercing gaze that could make a person think he or she was the most important person in his life. "He also told me how important it is that somebody gets Molly talking as soon as possible."

Haley leaned forward and for a moment smelled the scent of him, a crisp clean male scent. "I was hoping she'd talk to me. I was hoping that no matter how awful things were in her head she'd trust me." She grabbed a strand of her hair and tugged in an effort to staunch the tears that threatened to erupt. She hadn't realized until this moment how utterly defeated she'd been by Molly refusing to talk to her.

"She needs to see a professional," Dr. Grey said, his smooth deep voice filled with concern. "She's obviously traumatized and has chosen for whatever reason to stop speaking. It's called elective muteness. I can't tell you whether it's just a residual form of posttraumatic stress or if there's another logical reason why she's decided not to talk."

"What logical reason could there be?" she asked.

"It doesn't have to be logical to you or me, just to Molly. And I don't know. What I do know is that she needs to be in therapy immediately."

Haley leaned back in the chair and released a sigh. "Whatever it takes to get her well. Whatever it takes to get us through all this."

He nodded and pulled a notepad from his shirt pocket. "I'll give you the phone number of a colleague of mine, Dr. Jerry Tredwell. He's excellent, especially working with children."

"Couldn't you do it? I mean, you've already seen her once. You're a psychologist. Why can't you do her therapy?" She liked him, and even though she'd only known him for about ten minutes, she already trusted him.

"I don't see patients."

"Couldn't you make an exception in this case?"

That gorgeous smile curved his lips but he shook his head. "You'll like Dr. Tredwell." He handed her the piece of paper with the phone number. "I'll give him a call and make sure he understands how important it is to get Molly in right away."

He stood, and she had the crazy impulse to throw her arms around his neck, to beg him not to leave just yet. She had absolutely nobody to talk to, nobody to help her through this ugliness that had become her life.

He seemed to sense something of what she felt. He smiled again, his eyes so kind she felt that familiar wobble of emotion in the pit of her stomach.

"You'll be fine, Haley," he said. With those words he left the office and she was once again alone.

Grey stepped out of the interview room and walked down to the break room, which at the moment was empty. He walked over to the coffee and poured himself a cup, his thoughts on the woman he'd just left.

It had been a very long time since any woman had affected Grey on any level, but something about Haley Lambert made him realize it had been too long since he'd had the pleasure of a woman's company.

She'd sparked something inside him the moment he'd stepped into the room. He'd always been a sucker for blondes, but it was more than just the color of her hair. She had ignited something inside him he'd thought long dead. He just wasn't sure what exactly it was about her.

Her pretty face had worn lines of stress, but she'd held herself together remarkably well. Still, he'd been able to feel the grief that emanated from her and sense a simmering terror just beneath the surface, a terror he understood.

The unexpected, violent death of a loved one stripped you down to the bones, took you to a place of utter aloneness, of sheer terrifying emotion.

Grey knew all about that place. He'd lived it. He'd breathed it.

It was why he didn't practice anymore.

Haley looked up as the door of the interview room opened once again. The tall, handsome dark-haired man who entered stopped short, his face paling at the sight of her.

"Jesus . . . you look just like her." He shook his head, one quick shake as if to steady himself. "Sorry." He held out a hand. "I'm Detective Frank Marcelli. You must be Haley."

She stood and grasped his hand. He held hers tight. "My wife and kids . . . we all live next door to Monica. She was a terrific person, a great mother." He finally released her hand as Detective Tolliver came back into the room.

"Ah, I see you two have met. Did Dr. Grey come in to talk to you?"

"Yes, he gave me the name of a psychologist to contact." She folded the piece of paper with the number on it and put it in her purse.

"I was just telling Haley that I live next door." Marcelli looked at her once again and his brown eyes burned with the fervor of a man possessed. "We're going to get the bastard. I promise you we aren't going to rest until whoever killed Monica is behind bars." Haley nodded, oddly comforted by the fervent zeal she saw in his dark eyes. "How's Molly?" he asked as he gestured for her to sit once again.

"Actually, I was planning on seeing her again in just a little while." She looked at Tolliver. "I thought you might want to be there."

Marcelli's eyes darkened with obvious torment. "Poor little kid," he said. "She must be terrified. She's best friends with my daughter, Adrianna, and the two girls were always back and forth between the houses."

Haley looked at him thoughtfully. "Maybe you

should come with us to see her. She'd probably feel more comfortable with you than with me. I mean, honestly, I don't even know her that well." She was embarrassed by the admission but figured they needed to know the real score.

"Maybe that's a good idea," Tolliver said to Marcelli. "You go with Haley to see Molly and I'll try to finish up those neighbor interviews."

Haley looked at him with interest. "Do you have a suspect?"

Tolliver quickly shook his head, his bald pate gleaming in the light overhead. "No, just some follow-up questions for the people in the area of your sister's home."

"One of the men in the cul-de-sac went out of town the afternoon of the murder. We haven't been able to interview him yet," Marcelli added.

"Here's the card of that cleaning service," Tolliver said. "And if you can't break through with Molly today, then I would recommend that you take Dr. Grey's advice and get her in to see somebody as soon as possible."

He leaned back in his chair and drew a hand across his lower jaw. "I'll be honest with you. At the moment we don't have much on this case except for the possibility that your niece saw or heard something. Unless she talks, we don't have a lead to follow or a chance in hell of breaking this open."

Marcelli looked at his partner in surprise and Tolliver grimaced. "Well, you know it's true," he said defensively. "We need that little girl to talk."

He leaned forward across the table and she could smell the scent of stale coffee wafting from his breath. "So far we've managed to keep it from the press that there was a possible eyewitness to the crime, but I don't know how long it might be before some nosy reporter finds somebody who might talk."

Haley's heart beat an unsteady rhythm. "So, is Molly in danger?"

"We don't believe so," Marcelli replied. "If the killer knew she was there, then we wouldn't have found her alive under the bed. As long as we can keep her under wraps, she should be safe."

Haley's head momentarily spun. She hadn't even considered the possibility that Molly might be in danger. But somewhere out there was a killer, and if that person discovered that a witness had been left behind, then Molly wouldn't just be a traumatized little girl. She'd be a loose end that needed to be addressed. Permanently.

A few minutes later she sat on the passenger side of Frank's car. "Tell me about Molly," she said as he pulled away from the police station. "You mentioned that she spent a lot of time at your house."

"What do you want to know?"

Haley frowned and stared out the passenger window. "Everything. Anything you can tell me. What she likes, what she doesn't like." She turned to look at him. "I haven't been around her much. What kind of kid is she? Tell me anything that will help me with her."

He shrugged. "I guess she's a pretty typical eight-year-old girl. Even though she was at my place a lot, I didn't spend a lot of time with her. Angie . . . Angela, my wife, would be able to answer you better than I can."

She tamped down an edge of frustration. "Then tell me about your daughter. Adrianna, didn't you say that was her name?" Maybe if she knew about Molly's best friend, she would learn something about Molly.

At the mention of his daughter's name all of his features seemed to soften. "She loves clothes and makeup, but still plays with dolls. Sometimes she loves to cuddle and sometimes she insists she's too big for such nonsense. She's smart and silly at the same time. She and her little sister are the reasons I get up in the mornings."

He flashed her an apologetic smile. "I guess that doesn't help you much. The one thing I can tell you about Molly is that she's really smart and she's a really good kid. Your sister was doing a terrific job in raising her."

"That's what scares me," she confessed. "I'm afraid that I'm going to take this smart, good kid and within a couple of years she'll be a neurotic teenager throwing up after each meal and popping antidepressants because I royally screwed things up."

He pulled into the driveway of the Roberts home, cut the engine and turned to look at her. "You know, if you're really worried about her, then whether she talks today or not, you should make an appointment with whoever Dr. Grey recommended for you. Get her some therapy."

Haley wondered if it wouldn't be a better idea to make an appointment with somebody and get herself some therapy.

Chapter 6

It promised to be a difficult day.

Haley stood in front of the bathroom mirror in her motel room and stared at her reflection. If she'd been in Las Vegas she would have been in bed until noon on a Wednesday. Tuesday nights were ladies' nights at Joey's Lounge and Haley always worked the late shift, not getting back to her apartment until after five in the morning.

But today wasn't a day to stay in bed. Today was the day she would bury her sister, but first she and Molly had an appointment with Dr. Jerry Tredwell, the therapist Dr. Greyson Banes had recommended.

Over the past couple of days she'd found herself thinking about the hunky consultant she'd met at the police station. Of course, thinking about Dr. Grey was much more comforting than thinking about the arrangements for a funeral.

The black slacks and gray blouse she wore seemed to reflect the dismal pall that had taken over her life, her very spirit, although each time she saw Molly she tried to be upbeat and cheerful, thinking that was what the grieving little girl needed most.

The past two days had been busy ones. Monica's lawyer had contacted her to let her know that Monica had a will on file. Haley shouldn't have been surprised that Monica had been as efficient in preparing for her death as she'd been in living her life.

She'd left all her worldly possessions to Molly and to Haley and had also left detailed instructions for her funeral.

Haley had not only taken care of those details, but first thing Monday morning she'd also hired the service to take care of the house. As of noon today the house would be ready, and Haley was checking out of Lazy Ray's that morning with the intention of moving into the house until she figured out what came next.

She assumed there would be people at the funeral who would want to congregate somewhere afterward, so she hoped the house was ready for friends and neighbors who wanted to mourn her sister.

Each day she'd gone to the Roberts house and visited with Molly, who still hadn't uttered a sound. She spent most of Haley's visits staring at the floor, her little shoulders hunched forward as if in preparation for another blow. Frank had even tried to get her to talk, but Molly wasn't having anything to do with him either.

The investigation into Monica's death had stalled and it seemed that all hope of anything breaking loose was in Dr. Jerry Tredwell's hands.

She turned away from the bathroom mirror and checked her wristwatch. It was time to go. She and Molly had a nine o'clock appointment. The funeral was set for three that afternoon and Haley had never dreaded anything more in her life.

She'd take Molly to her mother's funeral, then return the little girl to the Robertses. She didn't want Molly at the house for the aftermath of the funeral. She wanted everything right when she brought Molly home. If and when she brought Molly home.

As she left Lazy Ray's parking lot she thought about how much she hoped the psychologist was not only able to help Molly, but would have some answers to some pertinent questions for her as well. She wanted some professional help to make the decisions that needed to be made concerning what was best for Molly.

Selma opened her front door with the usual smile and small shake of her head to indicate that nothing had changed with Molly overnight.

Molly greeted Haley with the same solemn gaze she'd had for the past four days. There was no welcome and no rejection, just a weary resignation on her little features.

"You ready to go?" Haley asked. Molly nodded. This was the first time she and Molly would be completely alone and she wished she could read Molly's thoughts. Was she afraid to be with Haley? Was she afraid to leave this house? It was impossible to tell by looking at her pretty but placid features.

Haley had left it to Selma to explain to Molly that she was going to see a nice man who was just going to talk with her. "Maybe we can get some pizza or something after you talk to Dr. Tredwell and before the funeral," she said once they were in the car and headed for the office in downtown Kansas City. She didn't expect a reply and didn't get one.

Molly stared out the passenger window and Haley gripped the steering wheel more tightly. She felt no more connected to the little girl than she had on the day she'd arrived in Pleasant Hill.

"Or if you don't like pizza we could go to Mc-Donald's and get one of those happy thingies," Haley said. Wouldn't it be nice if a Happy Meal really could make Molly happy again? If Haley thought it would work, she'd buy Molly a dozen of the special sacked meals with the surprises inside.

Immediately after making the suggestion Haley wanted to kick herself. No Happy Meal from Mc-Donald's could take away the trauma of going to your mother's funeral.

Haley chattered the entire thirty-minute drive to downtown, hoping to elicit some sort of response from her niece. She talked about the weather and how nice the Robertses seemed to be. She talked about what she'd had for breakfast and how much she loved fast food.

All the while Molly remained rigidly straight in the passenger seat, her gaze focused out the side window. Haley sighed in frustration and finally fell silent as they entered the downtown area.

Dr. Jerry Tredwell's office was located just off Broadway in an eight-story steel and glass building. She lucked out and found a parking space on the street a block away. Haley fed the meter enough quarters to give them a little over an hour. Then together she and Molly took off walking.

As they walked the block, Molly kept her hands in her jeans pockets, her shoulders hunched forward: a tiny island alone in a sea of grief and fear.

In the time that Haley had been in town Molly

hadn't reached for her again since that first desperate hug they had shared. It was as if she knew not to depend on Haley.

Dr. Tredwell's office was on the seventh floor. They entered a small waiting room and a middle-aged receptionist smiled a greeting. "I have some forms for you to fill out," she said, and handed Haley a clipboard with several sheets of paper attached.

As Haley sat in one of the chairs to fill out the required forms, Molly sat next to her with a children's magazine in her lap.

It took exactly two minutes for frustration to well up in Haley as she tried to fill in the blanks to questions that were difficult to answer, questions about changes in behavior, schoolwork and social play of the little patient.

Once again she was struck by all the things she didn't know about Molly. What did she like to do in her spare time? What kind of student was she? Did she wet the bed? Have nervous habits? How was her appetite?

She filled out the forms as best she could, then returned them to the receptionist. As they waited to be called back to see the doctor, Haley looked around the room with interest.

At least the office gave the aura of success. The chairs were cushioned and covered in a dark cranberry cloth material that looked rich and was complemented by the soft beige walls. Pastoral scenes in thick gold frames hung in a grouping.

Haley suspected most people would find it a soothing room, but she was nervous as hell. More than once Monica had said that Haley should see a therapist to find out why she couldn't make a commitment to anyone, why she indulged in fleeting superficial relationships not only with lovers, but with friends as well.

But the last thing Haley wanted was some stranger poking around in her head. She was doing this for Molly, because she obviously needed more help than Haley could give, but she wasn't about to open herself up for being analyzed.

"Dr. Tredwell will see you now," the receptionist said, then opened the door that separated the waiting room from the mysterious inner office where the doctor practiced his head-shrinking.

The receptionist led them down a long hallway. They came to a room with glass windows. Inside the room was a child-sized table and chairs and shelves of toys. "Molly, honey, why don't you play in here for a few minutes while your auntie visits with the doctor," the receptionist said and opened the door to the room.

Molly nodded, her gaze meeting neither Haley's nor the receptionist's. She went directly to the small table and sat, not showing an interest in any of the toys or books on the shelves.

"Don't worry, I'll keep an eye on her," the receptionist said, then pointed to a second door down the hall. "Dr. Tredwell is waiting for you."

Haley assumed her conversation with the doctor would be brief, but that didn't make her dread any less intense. All she wanted was for him to fix Molly so the cops would be able to arrest the person who had killed Monica.

The door was closed and when she knocked a deep voice bid her to come in. When she entered she was surprised to discover the office was like any other she'd ever been in. No traditional analyst's couch, no hypnosis tools or new age crystals, nothing but an office that could have belonged to a bookkeeper or a stockbroker.

Dr. Jerry Tredwell got up from his chair behind his desk and held out a hand in greeting. He was a tall, lanky older man with curly gray hair that fell almost to his shoulders and wide brown eyes that held both warmth and curiosity.

"Ms. Lambert, it's nice to meet you."

"It's nice to meet you too." She gave his hand a perfunctory shake.

"Please." He gestured her into a chair across from his desk. He waited until she sat, then returned to his chair behind the desk. "I understand you've had a loss in your family."

For the next few minutes Haley told him about Monica's murder, Molly's silence and the need for somebody to help Molly gain her voice again.

He listened, and nodded, and took notes. Occasionally he'd ask a question, but for the most part he simply listened as she chronicled everything that had happened since she'd arrived in Pleasant Hill.

"Why don't I have a little conversation with Molly," he said when she'd finished.

"Good luck with that," she replied dryly.

He smiled and she thought it might just be a smile of condescension. "Conversation doesn't always have to be verbal." He stood and gestured toward the door.

Haley preceded him out of the office and back into the hallway. "The room where Molly is right now has windows that allow the people on the outside to see in, but she can't see out. Although I don't allow parents or others in while I'm conducting a session with a patient, I encourage you to watch."

Haley nodded. She assumed the viewing was as much for his own protection as that of his little patients. In the litigious society in which they lived, a male doctor of any kind alone with young girls or boys was just asking for problems.

As they approached the room where Molly waited, Haley saw that a chair had been placed in front of the window so she could sit and watch in comfort.

"Usually I work for about an hour, but with the younger children it's often shorter sessions." He gestured her toward the chair, then went into the glass-enclosed room where Molly still sat at the little table, looking as if she hadn't moved a muscle since she'd been led into the room.

Haley sat in the chair and watched as the doctor greeted the little girl. Although she couldn't hear a word that was being said, she noted that Dr. Tredwell's features held a softness that had been absent before.

Molly looked at him as he spoke to her. She nodded several times, then got up and went to the shelves. She grabbed a box of crayons and sheets of paper and returned to her seat.

As she withdrew first one crayon, then another, from the box and applied them to the paper in front of her, Dr. Tredwell continued to talk to her.

Haley had never met a psychologist in her life, but in the last three days she'd met two. Her thoughts drifted to the other one, Dr. Grey Banes.

It was crazy. She'd only spoken with him for a

few minutes, but since that time she hadn't been able to get him out of her head. Those kind, gorgeous eyes of his had pulled her in, made her want to know him better, somehow had made her feel safe, for at least a minute or two.

Or maybe she hadn't been able to get him out of her head because for just a moment he'd made her feel decidedly unsafe. As he'd spoken to her, she'd caught his gaze giving her the once-over, looking at her not as a victim, but as a woman.

She frowned and focused her attention back to the glass room, consciously dismissing thoughts of the police consultant from her mind.

The tension that had ridden Molly's features, that had kept her rigid and taut, seemed to fade away as she colored. The tip of her tongue moved back and forth across her upper lip as she worked.

A wave of grief stabbed Haley as she remembered Monica used to do the same thing when in deep concentration. *Oh, Monica, I can't do this. How could you leave me alone with your daughter? How am I supposed to do all the right things for her, all the things you would have done?*

She pulled on a strand of her hair, a nervous habit that used to drive her mother crazy. "You'll be bald before you're thirty," her mother had often said when Haley had been a young teenager.

"Maybe I should just shave my head bald now," Haley had replied defiantly.

Her mother had stared at her in horror, a frequent look on her face whenever she dealt with Haley. "Don't you dare do such a thing. If you shave off even one strand of hair you'll be grounded until you're twenty-one."

A fierce longing for her mother filled her. Ann Lambert and her youngest daughter had rarely seen eye to eye on anything. They had disagreed with each other on every topic, from the appropriate dress for school to what food constituted a healthy meal.

Even though their relationship had been stormy, Haley had never doubted her mother's love. How she wished her mother were here now to tell her what to do.

Even though Haley had never listened to her mother before, she would have listened now.

Dr. Tredwell worked with Molly for about forty minutes. Then he left the room and walked into the hallway where Haley stood and greeted him with a worried frown. "You didn't get her to talk." It was a statement, not a question.

"I didn't try to force her," he replied and gestured for her to go back to his office. When they reached the office he once again gestured her into the chair, then sat at the desk, Molly's drawings in front of him.

"I know how important it is that Molly talk about what she might know about her mother's murder, but my main concern at the moment is Molly's well-being," he said. "She's fragile and I don't want to push. It's important that I build some trust with her and that takes time."

"How much time?" Haley asked.

"I can't answer that. Psychotherapy isn't an exact science. It takes as long as it takes. I asked Molly to draw pictures of the three things she missed most in the last week." He held up the first drawing. "This is the first one she drew."

Haley leaned forward and took the paper from him. Her heart squeezed so tight it forced the air out of her. Her fingers trembled as she held the paper. "Her mommy," she said softly. There was no mistaking what the picture depicted.

He showed her the second drawing. "I'm assuming that's her home?" It was a picture of a white ranch house with a bright red door.

"Yes, yes, it's the house."

"And this is the third picture she drew." He handed her the final drawing of a big tree with a tree house nestled amid the branches.

"It's in the backyard," she said. "My father built the tree house for Monica and me when we were kids." She handed him the three drawings.

He placed them in a file folder, then leaned back in his chair. "You mentioned you were staying in a motel and Molly is in foster care. I think it's in her best interest for you to get her out of foster care as quickly as possible. What are your plans?"

"That's part of why I'm here. I was hoping you could tell me what my plans should be." She fought the impulse to reach up and grab a piece of her hair.

"My recommendation would be that what Molly needs more than anything at the moment is stability and routine. It's obvious from the drawings that she misses her home. What's the status of the house?"

"It's now in my possession. I had a cleaning crew come in and . . . uh . . . take care of things."

"So you could move Molly back into the house at any time."

Haley stared at him. "But would that be a good idea? I mean, she was there when her mother was brutally murdered."

"Be that as it may, she indicated to me that she misses her friends, she misses her room. She wants to go back to school. I think the best thing for her right now is to get back into the environment where she feels safe, and despite what happened to her mother she wants to be home."

"Then I'll bring her home," Haley said, fighting against the whisper of terror that threatened to take hold. "Tomorrow. I'll get her home tomorrow."

"Good, and make an appointment with Sherry for tomorrow afternoon. We can discuss how the transition went." Dr. Tredwell stood in obvious dismissal and Haley got up as well. "Structure, that's what all children need," he said.

Terrific, Haley thought. The one thing Molly needed most in her life was the one thing Haley had never managed to have in her own life.

Chapter 7

It should be raining. As Monica was lowered into the ground Haley wanted the sky to blacken and rain to pelt down. She wanted God to weep the tears she found difficult to release.

Instead of rain the sun shone bright in a cloudless blue sky. Birds sung sweet hymns from the nearby trees and the air was filled with the scent of flowers.

She was astonished by the turnout. There must have been fifty or sixty people in attendance. Names and faces blurred together as Haley and Molly were met in sorrow.

Despite the crowd, she'd never felt so alone and her heart ached for Molly who seemed equally alone. The little girl stood next to Haley, crying without a sound. Her quiet tears ripped at Haley's heart more deeply than hysterical sobs could ever do.

It was difficult to find comfort in the hugs of well-meaning strangers, in the sorrow of people she'd never met before in her life. And it was difficult to give comfort to Molly, who stood stiff and silent beside her.

The preacher did a wonderful job, speaking eloquently about Monica's service to the church and her community. He not only talked of the loss of Monica and how many lives she had touched, but also encouraged everyone to pray for strength for those Monica had left behind.

The tears that had never been far from the surface for so many days seemed trapped in a deep place inside her, a place that today, of all days, she couldn't access. She endured the ceremony with the familiar numbness that had consumed her in the hours just after learning of her sister's death.

After the ceremony she was surprised to see Dr. Grey Banes walking toward where she and Molly stood. Despite her grief and the somberness of the occasion, a small spark of pleasure swept through her at the sight of him.

"Haley." He nodded a greeting to her, then bent down to Molly. "Hey, Molly. Remember me? Dr. Grey?"

She raised her face to look at him, her cheeks still shiny from her silent tears. She nodded, a faint little movement of her head.

"I know this is tough, but you're a very brave little girl," he said, then straightened and looked at Haley. "How are you?"

"I'm hanging in there," she replied. She tried not to notice how handsome he looked in a somber black suit and a white shirt.

Molly walked over to a nearby stone bench and sat and stared down at her hands clasped in her lap. "How's she doing?" he asked.

"The same. We saw Dr. Tredwell this morning. He said it's going to take time to break through to her. He's recommended that I get Molly home as soon as possible."

"Are you taking her back to the house when you leave here?"

She shook her head. "No, I didn't want to do it knowing that there might be all kinds of people there. My plan is to bring her home around noon tomorrow." She was surprised to hear her voice tremble slightly. "I'm terrified at the very thought," she admitted. "I called Dr. Tredwell right before the funeral to see if maybe he'd be available to be at the house when I bring her home, but he has patients all day."

Grey hesitated a moment and looked over at Molly, then back at Haley. "I could be there," he said. "Not in any official capacity," he hurriedly added. "But simply as support."

A rush of relief swept through her. "Really? You wouldn't mind?"

"As long as you understand I'm there strictly for support, not as a therapist or an officer of the court."

"I totally understand and I really appreciate it." Her words were an understatement. At least for the moment she didn't feel quite as alone as she had before. "I need to give you my address."

She fumbled with her purse to find a pen and paper, but he placed a hand on her arm to stop her. "I'll get it from Tolliver." She felt the heat of his touch through the silk of her blouse, felt instantly bereft as he dropped his hand back to his side.

"Haley."

She turned to see Officers Tolliver and Marcelli approaching her, both clad in dark suits and grim expressions.

"Why don't I go sit with Molly so you can speak to the two detectives," Grey said. He greeted the two officers, then walked over to the bench and sat beside Molly.

"You didn't have to come today," she said to the two men. "It wasn't necessary. I'd rather you be working the case than be here."

"Actually, we are working the case by being here." Tolliver rocked back on his heels and looked at the dispersing crowd.

"It's not uncommon for the guilty party to show up at the funeral of the victim," Frank said.

Haley looked at him in surprise. "What kind of a monster could kill her so viciously, then come here and pretend to grieve?"

"A smart one," Tolliver replied. "If what we believe is true and Monica was killed by somebody she knew, then it's possible that person was here."

Haley gazed around as a chill walked up her spine. "Did you see anything suspicious? Did anyone do or say anything that might have given you a clue?"

Frank appeared dismayed. "No." He straightened and smiled as a slightly plump, attractive dark-haired woman approached them. "Haley, this is my wife, Angela. Angie, this is Monica's sister."

Angela Marcelli reached out for one of Haley's hands and grabbed it tightly, her large brown eyes misting with tears. "I've heard so much about you. Monica talked about you all the time." She dropped Haley's hand and instead hugged her tight. "I don't know what I'm going to do without her. She was one of my very best friends."

The hug lasted too long and for a moment Haley

felt as if Angela was sucking the very air from her lungs.

"Honey," Frank said with an embarrassed tone. "I think you're choking her to death."

Angela instantly dropped her arms and stepped back. "I'm sorry," she exclaimed and pulled a tissue from her purse to dab her eyes. "I just can't believe we're here and she's gone. She was such a wonderful friend and neighbor. I don't know what I'm going to do without her. If there's anything I can do for you, anything at all, you just have to call. You know I'm right next door."

Angela looked over at Molly, who sat next to Grey on the stone bench. "Poor little thing. I just can't imagine what she's been through."

"Are you coming to the house?"

"Of course. I'll see you there." With an audible sniff and another dab at her eyes, Angela touched her husband's arm, then turned and walked away.

Tolliver glanced over to Grey and Molly. "You had an appointment this morning with a therapist. How did it go?"

"Okay, but if you were hoping for a miracle where Molly talking is concerned, then I can tell you miracles seem to be in short supply."

"He didn't get her to say anything?" Tolliver's voice held his obvious disappointment.

"No, and he told me it's going to take time. He thinks Molly isn't going to talk until she feels safe again, until she has some stability back in her life."

Stability. God, that word terrified Haley.

"Then we'll have to do what we can without her," Tolliver said, although it was obvious he wasn't pleased. A new wave of depression swept over

Haley as she realized once again that without Molly they had nothing.

Molly had liked Dr. Tredwell, but she really liked Dr. Grey. He had pretty blue eyes and when he smiled at her he made her feel a little bit warm inside. And he didn't even try to make her talk.

She knew everyone wanted her to tell about that morning. That awful morning. But she didn't want to talk about it. She didn't even want to think about it. If she tried real hard she could almost forget the sound of her mommy's screams.

Shush, Lollipop. Don't move. Don't make a sound. She forced her thoughts away from her mommy's last words.

She looked over to where her Aunt Haley was talking to the two men. She wasn't sure what she thought about her aunt. Her mommy used to say that for a smart woman Aunt Haley didn't have the common sense that God gave a toad. Molly wasn't sure if that was good or bad. She didn't know how much common sense a toad had.

Molly was scared. She knew her mommy was dead and wasn't ever going to come back again. Molly knew all about being dead. She'd had a hamster that had died last year and her mommy had said that Snuggles had gone to heaven to be with Molly's daddy, who was also there. Her mommy was in heaven now with Snuggles and with Daddy.

Molly's heart hurt.

Who was going to fix her waffles and use chocolate chips to make happy faces? Who was going to take her to Brownies and wake her up in the morning with kisses and hugs? Who was going to call her Lolly and just love her?

She knew everyone wanted her to talk. She knew everyone wanted her to remember what had happened in Mommy's bedroom. But she didn't want to remember. She couldn't remember because it scared her too much.

Besides, even though she knew her mommy was gone forever, sometimes late at night before she went to sleep she could hear her mommy whispering in her ear.

Shush, Lollipop, her mommy said. *Don't make a sound. It's not safe yet.*

And when Molly heard her mother's voice she knew that if she talked something bad would happen again.

Chapter 8

As Haley drove away from the Roberts house after saying goodbye to Molly she found herself marveling at how many people had attended the funeral. Monica had apparently touched a lot of lives.

And who will come to your funeral when you die? she asked herself. The answer was definitely depressing. Other than a few drunken regulars at Joey's Lounge who might raise a glass to her memory, she could think of nobody who would mourn her passing.

She pulled into the driveway, glad that no other cars were parked out front, although she knew that situation would change within the next hour.

She'd been disappointed that Grey had said he wouldn't be coming to the house, that he had a prior engagement. She told herself it was ridiculous to be disappointed over a man she barely knew. But something about Grey Banes attracted her like no other man had in a very long time.

At least he would be here tomorrow when she brought Molly home. Even though he wasn't

Molly's therapist, he'd be here with Haley if Molly had some sort of a meltdown.

Maybe his attractiveness came from the fact that he was the only person who was offering support. Maybe it was nothing more than her grasping on to anyone who had eyes as kind as Grey's.

She stared at the house. She hoped it was ready, that the cleaning crew she'd hired had done their job. She should have come by earlier to check, but there hadn't been enough time with Molly's morning appointment and then the funeral.

She got out of the car and headed inside, wishing she could change into a pair of sweats, curl up on the sofa and weep for the next ten years. Other than her brief breakdown on the first day with Tolliver, she had yet to weep the tears that filled her heart.

She stepped through the front door and was greeted by the scent of new paint and furniture polish. A quick glance around let her know that the crew had done what they'd been paid to do. There appeared to be no crime scene left, at least not from what she'd seen so far.

In the years since their mother's death, Monica had made significant changes to the house. The frilly, cluttered look their mother had loved had been replaced by a soothing style of clean, elegant lines.

Haley picked up a cobalt blue vase with a delicate butterfly crest from one of the shelves of the entertainment center. The glass was cool to the touch and somehow calmed the nerves that flittered through her as she thought of the next couple of hours.

She remembered the day Monica had bought this

particular piece. She and Monica had been shopping at a nearby mall and had stumbled onto a little boutique that sold lamps and clocks and a large array of the Fenton glass in various colors and styles.

The saleslady in the store had explained to them that Fenton glass pieces were considered collectibles and known for beautiful colors and designs. Monica hadn't been thinking of starting a collection, but she fell in love with the soothing blue glass and had bought her first piece on the day the doctor had told her she was pregnant with Molly.

"I'll mark every momentous occasion in my child's life with a new piece," she had proclaimed.

And she had. There was a blue bell that had been bought for Molly's first smile, a bluebird of happiness for her first step. Monica had even bought a hurricane candle to commemorate Molly's first real audible fart. The two sisters had laughed themselves silly over that particular momentous occasion.

She carefully placed the vase back on the shelf, a lump of emotion growing big in her throat. She left the living room and walked down the hallway.

The first bedroom was Molly's, an explosion of pinks and oranges and lime greens. Fuzzy throw pillows shared space with stuffed animals on the bed. Books and dolls filled the shelves. The room was neat and tidy and Haley wondered if one of the last things Monica did in her life was straighten her daughter's room and neatly make the bed.

A bathroom was across the hall from Molly's room. Guest towels hung straight and a sleek beige soap dish held a fresh bar of soap.

The second bedroom was the one where Haley would stay, a guest room decorated in pastel colors. The last bedroom had been Monica's. Haley opened the door and stepped inside the empty room.

The scent of new paint and carpeting greeted her. She'd had the specialized cleaning crew remove the bed and dresser and pack away the personal items that had been in the room. There were several boxes in the closet, but most of the things had been stored in the basement.

The master bathroom still held her sister's things. The lump in her throat nearly choked her as she turned back and stared at the empty room, a room where her sister had slept and dreamed.

Haley reeled out of the room and slammed the door with enough force to raise the dead. Suddenly she was angry. She was as good and pissed off as she'd ever been in her life. She opened the door and slammed it again . . . and again . . . and again.

She only stopped when she realized the phone was ringing. She leaned with her back against the hallway wall and drew a deep breath to steady herself, to stuff down the anger that had exploded so unexpectedly, then hurried back into the living room.

She grabbed up the receiver of the cordless phone. "Hello?" she said.

"Whore." The voice was low and barely audible.

"Excuse me?" Surely she'd misunderstood. There was no reply, only an audible click that indicated the caller had hung up.

Haley replaced the receiver and sank down on the edge of the sofa. Had she really just been called a whore or had she not heard correctly? She didn't even know if the caller had been male or female: the voice had been sexless but filled with venom. She shook her head. Less than a week in town and already somebody thought she was a whore.

Before she had much of a chance to think further about the phone call, somebody knocked on the front door. The knocking fell silent, then began again, this time more loudly. Haley hurried toward the door and pulled it open to see Angela Marcelli.

"Haley." She bent down to pick up a large baking dish that she'd apparently set down so she could knock. "Lasagna," she said as Haley opened the door to allow her in.

She went directly toward the kitchen and Haley followed, just wanting this day to finally be over. Angela stopped short in the doorway and gazed around the tidy kitchen. "Honey, there's going to be lots of food brought in and lots of people eating. Do you have some paper plates? Napkins?"

Haley stared at her, a well of emotion once again knotting in her chest. She hadn't even thought about plates and utensils. Already it was beginning, the expectations and the failures.

"It's all right." Angela's dark eyes held a wealth of sympathy. She smiled. "I'm a Brownie leader, among other things. I have tons of paper plates and stuff at my house." She set the baking dish down on the table. "I'll be right back."

Haley frowned and looked around the kitchen. Surely she should do something to prepare for the onslaught of people she suspected would begin arriving at any moment.

Coffee. She could make coffee. She grasped on to the task, grateful to have something, anything to do to feel useful. The brew had just begun to fill the glass carafe when Angela reappeared carrying a large plastic bag.

"You sit, have a cup of that coffee and I'll take care of things," she said.

Haley did just that. It was a relief to let somebody else take over at least for a little while. And Angela seemed to be a take-charge kind of woman.

"I should have taken care of this," Haley said as Angela pulled plates and cups and plastic utensils from her bag.

"Nonsense, you've had other things to think about." She stacked all the items on the edge of the countertop.

"Monica would have remembered to have all this ready."

Angela flashed her a sympathetic smile. "Yes, she probably would have. Your sister was definitely efficient. We were alike in that way." She looked around the kitchen. "I think the best plan would be to lay out all the paper goods and utensils here on the countertop and leave the table for the food that comes in. Is that all right with you?"

Haley nodded, just grateful at the moment that she didn't have to make any decisions. She watched as Angela busied herself, once again noting that she was a pretty woman in a traditional Italian sense. Her olive skin was without blemish and her long dark hair framed her plump face. Her nose was a little big, but seemed a perfect fit with her large doelike eyes and full sensual lips.

"Your husband is nice. I'll bet he's a good detective," Haley said.

"He is. He's also a great dad and husband. Everyone loves Frank. I'm a lucky woman." She finished arranging things, then sat at the table opposite Haley. "Frank told me you're moving back in here. Does that mean Molly will be coming home?"

"I'm going to bring her home tomorrow," Haley replied.

Angela shook her head. "Poor kid. And she's still not talking?"

"Not a word." Haley took a sip of her coffee, then asked, "Do you know if Monica was seeing anyone?"

"Seeing anyone? You mean like dating?" Haley nodded. "No, as far as I know your sister wasn't dating, although it wasn't from lack of opportunity."

"What do you mean?"

Angela's full lips curved into another smile. "Your sister was pretty, had a good figure and was single. She was always getting asked out to dinner or for a drink or something, but to my knowledge she never went."

The ringing doorbell interrupted any other conversation they might have shared. For the next three hours Haley scarcely had time to think as the house filled with people.

In those hours she began to put faces with names and figure out what part they had played in her sister's life. Angela helped, staying close to her and occasionally whispering a tidbit of gossip in her ear.

"Richard and Kim Brown," Angela said as a new couple entered the fracas. "They live in the brick house at the end of the cul-de-sac. He's an attorney and she's a nurse. They have a fifteen-year-old son named Dean who's in trouble all the time."

"What kind of trouble?" Haley asked.

Angela shrugged. "Mostly teenage stuff, breaking curfew, underage drinking, smoking pot." Her eyes flashed darkly. "Frank says he's really not such a bad kid, but he definitely gives me the creeps."

"Haley, can I talk to you for just a minute?"

Haley turned away from Angela to see Grant Newton, a man who had the distinction of being the cul-de-sac's only single male.

Haley guessed the short man was in his late forties, although his hair was almost completely gray. His suit was slightly ill fitting, as if it had been bought when he'd weighed twenty or thirty pounds less than he did now.

He placed a hand on her arm and led her out of the kitchen and to a corner in the living room where they could speak more privately. "You probably know by now that the police have interviewed me several times concerning your sister's death."

Haley realized he must be the man Frank Marcelli had mentioned who had left town on the day of Monica's murder. Newton frowned and shifted from foot to foot in obvious discomfort. "Look, you might as well know . . . I asked Monica out several times, but she turned me down each time. I guess the cops think maybe I had something to do with her death because I didn't like her rejection."

He flashed Haley a smile that exposed pointy, unattractive eyeteeth. "If I killed every woman who rejected me, I'd leave a trail of dead women that would make Ted Bundy jealous." A small, almost girlish giggle escaped him.

Haley stared at him, unsure what to say, what he expected from her. He took a step closer. "I just wanted you to know that I'd never harm Monica and I sure as hell didn't kill her. You've got to believe me." He took her hand in his, his hot and sweaty.

At that moment Frank walked over and saved Haley from having to make any kind of reply. "Grant," he said and nodded his head to the man.

"Detective Marcelli." Grant bobbed his head in greeting and dropped Haley's hand. "Tough day."

"Yes, it is." Frank touched her shoulder. "You look like you could use something to eat," he said. It was an obvious rescue from an uncomfortable situation.

"Mr. Newton, it was nice meeting you," she murmured, then allowed Frank to lead her back into the kitchen.

"Thanks," she said to him as she grabbed a plate, then stared at the vast array of food on the table. She immediately set the plate back down. She wasn't really hungry. The brief conversation with Grant Newton had unsettled her.

Frank picked up the plastic plate and held it out to her. "You have to eat something."

Reluctantly she took the plate from him. "Thanks for the rescue. That was just too weird." She scooped up a spoonful of potato salad. "Is he still a suspect?"

Frank leaned against the cabinet and frowned thoughtfully. "Everyone is still a suspect."

She added a slice of ham to her plate, then looked at the detective. "Grant Newton doesn't look like a killer."

Frank smiled. He had a flirtatious smile, one that warmed his features and made him look wickedly charming. "And what exactly does a killer look like?"

"Oh, I don't know. I always thought that if somebody was capable of murder you'd be able to see a hint of that in their eyes, sense it in their behavior."

"That would certainly make my job a hell of a lot easier. Unfortunately in all the years of working as a cop, I've never arrested a killer who I thought looked like one."

Angela bustled into the kitchen and smiled at her husband and Haley. "You both doing okay?"

"I was just encouraging Haley to get something to eat," Frank replied.

"Absolutely, you need to keep up your strength for the days that lie ahead." She threw several dirty plastic plates into the garbage. "I think people are starting to leave."

Haley put down her plate. "Then I should go and stand at the door and thank them for coming."

The darkness of night had fallen by the time Haley shut the door after the last guest. Angela had offered several times to stay and help with the cleanup, but Haley had declined her offer.

The silence of the empty house was almost a relief as she locked the front door and went back into the kitchen to face the mess.

Funerals brought out the best in people, not only in offering grief, but in giving food to the bereaved. Although a ton of food had been consumed in the past several hours, a ton had been left behind.

She opened a cabinet to find a collection of Tupperware containers in every size, shape and color. It was another indication of how different she'd been from her sister. Haley's food storage containers consisted of old butter and whipped cream tubs.

It took her nearly an hour to store all the leftover food. Then she stood at the kitchen sink and hand washed the items that couldn't be thrown away.

Tomorrow at two she would be bringing Molly home. Was it the right thing to do? Was Dr. Tredwell right to believe that's what she needed? Thank God Grey would be here to help with the transition.

Too bad he couldn't be here 24/7 for the next month to help Haley with the transition from single, wild female to surrogate mom and caretaker.

She pulled a glass platter out of the soapy dishwater and rinsed it. She began to dry it as she looked out the window. She didn't know what was louder, the crash of the platter as she dropped it to the floor or her scream as her gaze met a pair of eyes staring in at her.

THE HUMMING WAS BACK.
INSIDE. IN THE MIDDLE OF THE BRAIN.
IRRITATING.
INCESSANT.
SHE LOOKED JUST LIKE HER SISTER.
THAT BLOND HAIR. BIG EYES.
JUST LIKE THE OTHER ONE.
THE HUMMING WAS BACK.
IT HAD STOPPED BEFORE, WHEN THE
KNIFE HAD SLASHED INTO MONICA'S
BODY.
IT HAD STOPPED WHEN HER BLOOD HAD
RUN RED.
THE HUMMING WAS BACK, BUT IT COULD
BE STOPPED.
JUST LIKE BEFORE.
SHE LOOKED JUST LIKE HER SISTER.
THE BITCH.

Chapter 9

"Could you tell if it was a man or a woman?" The uniformed police officer looked a little bit bored and a little bit irritated at having been called to the house on what he obviously considered a waste of his time.

"No, I just saw eyes. They were there a minute, then I screamed and they were gone." Haley stood on the front porch, her arms wrapped around herself as her gaze shot down the quiet, dark street.

Maybe it was the fact that her sister had been murdered in the house, or maybe it was that Haley had never felt so alone in her life, but the window peeper had shaken her to the core.

She had stumbled away from the sink and to the phone and dialed 911, not particularly pleased when it had taken nearly twenty minutes for the officer to show up.

In retrospect she realized she should have called Frank Marcelli, who could have been at her house in a matter of seconds, but when she'd grabbed the phone all she could think about was dialing the emergency number. She'd hoped that an army of police officers would respond instead of this single officer who looked bored.

"So you can't give me any kind of a description of the person you saw looking into your window?" the officer asked with a touch of impatience.

"I was in the light inside. He was in the dark outside. I'm sure he could give you a great description of me, but I couldn't see him."

"You're saying him. So you think it was a man?"

"Haley?" The porch light next door went on and Frank stepped outside. "Is everything all right?" He jogged the short distance between the houses and quickly introduced himself to the officer. "What's going on?"

"I had a peeper," she said. "I was drying dishes at the kitchen sink and looked up to see somebody looking into my window."

"Unfortunately, she couldn't tell if it was a man or a woman or anything else," the cop said.

"There have been several reports in this neighborhood of a window peeper," Frank said.

"I'll file the report, but there's not very much we can do without more substantial information. Is there anything else I can do for you tonight, Ms. Lambert?" the officer asked. Amazing how solicitous he had become when Frank had arrived on the scene.

"No, I guess that's it." What else could she say? That she wanted him to sit outside the house with his gun drawn for the rest of her natural life?

"Are you okay?" Frank asked as the officer headed back toward his car.

"I'm just a little freaked out." She tightened her arms around herself.

"Under the circumstances anyone would be a little freaked out," he replied.

She dropped her arms to her sides. "So, were you telling the truth? There have been other reports of peeping toms around here?"

"Yeah, even Angela had one a couple of weeks ago. She was watching television in the living room and glanced toward the window and saw somebody looking in."

Some of the frightened tension that had whipped through her began to relax a bit. "Do you have any idea who it might be?"

Frank frowned and his gaze went up the street toward the Browns' place. "I have my suspicions."

"And those suspicions run to a certain teenage kid named Dean?"

He looked at her once again and smiled. "I see somebody has been filling you in on the neighborhood personalities."

"Angela mentioned the Browns and their son earlier this evening."

"Dean also has a lot of friends who hang out at his house, one of whom might just be a little pervert trying to see a naked woman through a window. My recommendation would be to pull your shades at night."

He reached out and took her hand in his, a gesture that might have seemed presumptuous coming from anyone else but the cop next door. "Are you sure you're going to be all right? First night in the house and all."

"I'm fine. Really." She offered him a smile. "It helps to know a detective lives right next door."

His frown deepened and he dropped her hand.

"That sure as hell didn't help your sister." He raked a hand down his jaw. "I still can't believe what happened."

"You can't feel personally responsible for that," Haley said softly. She frowned as she remembered something else. "I also got a weird phone call earlier."

"Weird?"

"I answered the phone and I thought the person called me a whore, then hung up." Once again her gaze swept the area. Strange phone calls, peeping toms and a murder: this quiet cul-de-sac had begun to take on the characteristics of a horror film neighborhood.

"Frank? Is everything all right?" Angela's voice drifted across the yard.

"Everything is fine, Angie," Frank called back. "You have our phone number?"

Haley nodded. "Angela gave it to me earlier."

"Call if you need anything."

"Thanks, I will." She watched as he walked back to his house, the night shadows swallowing him up; then she went inside and carefully locked the door behind her.

It took her only minutes to finish up in the kitchen. She turned off all the lights and went into the guest bedroom. She carefully pulled the shades down tight and changed into an oversized T-shirt that had been left at her place by a former boyfriend. She hadn't particularly liked him by the end of their brief relationship, but she still loved his shirt for sleep.

The guest bedroom seemed to be the only room in the house that still looked as if it had been decorated by Ann Lambert. An old rocking chair sat in the corner and the double bed was the same one that Haley had grown up sleeping in.

As she sank into bed, the mattress lumps shifted to embrace her body in familiarity. Unexpectedly, exhaustion trumped tension and it was morning before Haley had time to wonder if she'd be able to sleep.

She opened her eyes to the sunshine that poured through the thin shades, and a glance at the clock jolted her awake. It was after ten already.

She hit the floor running for the shower. She had tons of things to do before bringing Molly home. The first and most important was she needed to return the rental car. Monica had a perfectly good vehicle parked in the garage and there was no sense in Haley keeping the rental.

A piece of leftover cake served as breakfast. Then she left the house and headed out. She was supposed to meet Grey at her place at twelve thirty. Before he'd left the funeral the day before she'd managed to talk him into going with her to get Molly from the Robertses and bring her back to the house.

She knew it was probably unusual for him to do such a thing and wondered what had prompted his offer. Not that she cared. She wasn't about to look a gift horse in the mouth.

At twelve fifteen she was back at the house, errands done and nervous tension making her fast-food lunch feel heavy in her stomach.

As she waited for Grey to arrive, she checked her reflection in the bathroom mirror. She brushed her hair and put on her lipstick and told herself she was insane to primp for a man who was probably just being kind because her sister had been murdered.

Torn between laughing and sobbing, she turned away from her reflection in disgust. It was a relief when the doorbell rang a moment later, bringing her self-recriminations to an abrupt end.

Her stomach started to flutter even before she opened the door. This man affected her on a level that had nothing to do with psychology or police work.

Haley loved men, loved the way they smelled, the way they felt. But when they started wanting to know what was going on in her head, when they began to look at her with a proprietary gaze, she kicked them to the curb. Ironic, of course, that she'd be attracted to a man whose very job was to learn what was going on inside people's heads. Maybe it was just a weird reaction to stress, this crazy attraction she felt.

Opening the door, she greeted him. "Grey. Come on in." As he stepped past her she caught the scent of him, clean and masculine with a hint of earthy cologne. The flutter in her stomach continued.

"How are you doing today, Haley?" he asked as they stepped into the living room.

"I'm fine, thank you."

He searched her face, those intelligent blue eyes of his seeming to peer into the depths of her. "Everything go all right after the funeral yesterday?"

Haley broke the eye contact. "As well as could be expected." She thought about telling him about the man peeping into her window, but then dismissed the idea.

She didn't really know this man. He'd merely offered to be here for her when they brought Molly home. He hadn't offered to be privy to her every thought, her entire life.

"Are you ready for this?"

"Probably not," she replied honestly.

He smiled. "If you'd answered any other way I would have doubted both your honesty and your grasp on reality."

"Yeah, well, I've never been a big fan of reality," she replied dryly. "Shall we go?" She pulled the keys from her purse and gestured toward the front door.

"Before we do, do you mind if I see Molly's room? I'm not trying to be intrusive, but I'd like to get a sense of her in case this doesn't go well."

Haley nodded and led the way down the hall to Molly's room. She stood at the doorway and watched as he walked around the room, his gaze seeming to take in every stuffed animal, every book and toy on the shelves.

"It's a nice room," he said.

"Molly was spoiled, but in a good way," she replied. The knot of emotion that had become a familiar companion pressed hard inside her chest. "As far as Monica was concerned the sun rose and set on Molly."

"That's the way it should be for every child," he replied. He stepped back out into the hallway and stopped as he saw the closed door at the end. "Is that where Molly was found after the murder?"

"Yeah, but I've had it all cleaned up. There's nothing in there now except a few boxes in the closet."

"I think it would be better if the door was left open. Terrible things can be imagined behind a closed one."

Haley nodded and walked down the hallway and opened the door. Avoiding the tree house out back had been relatively easy. How would she be able to avoid entering the master bedroom? One brought back memories of the sister she mourned; the other brought back memories of the only man she'd truly loved, the only man who had truly understood her.

"Let's get this over with," she said briskly, needing action to take away the press of uncomfortable emotions.

A few minutes later they were in Monica's car and headed for the Roberts place. "When is your next appointment with Dr. Tredwell?" he asked.

"This afternoon at four thirty."

"Good. So if there's any problems he'll be seeing her. He's good at what he does."

"He seemed okay," she replied.

"I understand you've been living in Las Vegas. What took you there?"

"The wind, a whim." She shrugged. "No real reason other than it was the last stop in a bunch of cities I've lived in over the years. The nice thing about Vegas is that you can have the flavor of dozens of other places just by visiting the strip."

"What did you do there? Showgirl?"

She laughed, flattered by the assumption; then on further thought she was slightly offended. Why hadn't he thought she might be a teacher or a high-powered corporate player? "Actually, I was a bartender. My . . . uh . . . assets weren't big enough to be a showgirl and I wasn't about to undergo plastic surgery so I could prance around on a stage half naked."

"I'll bet you were a good bartender," he observed.

"I was," she said with a touch of defiance. "There isn't a drink that I don't know how to make."

"But that's not what made you good. I'll bet you're great at listening to other people talk. Isn't that the mark of a really good bartender?"

"Definitely," she agreed. "But that's the mark of a good psychologist too." She flashed him a quick glance. "It must be interesting, being a consultant for the police department. Do you do that full-time?"

"No, part-time. I also teach at Maple Woods Community College. So, what do you plan to do now?"

Haley tightened her hands on the steering wheel. "To be honest, I haven't thought about it. I'm just taking it one minute at a time right now. I've got some money in savings and that, along with Monica's life insurance policy, makes it so I don't have to make any major decisions for a little while. Right now my priority is to get Molly mentally healthy."

"While you're working on that, don't forget your own mental health."

She flashed him a quick glance. "You aren't somehow analyzing me, are you?"

Again he smiled and she felt the power of that attractive gesture in a whirl of heat that suffused her. "Maybe a little," he replied.

She pulled to a stop in front of the Roberts home, then turned in her seat to stare at him. "Dr. Grey, according to my mother and my sister I should have been in therapy years ago. I'm rebellious, defiant and supposedly have issues with intimacy. But I like who I am. I'm not interested in getting fixed. Molly is the one who needs to get fixed."

Once again she had the feeling that those piercing blue eyes of his were seeing into her brain, finding secrets she didn't want told, assessing wounds that hadn't healed. "Let's get Molly home," he said and opened his car door.

As Haley got out of the car she eyed the handsome doctor with narrowed eyes. He was obviously good at what he did to be a consultant for the police department, but that didn't mean she wanted him doing any sort of therapy on her.

All thought of anything else fled as Selma Roberts greeted them. Molly sat on the sofa, a small suitcase at her feet. Haley's heart felt as if an iron vise squeezed it as she looked at her niece.

Molly seemed disconnected to her surroundings, so small and so alone, and it ached in Haley that Molly made no attempt to reach out or even make eye contact with her.

And why should she? Once again Haley wished she'd spent the last couple of years forming a real relationship with her niece instead of making small talk with strangers in a Vegas lounge.

"Hi, honey." Haley sat on the sofa next to Molly. "You remember Dr. Grey from yesterday?" Molly looked up at Grey and half raised a hand in greeting.

"Hi, Molly," he said. "I see you have your bag all packed. Are you ready to go home?"

She nodded and stood. Selma walked over to the child and gently swiped a strand of her pale blond hair away from her face. "We enjoyed having you here with us, Molly. I'm sure your aunt is going to take very good care of you."

For the first time since they had walked in Molly looked at Haley, and in the depths of those childish eyes Haley saw doubt.

"We're going to be just fine," Haley said with more confidence than she felt. "Thank you, Selma, for taking such good care. And now I guess we'll be on our way."

Molly picked up her small suitcase and together she, Haley and Grey left the house. Haley stored the suitcase in the trunk while Molly got into the backseat and buckled up. Grey slid into the passenger seat.

Haley slammed the trunk, her heart taking on an unsteady rhythm. For the first time since those officers had appeared at the door of her Las Vegas apartment, the consequences of Monica's death hit home.

She wasn't just taking Molly home for a visit. For at least the next ten years Molly would be dependent on her for every need. Haley couldn't get bored or frustrated and just pick up and leave. Of all the things she'd done in her life, this was the one thing she didn't want to screw up.

She was grateful to Grey, who kept up a running monologue as they drove back to the house. Molly, as expected, remained silent.

Grey seemed to be soft-spoken but she sensed an energy in him, a hint of something slightly dark that was as appealing to her as his low, melodic voice.

She sure as hell hoped Dr. Tredwell was right about Molly wanting to be home. She pulled into the driveway, half expecting Molly to take one look at the house and run screaming from the neighborhood.

But as they all got out of the car the only indication that Molly felt anything was the fact that she reached for Grey's hand as Haley got her suitcase from the trunk.

As Haley saw Molly take Grey's hand, she felt the strain of rejection deep in her soul. Her niece would rather hold on to a relative stranger than reach out to her.

"You squeeze my hand if you feel uncomfortable, okay?" Grey said to the child as Haley unlocked the front door.

Molly nodded and together they all stepped inside. Almost immediately Molly dropped Grey's hand and walked down the hallway. The two adults followed her.

She went first into her bedroom where she walked around, touching items here and there as if to assure herself that the room was exactly as she'd left it.

She then left her bedroom and walked down the hallway to Monica's room. Haley's stomach clenched as Molly stood in front of the open door and stared inside.

What horrors were replaying in Molly's mind? She wanted to scoop Molly up in her arms and carry her away from the visions that must haunt her as she stared into the place where her mother had died.

She started forward, but Grey touched her arm to hold her back. Molly stood for what seemed like an eternity in the threshold and when she finally turned to face them, tears streamed down her cheeks.

"Oh, honey." Haley fell to her knees in front of Molly and drew her into an embrace. For a long moment, Molly remained rigid in her arms. Then her warm little body melted into Haley and her arms wound around Haley's neck.

Haley held tight. *I can do this, Monica. Maybe I've never done anything else right in my life, but I promise that somehow, some way I'll do this right.*

Molly finally pulled away and wiped her eyes with the back of her hands, then drifted into her bedroom where she curled up on the bed and closed her eyes.

Grey motioned Haley away from the room and back into the living room. "She seemed to handle this all right," he said. "Her reactions were what I would consider normal. I think she'll be fine, but it's good you have an appointment for her with Dr. Tredwell later this afternoon."

"Thank God it seemed to go okay. If I put on a pot of coffee would you drink a cup?" she asked. She wasn't ready for him to leave. Not yet.

He smiled. "I never turn down a cup of coffee."

Together they went into the kitchen where Grey sat at the round oak table and Haley prepared the coffee. "When do you plan on getting her back into school?" he asked.

"I wanted to see how she'd do coming back here before I decided. Dr. Tredwell said he thought she missed school, missed her friends. I'll talk to him this afternoon and maybe I can have her back to school first thing Monday morning."

He nodded and glanced out the window. "Nice tree house."

Haley followed his gaze out the window. "My dad built it when Monica and I were kids. Three nights later he died in his sleep from a heart attack."

For a moment the only sound in the room was the gurgle of the coffee filling the pot. Haley stared at the tree house. "After he died, I couldn't go back up there. I tried a couple of times, but I'd get one step up the ladder and my heart would start to pound, my mouth would go dry and I couldn't catch my breath."

"Panic attack?"

She shifted her gaze back to him and nodded. "Yes. Thankfully I don't get them often. Anyway, Molly seems to have found the joy in the tree house that I never could find."

She joined him at the table as they waited for the coffee to brew. "Thank you for doing this today," she said. "I know this is not exactly business as usual for you. I'm sure you're a very busy man."

"Not as busy as I used to be. I retired from private practice two years ago and even working part-time teaching and for the police department, I still have time on my hands." He leaned back in the chair. "Have you ever been married, Haley?"

She blinked in surprise at the change of topic. "No, never even came close."

"Why is that?"

"Depends on who you ask. If you'd asked my sister that question she would have told you that I have commitment issues, that I never hang around long enough in one place to get close to anyone."

"Is that true?"

She narrowed her gaze. "Are you trying to analyze me again?"

He laughed. "Perhaps."

She got up from the table to pour the coffee. "What about you? Are you married?" She was far more comfortable with the conversation on him than on her. Even though he wore no ring, that didn't mean there wasn't a wife at home.

"I'm divorced."

"Any kids?" She set the mugs on the table.

"Thanks, and no."

She sat at the table once again. "What made you decide to go into psychology?"

"I knew early on that psychology was where I wanted to be. The workings of the human mind fascinate me. Always has."

"I'll bet you've seen some scary things in people's heads."

"Some," he agreed.

"Still, it must be rewarding too."

Those gorgeous eyes of his darkened and again she sensed something dark inside him. "Sometimes. It can also be heartbreaking."

"Ever seen a case like Molly's?"

He took a sip of the coffee, then set the cup back down. "Not specifically, no. But before you know it things will return to normal."

"I've never been so terrified in my life," Haley confessed. "I wouldn't know a normal life if one stepped up behind me and kicked me in the butt."

Grey laughed and for the first time she noticed the fine lines that radiated out from the corners of his eyes, lines that only added character and in-

creased his attractiveness. "I think you underesti-
mate yourself, Haley."

"I think you're underestimating how terrified I
am," she said in a burst of utter honesty. "I know
parenting is the most important job anyone can do,
but I don't know how to parent. I'm terrified I'm
going to screw this up and Molly will need therapy
for the rest of her life."

He leaned forward and smiled once again. "If
you're worried about screwing this up, then the
odds are good that you won't." His smile fell away
and a thoughtful frown creased his forehead. "You
have friends, Haley? Somebody you can talk to,
somebody who has kids of their own? Maybe someone who can give you advice on the daily care and
feeding of children?"

She wrapped her fingers around her cup. "No,
but there is the woman next door, Angela Marcelli.
Her husband is one of the detectives on Monica's
case. Oh, you probably know him. Frank Marcelli."
She offered him a wry smile. "Anyway, Angela is a
little too Stepford perfect for my taste, but I think
she'd be a friend if I let her, and she seems to be a
great wife and mother."

Grey finished his coffee, then pulled a small
notepad and a pen from his shirt pocket. "I'm going
to give you my home and cell phone numbers." He
wrote the numbers down, ripped off the piece of
paper and held it out to her.

She looked at the paper dubiously. "Is this in case
I need therapy?"

He laughed. "No, Haley, it's in case you need a
friend."

His words touched her more than anyone had

touched her in a very long time. "Thank you." She studied him thoughtfully, ignoring the fluttering in the pit of her stomach. "You wouldn't reconsider and do Molly's therapy sessions, would you?"

"Why? You don't like Dr. Tredwell?"

"No, it's not that. He seems fine and he seemed to get along well with Molly. It's just that I feel more comfortable with you." The warmth of a blush swept up her neck.

"But it's about Molly," he said gently. "Besides, I can't do therapy with her. It would be unethical."

She looked at him in surprise. "Unethical?"

He nodded. "I can't be Molly's therapist and ask you to have lunch with me."

The blush that had momentarily warmed her was replaced by a new warmth and the flutter in her stomach grew stronger. "Are you considering asking me to have lunch with you?"

He took a sip of his coffee, his gaze holding hers intently. He placed the cup back on the table and smiled. "I'm definitely considering it."

"You'll let me know when you've made a decision?"

His smile widened, flashing those impossible dimples. "Okay, I've decided. Would you like to have lunch with me on Monday?"

"I don't know, I'll have to think about it," she replied.

"You'll let me know when you've made a decision?"

They were flirting. The thought stunned her and also thrilled her more than a little. "Okay, I've decided. I'd love to have lunch with you on Monday, but can I call you to confirm? I won't be available if I don't get Molly back in school by then."

"Just let me know." He got up from the table. "And now it's time for me to get out of here. I have a class in an hour."

She walked with him to the front door. "Thank you again. I can't tell you how much I appreciate you being available today to help me with Molly's transition."

He stepped out the front door and turned back to her. "No problem. You'll call me about Monday?"

"As soon as I know what's going on."

He started to leave, but stopped and turned back to face her, a gleam in his eyes. "Oh, and Haley, I'm glad you didn't opt for plastic surgery because your assets look just fine to me."

He left then and she stood on the porch openmouthed in shock and warmed by a swirl of feminine pleasure she hadn't felt for a long time.

It was after six by the time Molly and Haley returned from their second session with Dr. Tredwell. This session had gone much the same as the one before, with Dr. Tredwell talking and Molly listening.

She now sat at the table as Haley warmed up some of the leftovers from the day before. "I know it's kind of an odd mix," Haley said brightly as she placed the plates and dishes on the table. "We've got leftover lasagna, some strange chicken casserole, baked beans and macaroni salad. But best of all, there's seven different kinds of dessert."

Molly was obviously too withdrawn to get excited about the prospect of chocolate cake, brownies and French silk pie, for she simply sat at the table and stared out the window into the backyard.

"Your mother loved that tree house," Haley said, guessing what held Molly's attention. "You love it too." Molly turned and looked at her and nodded. Her eyes were so sad. Haley wished there was something she could do to erase that sadness, but it was an emotion that resonated deep in Haley's heart as well.

Just be cheerful, she told herself. "You need to eat," she said. She picked up Molly's plate and filled it with a small portion of everything she had zapped in the microwave. "We'll both feel better after we have something to eat."

She set the plate back in front of Molly. Molly stared down at it for a long moment, then pushed it away. When she looked up at Haley there was a touch of defiance in her eyes, something Haley hadn't seen before.

"Molly, honey, I know all of this has been upsetting to you, but it's really important that you eat something." Haley pushed the plate back in front of her.

Molly got up from the table, went to a kitchen drawer and pulled out a pad and pencil. She sat back down at the table and used the pencil to write a big, fat *NO* on the paper. She shoved it toward Haley, then crossed her little arms over her chest.

"Molly, I don't want to fight with you. It's dinnertime, that means we eat." This was the first real thing Haley was responsible for and she didn't want to screw it up. She pushed the plate back in front of Molly.

Molly stared at her for a long moment, then

pushed back from the table and ran from the kitchen. A moment later Haley heard the violent slam of her bedroom door.

"That went well," Haley said to the empty room, then pulled the chocolate cake in front of her and burst into tears.

It wasn't supposed to be like this. Everyone Haley had ever loved was gone. She'd thought her father's death the most difficult thing she'd ever lived through.

Charles Lambert had been Haley's hero. While Monica and their mother had baked cookies or worked on crafts, Haley had been her father's shadow, helping him build things in his woodworking studio in the garage. And while they worked, he'd talk.

"There are two kinds of people in this world, Haley girl," he'd said one day not too long before his unexpected death. The two of them had been in the garage building a birdhouse for the backyard. Haley had just had a fight with her mother over something stupid.

"There's the rocks and there are the kites," he'd said. "Your mother and your sister, they're rocks. They're most comfortable with solid ground beneath their feet. Rocks are happiest when they're building nests and have routine in their lives. You and me, we're kites. We like the wind beneath our wings, we like surprises and adventure. The world needs both, and kites need rocks so they don't fly too high."

He'd given her a quick hug, smelling of sawdust and varnish. "You know your mother loves you. It's just hard sometimes for rocks to understand kites."

The memory whispered through her, bringing more tears as she cleaned up the kitchen. Her mother's death had been just as hard, but in a different way. Ann had been sick for some time before she'd finally succumbed to death, and when she was gone Haley had been filled with the regret that she and her mother had never really understood each other.

She was too young to feel this kind of grief. There had been too much death in her life. She wanted her mother here to tell her what to do. She wanted her sister alive and well to take care of Molly, who obviously wanted nothing to do with her Aunt Haley.

Molly remained in her bedroom for the rest of the evening. Several times Haley cracked open the door to check on her. She had the little portable television on top of her dresser tuned to sitcoms and hugged a stuffed lion in her arms. She refused to look at Haley.

Haley left her alone, unsure what else to do. At eight thirty she went into the room and shut off the television. "It's time for bed, Molly." She had no idea what bedtime Monica had observed for her daughter, but she suspected it was about this time.

Once again there was a flash of defiance in Molly's eyes and Haley feared she was about to indulge in another battle of wills. But thankfully Molly got off the bed, pulled a pair of pajamas from a dresser drawer and disappeared into the bathroom across the hall.

A few minutes later she came back out clad in a pair of pink pajamas and smelling of toothpaste. She ignored Haley's presence as she turned down her bed and got beneath the covers.

Haley went over to the bed and bent down to give her niece a kiss good night, but Molly turned her face into the pillow, refusing the kiss.

Maybe things would be better tomorrow, Haley thought as she left Molly's bedroom. Maybe she was expecting too much from the little girl.

At nine when Haley checked on Molly, she was asleep. Haley watched her from the doorway for several long minutes.

What if things weren't better the next day? What if things never got better? She thought of the phone number Grey had given her earlier in the day. She could call him, let him know that Molly hated her and ask him what to do.

She immediately dismissed the idea. They had another appointment with Dr. Tredwell the next day. She'd talk to him about Molly.

She'd tell him that what worried her most was that Molly needed a rock in her life . . . and she'd been stuck with a stupid kite.

Chapter 10

Haley awoke slowly, shifting positions in the bed as consciousness pulled her from her dreams. For just a moment as she lay there with her eyes closed, she had a sense of utter well-being.

From the nearby window she could hear bird-song, and the scent of spring flowers drifted in. The fresh-smelling sheets on the bed embraced her with warmth and she thought her dreams had been pleasant ones.

Then she remembered.

Monica was dead, murdered on a beautiful spring Friday.

She opened her eyes and screamed.

Molly, seated on the edge of the bed, slapped a hand over her mouth, but not before a giggle escaped.

"Jeez Louise, Molly, you scared me half to death," Haley exclaimed. She rolled over and glanced at the clock next to the bed, dismayed to see it was after ten.

No wonder Molly was in her bedroom. She was

probably curious to find out if her Aunt Haley would ever get out of bed.

"Guess I overslept," Haley said as Molly stood. She was already dressed in a pair of jeans and a bright blue T-shirt. Her hair was neatly brushed and now that the giggle was gone, she gazed at Haley with slightly accusing eyes.

She must be starving, Haley thought as she got out of bed and headed for the bathroom. She'd eaten nothing the night before and she was probably used to eating breakfast before noon.

Tomorrow you set the alarm, Haley, she said to herself firmly. It doesn't matter what you did before; this is a new life with new rules.

It took her only minutes to pull on a pair of sweatpants and a T-shirt. Then she and Molly went to the kitchen where Haley realized Molly had already fixed herself a bowl of cereal for breakfast. At least Molly was somewhat self-sufficient.

Molly slid into a chair at the table as Haley tried to figure out what of the leftovers might serve as an adequate breakfast for herself. She didn't feel like cooking and didn't see any convenience food in the freezer or cabinets. She knew Monica had preferred a healthy diet for herself and Molly that had included convenience or fast food only on rare occasions.

In Las Vegas, Haley had rarely gone to the grocery store. Food was cheap and easy to obtain along the strip. She could get a ham steak and eggs for $2.99 or a breakfast buffet for under ten bucks.

But you aren't in Vegas anymore, she told herself. And you no longer have just yourself to think about. Molly's gaze bored holes in her back as she stared at the contents of the refrigerator.

Chicken casserole, maybe that would work. After all, chickens laid eggs and eggs were breakfast food. Thank goodness Molly had already eaten, she thought as she pulled out the cold chicken salad.

A knock on the front door interrupted the breakfast debacle. Haley went to answer and found Angela on the porch, her hands filled with a baking dish and a basket.

"I knew this was the first morning that Molly was home, so I thought I'd bake a little welcome-home breakfast," Angela said as Haley gestured her inside. "I knocked earlier but there was no answer." There was a slight note of censure in the words.

"We overslept a bit this morning," Haley replied, fighting the impulse to apologize to the neighbor for her sleeping habits.

"Well, I've got a bacon and egg casserole and cinnamon muffins."

"You're a godsend," Haley exclaimed as she followed Angela into the kitchen. "Molly already had a bowl of cereal but I was just about to warm up some chicken casserole left over from yesterday for myself." Haley offered the woman a weak smile. "I'm not much of a cook."

Angela set everything on the countertop, then went over to Molly and bent down on one knee. "Hi, sweetie," she said softly. "I didn't get much of a chance to visit with you yesterday. We've missed you around here. Adrianna and Mary have asked about you every single day."

Molly nodded, her gaze somber as it lingered on

Angela. Angela stood and smiled at Haley. "That casserole should still be warm."

"Then let's eat," Haley said with forced brightness. As she got the plates and set the table, Angela took the foil off the top of the casserole dish and set both it and the basket of muffins on the table. Haley made coffee while Molly filled her plate and began to eat, apparently not completely satisfied by the earlier bowl of cereal.

Haley was grateful for Angela's presence to fill the silence of the meal. Angela kept up a running conversation, talking about her daughters and harmless neighborhood gossip and the weather.

When Molly was finished eating she left the kitchen and went back into her bedroom, leaving the two women seated at the table.

"How's she doing?" Angela asked, her brow wrinkled in concern.

"I don't know. It's hard to tell." Haley grabbed a second muffin. "I think she hates me."

"Oh, Haley, why on earth would you think that?"

Haley explained about the dinner drama the night before and when she finished Angela smiled sympathetically. "You know, I'm not a child psychologist or anything like that, but I'd say you'd better be prepared for a few power struggles. All kids test, and it sounds like that's what Molly was doing with you last night."

"If it was a test, then I'm pretty sure I flunked," Haley said wryly.

Angela laughed. "I've got news for you, it probably won't be the last test you flunk where Molly is concerned. I also think that her little temper fit was a good thing because it's wonderfully normal for an eight-year-old."

"Really?" Angela's words helped ease some of Haley's worry.

Angela laughed again and reached over to pat her hand. "You're going to be fine, Haley. I just know it. Do you plan on getting her back into school or are you going to just hold her out for the rest of the year?"

"Dr. Tredwell thinks it would be best for her to get back into school right away." Haley got up to pour herself another cup of coffee. "I'd planned on calling her teacher sometime today to explain things and see about getting her back into class on Monday."

One of Angela's dark eyebrows rose. "Dr. Tredwell?"

"Dr. Jerry Tredwell. He's a child psychologist I'm taking Molly to." She couldn't help the wave of heat that swept through her as she thought of the other psychologist in her life.

"If you want to talk to Molly's teacher, then tonight would be a perfect opportunity. There's a parent-teacher meeting tonight, kind of a near-the-end-of-the-year social gathering."

"I don't even know Molly's teacher's name," Haley replied.

"Miss Jackson, Sondra Jackson. She's a cute little blonde. The kids adore her. Look, if you want to make the meeting tonight, I've got a babysitter coming to sit with my girls. Molly could come over and stay with them. She knows the babysitter, Belinda Carson. Monica used Belinda on occasion."

"I don't know," Haley said. She wasn't particularly comfortable leaving Molly after just getting her home.

At that moment Molly walked back into the kitchen.

"Molly, honey, tonight is a parent-teacher meeting at your school. Belinda is going to come to my house and babysit Adrianna and Mary tonight. Would you like to come over and spend a little time with them so your Aunt Haley can meet Miss Jackson?" Angela asked.

For the first time Haley saw a spark of life in Molly's eyes. She nodded her head vigorously, then looked at Haley with appeal.

"You'd like to stay with Belinda and the girls for a little while?" she asked. "Just long enough for me to go to your school and have a little chat with your teacher?" Molly nodded again.

"Okay." Haley looked at Angela. "So, what time does this thing start this evening?"

"Seven o'clock," Angela replied. "Do you know where the school is?"

"Pleasant Hill Elementary at the corner of Third and Magnolia. I went there myself."

"That's right, I keep forgetting that you grew up here." Angela stood. "And now it's time for me to get back home. I've got tons of cleaning to do."

Haley got up to walk with her to the door. "I can't thank you enough for breakfast. As soon as I clean up the mess, we're heading straight to the grocery store."

"Just send Molly over around six forty-five tonight. I might already be gone, I've got some errands to run before I meet Frank at the school."

With a waggle of her fingers Angela left, seeming to take all the energy in the house with her.

Molly sat at the table and watched as Haley stuck the dirty dishes in the dishwasher, then wiped down the table. "How about we go to the grocery store and buy some things so we don't have to depend on the neighbors or crummy leftovers to eat."

She thought she saw a ghost of a smile lift Molly's lips. She decided to take advantage of the moment. "Molly, I've got to be honest with you. I don't know a lot about cooking and taking care of somebody, but I promise you I'm going to do the very best I can. I'm probably going to mess up occasionally, but maybe if you help me a little bit we'll do okay."

She held her breath as Molly eyed her soberly. Give me a chance, Molly, she thought. I know I'm not your mother, I know I'm not the one you want to take care of you, but just give me a chance.

Molly released a tremulous little sigh and gave a short, curt nod of her head. Haley had a feeling she was on probation. "Come on, let's get to the grocery store."

Minutes later Haley was trying to find her car keys when a loud knock sounded on the front door. She opened it to see a lanky teenager. Oily brown hair hung to his shoulders and was tucked behind his oversized ears. A gold eyebrow ring drew attention to his hazel eyes.

"Yeah, uh . . . I'm Dean Brown from over there." He pointed in the direction of his house. He jammed his hands into his jeans pockets, his gaze not quite meeting hers. "I was, like, wondering if maybe you need somebody to mow the yard."

"Shouldn't you be in school?" Haley frowned at the teenager Angela had told her about.

"I'm sort of not for the next two weeks."

"Suspension? Two weeks, huh? I'd say you were either caught smoking on school property or you had a fight."

His gaze met hers in surprise. "Smoking," he admitted.

"Pot or regular cigarettes?"

"Just tobacco. Contrary to what some people believe in this neighborhood, I don't smoke dope."

"Don't you know that smoking cigarettes will give you lung cancer? What else do you do in your spare time, Dean? You like to peep into windows?"

The tips of his ears turned red. "I don't know what you're talking about. I'm just looking for a little extra cash and thought maybe I could do your mowing."

"Did you mow for my sister?" Haley asked.

He hesitated a moment, his gaze once again sliding away from hers. "No, she had one of those fancy services come out a couple of times a month. She never thought I could do a good enough job."

"And what do you think?"

He pulled his hands from his pockets and straightened his shoulders. "I could do as good as anyone else and I'm a lot cheaper. I'd only charge you twenty a pop for mowing, weeding and edging."

Angela had told her this kid was trouble, but something about his slight belligerence reminded her of herself when she'd been that age. Haley looked beyond the porch and realized the lawn did need tending, and she had no idea what service Monica had used.

"I'll tell you what, I'll give you a chance. If you do a good job I'll hire you for the remainder of the season," she said.

"Thanks, I'll start right now." He backed off the porch. "I'm glad you aren't as uptight as your sister was."

Haley stared after him as he took off across the lawn. So Dean thought Monica had been uptight. Had she and the teenager had words? Had there been a run-in between them in the past?

Had she just hired Monica's killer to mow her grass? Was it possible Monica had been murdered because she was uptight and wouldn't let the neighborhood punk do yard work?

Surely a kid couldn't have done what had been done to Moncia, could he? She went back to searching for her keys, troubled by the mystery of her sister's murder.

By the time Haley and Molly were ready to take off for their trip to the grocery store, Dean was pushing a lawn mower toward their house. Haley stopped the car next to him and told him they'd be back soon.

As she pulled away once again she glanced over at Molly. A wave of relief went through her as she realized an important fact. If Molly had seen her mother's murderer, then surely she'd react in some wild, negative way to seeing that person once again.

Surely if Dean had killed Monica and Molly had seen him or heard him from her hiding place under the bed, she would have freaked out at seeing him now. But she hadn't freaked out. She looked out the window, calm and silent.

"We need to make this a fast trip," Haley said. "You've got an appointment with Dr. Tredwell at two. You like him, don't you?" Molly's head bobbed up and down. "Yeah, I like him too."

Molly liked Dr. Tredwell and that was good. Maybe he made her feel safe. Haley preferred Dr. Grey because something about him made her feel decidedly unsafe.

Most of Haley's grocery shopping took place in the frozen, already prepared section of the store. She filled the cart with potpies and Salisbury steaks, with pizza and chicken nuggets.

It was Molly who grabbed the front of the cart and led her to the produce aisle, where the little girl added lettuce, cucumbers and carrots, apples and bananas.

It was after noon when the two got back home. The lawn work was done and Dean sat on the front porch smoking a cigarette. He stood and tossed the butt in the bushes as the car came to a halt.

Haley and Molly got out and Haley looked around the yard. "Not bad," she said to him.

"What do you mean, not bad?" His eyes flashed with a hint of anger. "It looks great. I worked my ass off, so don't think you're going to get out of paying me."

"Whoa. Who said anything about not paying you?" Haley opened her purse and withdrew a twenty-dollar bill. "You did a good job."

He took the money from her. "Good enough that you'd hire me to do it again?"

"I said I would. Nice work, Dean. We'll see you next week, okay?"

He gave her a curt nod, tucked the money in his jeans pocket, then headed up the street toward his house. Haley watched him go. The kid had a temper. She glanced at Molly, who stood nearby.

Earlier she'd been comforted by the fact that Molly hadn't had any adverse reaction to Dean. But was it possible Molly hadn't seen her mother's killer? Hadn't heard his voice? Were they waiting for her to speak only to discover that she had nothing to say?

"Come on, kiddo," she said to Molly, "let's get our food inside before everything thaws and we have to eat it all tonight."

While Haley put the food away, Molly sat in front of the television in the living room and watched cartoons.

After putting the dishes away Haley stood at the kitchen window and thought about Dean. Had he been the person who had peeked in her window two nights before? Was he just a rebellious teenager or was he something more sinister?

Haley wanted answers. She wanted to know who had killed her sister, but more than anything else she wanted to know why.

At two o'clock she once again sat outside the windowed room, watching Dr. Tredwell work with Molly. It looked like he was giving Molly some kind of written tests, for her focus was on paper he'd given her and she'd read for a moment, then mark something down.

Haley sat up straighter on the chair. Why hadn't

anyone thought of it before? Molly could communicate by writing. She'd certainly had no hesitation
about writing *NO* the night before at the dinner
table.

How good were her written skills? If Detective
Tolliver asked her some questions, maybe she could
answer them without actually saying a word. Surely
third graders could write simple sentences.

"What do you think?" she asked Dr. Tredwell
half an hour later as she sat in his office. "Couldn't
Tolliver question her and ask Molly to write down
her answers?"

"That might work, although if she balks I don't
want anyone pushing her."

"Believe me, as much as I want the police to catch
Monica's murderer, I don't intend to sacrifice Molly
in the process."

He nodded and leaned forward in his chair. "So,
how is everything else going?"

"Today has been all right. Last night was a little
dicey." She explained about Molly's silent temper
tantrum. "She might not be talking but she certainly
managed to communicate to me that she wasn't a
happy camper."

"My best advice to you is not to take anything too
personally. Molly is not just hurt and grief-stricken,
she's also angry, and you're going to be a conven-
ient target for that anger." He leaned back. "So,
you're planning on getting her in school Monday?"

"I'm going to a parent-teacher meeting tonight
and speak to her teacher so that she can get back to
school routine first thing Monday morning."

"Good, then I'll see her Monday at five o'clock."

The rest of the afternoon seemed to fly by. Molly

watched television while Haley sat at the kitchen table and tried not to feel overwhelmed by the sudden turn her life had taken.

So far she'd had Molly in her care less than twenty-four hours and she'd already failed at feeding her two meals, overslept and twice planted her in front of the television. She had to pull it together.

She'd left two messages for Detective Tolliver to call her, eager to tell him that maybe they could get Molly to write down what she'd seen, what she'd heard on the morning of her mother's murder. So far he hadn't called back.

They ate chicken potpies for supper; then at six thirty Haley walked with Molly to the Marcellis' house. A plump teenager with kinky red hair and a face full of freckles answered the door. "Hi, you must be Haley." She offered Haley a bright smile as she allowed the two inside the front door.

"And you must be Belinda," Haley replied.

Before they could say anything else, two little girls came into the room. They were all dark hair, sparkling eyes and giggles. Belinda introduced them as Adrianna and Mary. The two girls grabbed Molly's hand and disappeared down the hallway.

"Don't worry, she'll be fine," Belinda said. "Angela explained everything to me, you know, about Molly not talking. I told the girls that Molly was playing a quiet game and might not talk tonight."

Haley nodded, unable to stop herself from looking around the Marcelli living room with interest. The room looked like it had jumped right out of the pages of some home decorating magazine.

She'd suspected that Angela might be a Stepford kind of wife and nothing in the attractive, spotlessly clean living room disabused her of that notion. Her mind boggled as she noticed that the movies in the entertainment center were shelved alphabetically.

Monica had flirted dangerously close to the edge of being obsessive-compulsive, but Haley suspected Angela Marcelli gave new meaning to the description.

"A place for everything and everything in its place," Haley remembered her mother saying often when she was growing up.

As she drove to the school for the meeting, she wondered if being compulsive somehow came with giving birth. Maybe it was a side effect of pregnancy that nobody ever talked about. She'd ask Grey on Monday.

She felt guilty, looking forward to having lunch with the handsome doctor while grief for her sister still swamped her whenever she let her guard down.

And yet Haley was well-adjusted enough to know that life went on for those death left behind. As difficult as it was to believe, she and Molly would once again have laughter in their lives, would once again know happiness. Monica would have wanted that for her sister, and more importantly for her daughter. Monica would have liked Grey Banes.

Haley's thoughts drifted again toward her lunch with Grey. He possessed the kind of chiseled features and square jaw that she'd always found attractive. She liked the humor that occasionally shone from his eyes, and she was intrigued by a darkness that sometimes flashed there as well.

Not too fast, Haley, she told herself. She knew she

was vulnerable at the moment, reeling from tragedy and isolated as never before. She'd be foolish to go too fast with a man she'd known less than a week.

She dismissed thoughts of Grey as she approached the school. The parking lot of the one-story brick school building was filled with cars. Haley found a parking spot on the row farthest away from the building.

She got out of the car and heard the bounce of a ball and young men's voices shouting from the nearby basketball court. There were about a dozen teenagers playing ball. She recognized Dean Brown as one of the players.

As she was walking toward the school, she spied Frank Marcelli just ahead of her. "Frank!"

He turned, a smile lighting his handsome face. "Haley." He stopped and waited for her to catch up with him. "How are you doing?"

"Hanging in there." It was funny: Frank was as attractive as Grey, but nothing about Frank Marcelli produced butterflies in her stomach. Nothing about the handsome detective caused her to feel the same slightly breathless anticipation as Dr. Greyson Banes did. "Anything new with you?"

He obviously knew she didn't want to know about a new car or a new problem. What she wanted to know was about the case, Monica's case. "Nothing specific." His frustration was evident in the curt reply.

"Have you been to a lot of these?" She gestured toward the school building.

"A couple a year since Adrianna and Mary started school. Angela takes care of almost everything, but she insists I come to the parent-teacher meetings whenever it's possible."

They stepped inside the door. The air smelled of chalk and floor wax and coffee. Haley paused, unsure in which direction to go to find Molly's teacher.

"Just stick with me," Frank said, obviously noting her hesitation. "Adrianna and Molly are in the same classroom."

It was ridiculous to be nervous about meeting Sondra Jackson, but Haley was a bundle of nerves. What if Miss Jackson didn't like her? What if she said something or did something that made things even more difficult for Molly?

Haley had never before worried much about what people thought of her. Once she'd realized she'd never meet her mother's expectations, it didn't seem real important to meet anyone else's.

For the first time in her life she had somebody to think about besides herself and she wanted to make a good impression for Molly's sake.

The halls were filled with parents and Haley found herself wishing she hadn't opted to wear jeans and a blouse a friend in Vegas had bought her that was patterned with sun visors, palm trees and margarita glasses. Unfortunately the clothes that worked well in Vegas didn't work so well in a conservative small town in the Midwest.

Got to do things right, Haley. Monica's voice whispered softly in her head. *You've got to step up. I'm depending on you.*

"I'm trying," she muttered, then flushed as Frank looked at her. "Just talking to myself."

"This is it," he said as they stopped before a classroom door. "Room 112, third grade with Miss Sondra Jackson." He smiled at her kindly. "Don't look so terrified. She's nice and she loves the kids."

She flashed him a grateful smile and together they went into the room. It was easy to see why the kids liked Miss Jackson. She was a petite blonde with big blue eyes and looked like she could pass for a twelve-year-old. She was seated at her desk speaking with a young couple.

There were other parents in the room, drifting from one bulletin board to the next, apparently seeking their child's work tacked up for public display.

Angela waved and hurried toward them. "Look who I found in the parking lot," Frank said to his wife.

Angela looped an arm with Haley and smiled brightly. "I'm glad you decided to be here. Come on, I'll show you some of Molly's work while we wait for Miss Jackson to be free."

She led Haley to a bulletin board where short essays were tacked up. She pointed to one with neat lettering. "That's Molly's." She squeezed Haley's arm with hers.

The essay was titled "My Mommy by Molly Ridge."

My mommy is nice. She cooks good. She takes care of me when I'm sick. She makes me laugh. I love my mommy.

Five sentences that ripped the very heart out of Haley. If Angela hadn't held her so tight, she felt as if she'd fall to the floor, for the grief that tore through her was almost incapacitating.

She squeezed her eyes closed for a long moment, fighting against the wave of tears that threatened to erupt. "Are you okay?" Angela's voice brought her back from the brink.

She opened her eyes and nodded. *It should have been me. It should be me lying in the ground, and Monica should be here with her daughter.*

"I'm fine," she told Angela and fought for the strength to see the night through.

"There's pictures that the kids drew over there." Angela pointed to a bulletin board across the room and together the two women went over. Angela showed her Adrianna's drawing of a pond with a cow drinking water; then they looked at Molly's drawing of a genie on a flying carpet.

"Ms. Lambert? Haley Lambert?"

Angela released her hold on Haley as a man hurried toward them. He held out a hand to Haley. "Hi, I'm Jay Middleton, president of the Parent's Association."

Haley looked at him in surprise and he smiled as if accustomed to that response. "Traditional rules have changed. Dads are now allowed to infiltrate the secrets of room mothering and fund-raising."

Jay was a tall man with an athletic build and blond hair neatly styled. His brown eyes radiated sympathy as he held on to Haley's hand. "I just wanted to tell you how much we're all going to miss your sister. I was out of town for the funeral, but I wanted to make a point of letting you know how very special we thought Monica was. You know she was my vice-president and right-hand woman."

By the time Haley got a chance to sit down and speak to Sondra Jackson she was ready to bolt. She knew the other parents were being kind in offering up accolades for Monica, but Haley's grief was still too raw, still too fresh to want to dwell in others' sympathy.

"How is Molly?" Sondra Jackson studied Haley with her huge blue eyes. "I've been so worried about her. The death of a parent is so tragic."

Haley explained about Molly not talking and that her doctor thought it best she return to school. "Maybe she'll surprise us and talk on Monday when she's here with all her friends."

"If that doesn't happen, then we'll deal with it just fine," Sondra assured her. "I can make sure the work I give her is all written until she begins to talk again."

"I appreciate that," Haley replied. "Her decision to stop talking is difficult." She didn't mention why it was so hard, that they suspected that somewhere in Molly's memory was a key to unlocking the mystery of Monica's death. So far they had been lucky that there had been no news reporting to the public that Molly had been present at her mother's murder.

Sondra smiled. "Your niece is very bright. She can be quite precocious. She also can be headstrong. If Molly has decided she isn't talking, then nothing and nobody is going to make her talk until she's ready."

By the time Haley finished speaking to the teacher, Angela and Frank had already left. Frank had gone back to work and Angela had headed home to relieve the babysitter.

After leaving the classroom, Haley went to the office and spoke not only to the principal, but also to the school nurse about her niece. She wanted to make sure that everyone was on the same page when Molly returned to class on Monday morning. The parking lot had emptied considerably as she walked toward her car. She felt good. She'd managed to interact with people who were important in Molly's life and she hadn't raised one single eyebrow or stuck her foot in her mouth.

Molly would start back to school on Monday, and hopefully being back in the class with the beloved Miss Jackson and her schoolmates would make her feel safe enough to talk.

She'd almost reached her car when another one squealed around the corner and roared across the lot, passing so close to Haley she dropped her keys and sprang backward.

She couldn't be sure, but as the car flew by she thought she recognized the driver: the neighbor with the too-small suit and sweaty hands. Grant Newton. Why would he be at the school? He had no children.

She picked up her keys and quickly got into her car and locked the doors, fighting uneasy chills that raced up and down her spine.

Jesus. That had been too close for comfort. She'd been able to feel the heat of the car. Another six inches and she would have been hit. She remembered the sweaty heat of Grant Newton's hand holding hers. The man gave her the creeps.

Was it possible he'd been watching her? Following her? Had he made that phone call to her? Peeked at her through her kitchen window?

Or was she letting her imagination run wild? Still, it took two tries for her trembling fingers to finally get her keys into the ignition.

*   *   *

It was almost ten o'clock when Sondra Jackson unlocked her front door and stepped inside. She was pooped. She always found the parent-teacher interaction exhausting. All the parents really wanted to hear was that their child was special.

As far as Sondra was concerned they were all special, but in the five years she'd been teaching she had only seen a handful of kids that were truly gifted in intelligence.

Poor Molly, she thought. Molly had been a favorite of Sondra's in the classroom. She was bright and full of life. It was hard to imagine the little girl not speaking.

Sondra couldn't fathom being so young and losing both parents. Sondra's parents had died in the past two years, each of a different illness, but she'd had a wonderful childhood of love and support before she'd had to tell them good-bye.

She was glad the evening was over. All she wanted now was a cup of hot tea and a good night's sleep. She dropped her purse on the sofa as she walked through to her kitchen.

This was her favorite room in the small house she rented. Decorated with curtains with sunflowers dancing across the border, the room was painted yellow and always felt warm and welcoming.

She grabbed an old teakettle from beneath the cabinet, filled it with water, then set it on the stove-top to boil.

While she waited, she got out her favorite red-flowered cup and saucer, a raspberry-flavored tea bag and a slice of lemon.

She'd just set all the items on the table when her

doorbell rang. Frowning, she glanced at her wrist-watch. Who could that be?

She hurried to the front door and opened it. There was no opportunity to express surprise. The knife caught her in the throat, slashing so quickly, so deeply, it took her a moment to realize she was hurt.

Tumbling backward, she gasped for air. Couldn't breathe! She couldn't breathe. The floor rose to meet her as darkness fell. She never felt the fists that pummeled her, nor heard the sound of the teakettle whistling that her water was ready for her tea.

Chapter 11

The morning was a success. Haley managed to get up early enough to fix Molly a bowl of instant oatmeal and make sure her socks matched and her hair was combed before walking her next door. Angela had offered to drive Molly to school with her girls and Molly had made it obvious that's what she wanted.

Several times over the course of the morning Haley had asked Molly if she didn't want her to take her to school, but Molly had looked horrified at the very idea. Even though Haley would have much preferred to take her niece to school herself, Molly seemed adamant about wanting to go with Angela and her girls. Haley had finally relented.

Angela greeted her at the door. It wasn't even eight yet but she had her makeup on and wore a pair of tailored beige slacks and a beige and dark brown blouse. Her long hair was French braided and gold hoops dangled from her ears.

Haley self-consciously threaded a hand through her disheveled hair as Angela invited her inside. She'd been so worried about making sure Molly looked presentable and was fed that the only thing she'd done to herself was wash her face and drag on a pair of sweats and a T-shirt.

"Usually they all take the bus," Angela said as she grabbed her purse from the table. "But this morning I've got a meeting and decided I could just drop them off on my way. Come on, girls. Molly is here and it's time to go."

"Do I need to pick them up or something this afternoon?" Haley asked.

"The bus can bring them home," Angela said, then smiled at Molly. "You can ride the bus home like you usually do, can't you, sweetie?" Molly nodded, then smiled as Adrianna and Mary ran out to meet her.

They all walked out the front door. "The bus stop is right here in front of my house and they usually get here about three forty-five each afternoon," Angela explained. "Okay, kids, load up," she said and pointed to the minivan in the driveway.

As the three little girls scrambled into the backseat, Angela smiled at Haley. "You'd better enjoy the last of these school days. It won't be long and they'll all be on summer vacation."

"Don't remind me," she said, half terrified by the very thought. It had been difficult enough getting through the weekend that had just passed. The hours had crawled by, filled with silence except for the sounds of the television.

Haley had smiled and joked, had practically tap-danced on the table to let Molly know she wasn't worried about anything, that she had everything under control.

She watched as Angela got into the driver's seat,

then waved and pulled out of the driveway and down the street. She had a sudden impulse to run after them, insist that she be the one to deliver Molly to school, but as she remembered the look on Molly's face when she'd made the suggestion, the impulse died. Maybe it was better this way, to try to keep things as close to normal as possible with the daily routines.

She went back into her house and into Molly's room. Sinking down on the edge of Molly's unmade bed, Haley picked up Molly's favorite stuffed lion and cradled it in her arms.

Eight days. It had been eight days since Monica had been killed. In some ways it felt like just a moment ago that Haley had been sitting in her Las Vegas apartment and the cops had arrived. In other ways, it felt like a lifetime had passed.

Eight days and nobody had come after Molly. No crazed killer had tried to get at the little witness who had hidden beneath her mother's bed. The police had done well keeping the fact that Molly had been home at the time of the murder out of the press. But that didn't mean that nobody knew about it.

Almost everyone Haley had spoken to at the funeral, then at the parent-teacher meeting, had known that Molly had been home and had stopped talking, which led Haley to believe that either the killer was certain Molly hadn't seen anything or he felt safe because she wasn't talking.

Thinking of the police, Haley got up, quickly made Molly's bed, then hurried into the kitchen to place another call to Tolliver.

She had yet to connect with him to discuss the possibility of questioning Molly and letting her write down the answers. She suspected Tolliver just assumed she had called for an update and his silence let her know there was no update for him to give her.

This time when she called and got his answering machine she left a message detailing her plan and the possibility that they wouldn't have to wait for Molly to speak to get some answers.

Once the call had been made she sat at the table and nursed a cup of coffee. The weekend hadn't been filled with just silence. Twice Molly had displayed her temper, once when Haley had insisted she take a bath and the other time when Haley had tried to give her a kiss good night.

The first had resulted in Molly stomping off to the bathroom and slamming the door. Then last night when Haley had leaned down to give her a kiss, she had pulled the covers up over her head and remained that way until Haley left the room.

That rejection had once again broken Haley's heart. What if Molly never accepted her into her life? What if they were bound together by blood but Molly never learned to respect or to love her?

Eight days, she reminded herself. It had only been eight days. She was expecting too much too soon. She'd hoped that in Molly's grief she'd turn to her aunt for comfort, but obviously that wasn't going to happen anytime soon.

The ringing phone pulled her from her thoughts. It was Tolliver. He listened as she explained her plan, then made arrangements to meet with her and Molly at four that afternoon.

It was going to be a full day: lunch with Grey and then an appointment with Tolliver. She couldn't help the flutter of pleasant anticipation that swept through her as she thought of lunch with Grey. She'd called him the day before to set up the lunch date. She was meeting him at a place called the Salad Shoppe, a restaurant he'd assured her served more than rabbit food.

She had no clue what it was about him that affected her. Certainly it wasn't just because he was good-looking. Maybe it was nothing more than that he'd made a genuine effort to reach out to her, and with the silence of her life with Molly, she needed somebody to talk to, somebody who would listen.

It was just after eleven when she stood in front of the dresser mirror in her bedroom. Behind her the bed was covered with clothes pulled out of the closet, then discarded as she'd tried to find something appropriate for a lunch date.

She'd finally opted for a pair of jeans and a long-sleeved, scoop-necked peasantlike blouse in shades of pinks and mauves. A coat of mascara and a dab of lipstick and she was ready, but as she stood in front of the mirror and checked her reflection one last time a new wave of sorrow struck her.

She was looking forward to meeting a man for lunch eight days after her sister had been brutally murdered. What was she thinking? Monica wasn't even cold in her grave, and Haley was fantasizing about what Grey Banes's mouth might taste like.

She had to cancel the date. It was one thing to tell herself that he offered her support with Molly; it was quite another to indulge in romantic fantasies. What on earth did she think she was doing dating anyone at a time like this?

She tried to get in touch with him but he didn't

answer his home phone or his cell. She couldn't very well just stand him up.

She got in her car and headed for Main Street where she searched for the address he'd given her for the Salad Shoppe. When she spied the restaurant with a bright green awning she pulled into an open parking space in front, right next to Grey's car.

She'd just go inside, tell him this was a bad idea, then leave. The interior of the place smelled not only of crisp salad greens and steaming vegetables but also of fried onions and juicy burgers. Haley's stomach gurgled, reminding her that although she'd managed to feed Molly that morning she hadn't eaten any breakfast herself.

Okay, so maybe she'd stay just long enough to chow down on a burger, but she absolutely, positively wasn't going to enjoy it.

Grey was seated at the back of the restaurant in a booth and he half rose as she approached. "I'm just going to grab a burger, then go," she said briskly as she slid into the booth across from him.

One of his dark brows rose. "Is there a problem?"

"No, I just don't feel right about this." She snapped open the menu and frowned down at the words, shocked to feel the hot press of unexpected tears.

His hand stretched across the table and covered hers. The physical contact shot off a spark deep inside her. "Haley, look at me."

His gentle voice made it impossible for her not to comply. She looked up at him and once again he smiled. "What don't you feel right about? Because I work for the police department?"

"No, that's not it." Once again she averted her gaze and pulled her hand from beneath his.

"Then what? You don't strike me as the type of woman who is afraid to say what's on her mind."

He was right. She'd never minced words. Her mother had often reminded her that not everyone spoke every feeling or thought out loud as she so often did.

"This feels bad because it feels good," she said and felt a blush warm her cheeks. "My sister has been dead just over a week. What kind of a monster am I that I was looking forward to lunch with a hunk?"

"A human one." He leaned back in the booth and eyed her soberly. "Grief is like most other emotions, it's impossible to sustain forever all by itself. Despite the fact that you hurt and sadness weighs heavy, life goes on and with life comes all the rest of the human emotions of living, like anger and frustration and joy."

"You sound like a therapist," she said wryly.

He grinned. "Imagine that." His grin fell away and his eyes darkened from clear sky to midnight blue. "Grief is also the most insidious emotion. Just when you think you've dealt with it and it's finally gone, you'll hear a song or smell a scent or entertain a memory that brings it all crashing back down on you."

She regarded him thoughtfully. "You sound like a man who knows what he's talking about."

He shrugged. "You can't get to be thirty-eight years old and not suffer some form of grief in your life."

Their conversation was interrupted by the appearance of the waitress at their table. "Now, tell me about your tattoo," he said as the waitress departed with their orders.

She looked at him in surprise and felt the warmth of another blush creeping up her neck to sweep over her face. "How do you know about my tattoos?" He must have seen the one on her ankle, but there was no way he could know about the one on the cheek of her ass.

One of his eyebrows danced upward again. "There's more than one?"

"Two. One on my ankle and one someplace else. Definitely not one of my finer moments. Legal age for getting tattoos is eighteen, so the day of my eighteenth birthday I got not one, but two."

"So you were a wild child."

She smiled. "I was wilder than my mother wanted me to be, but not quite as wild as she thought I was. Monica was the good daughter. She always got good grades, cleaned her room, did what she was told without arguing. I, on the other hand, struggled to conform."

"Were the two of you close when you were growing up or was there a lot of sibling rivalry?"

"Close. Monica was one of those people it was impossible to be angry with. She had the sweetest temperament and would never hurt a fly." Haley picked up her fork and toyed with it. "That's why all of this is so hard to understand."

"There is no understanding death, particularly sudden, violent death."

Once again their conversation halted as the waitress returned with their orders. "Enough about me,"

Haley said, then popped a French fry into her mouth. "Tell me about Dr. Grey Banes."

"What do you want to know?"

"What do you do when you aren't teaching or head-shrinking criminals?"

"For the past year I've been transitioning from a married man to a single one."

"I didn't realize your divorce was so recent." He nodded. She wasn't surprised that he'd been married before. There was no way a man like Grey could have lived thirty-eight years without some smart woman snapping him right up. "Just what is involved in making the transition from married to single?"

He took a bite of his burger, chewed and swallowed before replying. "The first thing I had to do was learn how to cook. I figured I could get my house cleaned, take my clothes to the cleaners, but eating was a number one priority and I like home-cooked meals. I took a couple of classes and now like to think I could give Emeril a run for his money."

"As far as I'm concerned there's nothing more appealing than a man who can cook. If you do windows and can fold a fitted sheet, then maybe we need to talk about a long-term relationship."

He laughed. It was a nice sound, deep and sexy. "I must confess, the folding of fitted sheets still eludes me."

"Then I guess we'll just keep this casual," she replied teasingly. There it was again, the flirting. It was so remarkably easy with him.

For a few minutes they focused on their food and

as they ate they made the small talk people did when they were getting to know one another.

On the surface it appeared as if they had nothing in common. They good-naturedly argued politics: he was a conservative, she was liberal. He liked psychological dramas when it came to books and movies. She preferred chick lit and action flicks.

He liked exercise, she abhorred it. She loved seafood. He loved steak. And yet, despite the differences, she liked him. Something about him both calmed her and excited her at the same time.

He talked a bit about his parents, who lived in Arizona, and she told him about her father, about what an important presence he'd been in her life and how devastating his death had been. She even told him her father's theory about people being one of two categories, rocks or kites.

"Your father sounds like he was a very wise man."

"He was more than that." As always, talking about her father created a pain in the center of her chest. "He was my world, and then in the blink of an eye he was gone." She cleared her throat. "You're right, this burger was awesome," she said in an effort to change the subject. She finished the last bite of the burger.

"Mine are much better, but these are definitely a close second." He glanced at his watch and smiled apologetically. "I hate to cut this off, but I've really got to get out of here. I've got an appointment at the police station in an hour, and I need to go by my place and pick up some files."

"I enjoyed this," she said as they stepped outside onto the sidewalk. "Thank you so much for inviting me."

"You probably didn't enjoy it as much as I did." His gaze was warm as it lingered on her. "In fact, I'd like to do it again. Would tomorrow be too soon?"

She laughed. He took her breath away, this man with his startling blue eyes and shoulders broad enough to carry the world. And he intrigued her with the shadows that occasionally flitted across his face.

"Tomorrow sounds great," she agreed. "Same time, same place?"

"I'll look forward to it," he replied. "And remember, Haley, it's okay to grasp at happiness wherever you can find it."

"You're a nice man, Grey Banes. How long were you married?" From the moment he'd told her he was divorced she'd been curious about his marriage.

"Sixteen years."

"Wow, that's a long time. What happened?"

For a brief moment something raw and wild flashed in his eyes. It was there only a minute, then gone. "Grief happened, Haley." His jaw clenched and he offered her a tight smile. "I'll see you tomorrow."

She watched him walk away, noting someplace in the back of her mind that he looked as good going as he did coming. It had been a long time since any man had intrigued her as much as Grey Banes did.

He was nothing like the men she usually chose to date. He didn't appear to have tattoos or piercings; he seemed relatively well-adjusted. There was a quiet strength in him, a self-possessed confidence that was so appealing. But she wouldn't be satisfied until she knew what made those shadows in his eyes. What kind of grief had Dr. Grey Banes experienced that had broken apart his marriage?

"What in the hell are you doing?" Grey asked himself as he drove away from the restaurant and Haley Lambert.

Was he really willing to risk his emotional stability for a woman who seemed to have so little of her own? He'd spent the last year trying to find a place of peace, some forgiveness for himself.

On the day Sarah had walked out on him, shouting accusations with rage and hatred burning in her eyes, he'd decided that never again would he risk his heart to anyone.

His hands pressed into the padded steering wheel as he thought of his ex-wife. Although logically Grey had known it was anguish that had transformed Sarah from a rational, caring human being into a screaming, sobbing shrew, emotionally he couldn't quite forgive her for not seeing his agony as well.

It had been at that moment that he'd seen all the flaws of his marriage, recognized the denial the two of them had lived with for far too long.

He hadn't tried to stop her when she'd left him. He'd known they would both be better off alone.

Alone. That's how he had expected to live the rest of his days and nights, and for the past year he'd been by himself with his thoughts, his regrets, and finally a quiet acceptance that happiness wasn't a requisite for drawing breath.

Then she'd walked into the police station with her sunshine-colored hair and wild energy and he'd felt a spark of something, a spark of excitement, a shimmer of desire, a burst of life that had been absent for too long.

He knew she was at a bad place in her life. She was reeling beneath the weight of new expectations and responsibilities.

This was the worst possible time for her to get involved with anyone new.

So what in the hell was he doing? "Damned if I know," he breathed softly.

"Something is wrong. I just know something is terribly wrong," Kate Morgan told Owen Tolliver. She'd caught him just as he was about to walk out of the station for his appointment with Haley and Molly.

He'd like to have blown her off, but unfortunately Kate Morgan wasn't just a cute brunette who taught second grade: she was also the mayor's niece.

"What makes you think there's a problem?"

"Every Saturday Sondra and I meet for lunch. Same place, same time, Micki's at one. She didn't show up on Saturday and she didn't call to cancel either."

"Maybe she made other plans and just forgot to contact you."

She shook her head vehemently, the gesture causing her shoulder-length hair to sway back and forth against her cheeks. "No way. Sondra wouldn't just forget to call. Besides, it's not just Saturday that worries me. I didn't hear from her yesterday and she didn't show up for work this morning. She'd never miss work and not call in to make sure there was a substitute teacher lined up. Nobody has heard anything from her since Friday night."

She opened her purse and withdrew a single key on a chain with a fuzzy red ball. "This is the key to Sondra's house. We exchanged house keys because we both live alone. Please, go over there and check on her. I would have done it, but I'm afraid. I'm telling you something isn't right."

Reluctantly Tolliver took the key from her. "What's her address?" As he wrote down the address, he considered his options. He could go over to Haley's and try to get a written statement from a traumatized eight-year-old and in the process possibly piss off his boss, or he could reschedule with Haley and go do a well check at Sondra Jackson's address.

He really didn't have a choice. "You'll call me? Please?" Kate asked as she stood.

"As soon as I know something," he replied. The moment she left the room he picked up the phone to call Haley and reschedule with her, then went to find Frank in the break room.

"Come on, Julie, tell me when you're going to go out dancing with me," Frank was saying to the female officer who sat across from him at the scarred old table.

"Does hell and freezing over mean anything to you?" Julie replied with good humor. Frank's flirting was legendary within the department, taken with good humor by everyone because they knew he was devoted to Angela and his kids.

"If she ever tells you yes, you'll crap your pants," Tolliver said from the doorway. "Come on, partner, we've got to take a ride."

"Later, Romeo," Julie said as Frank got up from the table and fell into step with Tolliver.

"Where are we going?"

"Morgan's niece stopped by, wants us to check on a friend of hers," Tolliver explained. "Nobody has seen or heard from the woman since Friday night. She missed a luncheon date on Saturday and work today."

"I thought you were meeting with Haley and Molly this afternoon."

"Yeah, right. I'm going to blow off the mayor's niece to work on a case that has gone stone-cold."

"So you don't think you can get anything out of Molly?" Frank asked as they got into the car.

"I think if that kid is scared so shitless that she refuses to talk, there's no way in hell she's going to write down anything we can use." He started the car and pulled out of the police lot. "I think Molly is a dead end. I think she probably didn't see the murderer and crawled under that bed after her mother was already dead."

"So, where are we going now?"

"Four-thirty-five Fourteenth Street. Sondra Jackson's residence."

Frank straightened in his seat. "Sondra Jackson? That's my daughter's teacher. We met with her at a parent-teacher meeting Friday night."

"Yeah, well, she missed a lunch date on Saturday and didn't show up for work this morning. Apparently she and Kate Morgan are good friends, and Kate insists something must be wrong. According to her Sondra isn't the type to blow off a lunch date without calling."

"Jesus, I hope it's nothing serious." Frank stared out the passenger window. "She's a cute little blonde. Maybe she met a guy, went off for the weekend or something."

"I'm sure it's nothing serious and Morgan is over-reacting," Owen said hopefully. Monica Ridge's murder lay heavy in his chest, haunted his sleep at night. The last thing he wanted or needed was something else to distract him from finding that killer.

He and Frank rode in silence until they pulled into the driveway of the small bungalow where Sondra Jackson lived. "If she went away for the weekend, you'd think she would have made it back in time to go to work today," Owen said as they got out of the car.

"I can't remember a day Miss Jackson has missed since school started last fall," Frank replied.

The house was small with a detached garage. As they approached the front door Owen saw nothing to give him concern. The small porch was neat and tidy, there were no broken windows and a twist of the knob let him know the front door was locked.

"I'll check the garage," Frank said and left the porch.

"Miss Jackson?" Owen knocked on the front door. "Hello? Miss Jackson, are you home?"

"Her car is in the garage," Frank yelled and for the first time since Kate Morgan had sat at his desk, Owen Tolliver had a bad feeling.

"Check around back, Frank. See if you find anything," Owen told his partner as he renewed his efforts banging on the door.

By the time Frank returned from checking the back of the house, Owen had pulled the key out of his pocket. He inserted it into the door, turned it and shoved the door open.

The smell hit him in the face. It was the stench of

death. "Oh shit," Frank muttered from just behind him.

Sondra Jackson lay in the doorway between the small entry and the living room. She might have been pretty, but whoever had taken her life had attempted to take her beauty as well.

Her throat was slashed and she'd been repeatedly stabbed, but she'd also been beaten. Her face had been pummeled nearly beyond recognition.

"Shit," Owen said, repeating Frank's sentiments. "We'd better call this in."

Frank made the call, getting the appropriate people in transit. As he did, Owen looked around the scene, trying to glean information that might help them understand what had happened, who was responsible.

There didn't appear to be any forced entry and it was obvious Sondra had been attacked immediately upon opening the door. "What time was that parent-teacher thing on Friday?" he asked Frank.

"I think it lasted until nine."

"I can't know for sure without the coroner's report, but we can assume she was killed either late Friday night or early Saturday morning."

Frank stared down at her body, a deep frown cutting across his forehead. "It's just like Monica's murder. Rage. You know, now that I think about it she even looks a little like Monica. You don't think we've got a . . . "

"Don't say it." Owen knew where Frank was going and he didn't want even a whisper of "serial killer" mentioned. For the last two years Owen's ulcer had been relatively silent, but now it burned like a bitch.

Even though he didn't want Frank to say the words out loud, he couldn't help but notice the similarities between the two murders.

In both cases, the victims had apparently opened their doors to allow their killers in, both bore the marks of a rage killing and both were pretty blondes.

"We'll need to canvass the area, see if anyone saw or heard anything." Owen rubbed his stomach and made a mental note to refill an old prescription. "We also need to check and see what kind of connection there might have been between Monica Ridge and Sondra Jackson."

"You mean other than the obvious? That Sondra was Molly's teacher?"

Owen looked at his partner in surprise. "I didn't realize she was Molly's teacher." He frowned thoughtfully and stared down at Sondra Jackson's beaten, broken body. "Is it possible maybe Monica's killer thought Molly had said something to her teacher?"

Frank blew out a breath of frustration. "I don't know. Until today Molly hadn't gone back to school since her mother's death. She wouldn't have had a chance to tell Sondra anything."

"We know that, but did our killer know that?" It was a rhetorical question because neither of them had the answer.

Chapter 12

Angela Marcelli's kitchen was a study in warmth and cheerfulness. Decorated in an apple motif, the room was obviously the heart of the house. Childish artwork hung on the front of the refrigerator and family photos were artfully arranged on the small built-in desk.

At the moment the air smelled not only of fabric softener wafting from the dryer that ran in the laundry room just off the kitchen, but also of the freshly baked cookies cooling on a rack on the counter.

"I hate it when Frank works late," Angela said as she got up to pour herself and Haley a second cup of coffee.

"Does he often work late in the evenings?" Haley asked. She'd been grateful when Angela had called a little after seven to see if she and Molly wanted to come over for some cookies and girl talk. Haley had jumped at the chance to break up the monotony of her night with the silent, withdrawn Molly.

"When things are quiet at work, he's usually home by six or six thirty so we all eat dinner together. But something must have happened today because he left me a message on my cell that he didn't know how late he'd be tonight."

"Did he say what's going on?" Maybe it had something to do with a break in Monica's case.

"No, but he definitely sounded tense." Angela placed a handful of the cookies on a small platter. "Girls, the cookies are ready," she called.

Almost immediately there was a pounding of feet as the three girls raced into the kitchen. Molly's cheeks were flushed and her eyes sparkled. At least here with her friends in the warmth of Angela's home Molly seemed to be able to forget, at least for a little while, the trauma that had transformed her life.

"Can we take them back to our room?" Adrianna asked. "We'll sit at our table and we promise we won't spill."

"We set the table for a tea party," Mary said. "We invited all our baby dolls. All we need is cookies."

"All right," Angela agreed and handed the platter to Adrianna. "Just make sure you eat them at the table and wash your hands when you're finished."

As the three girls ran for the bedroom, Angela prepared another platter and set it in front of Haley. "Help yourself," she said. "There's nothing better than cookies that are still warm from the oven."

"It's been a long time. The cookies I usually eat come from a bag." Haley leaned forward, grabbed one of the cookies, then leaned back and looked around.

Besides the artwork and school papers held neatly on the refrigerator with apple-shaped magnets there was also a dry erase board, and written in neat lettering was the week's schedule of activities both for Angela and the girls.

"You're so organized," Haley said. "Is that an apron hanging on the hook over there? I didn't know anyone wore aprons anymore."

Angela smiled. "I do so much cooking and aprons are still the best defense against spilling on your clothes. They're kind of hard to find anymore but I have them in almost every color. I make them myself."

Haley shook her head. "The only way I can see myself wearing an apron is if I'm naked underneath it and serving the man of my dreams."

Angela grinned. "There was a night when I met Frank at the door . . ." Her grin faded, transforming into a frown. "But that was a long time ago. Things get a little more complicated after kids."

Haley sighed as she thought of Molly. "She's like a different child when she's over here with your girls. I've been trying so hard to stay upbeat and cheerful, but she rarely even cracks a smile when she's with me."

Angela reached over and touched Haley's hand lightly. "You need to be patient. She hasn't had enough time with you yet. You have to remember she and the girls have played together almost every day for the last two years. From the day we moved in here they have been almost inseparable."

"Where did you and Frank live before you moved here?" Haley took a bite of the warm, gooey cookie.

"St. Louis."

"You have family there?"

Angela shook her head. "My family lives in Vermont. We aren't close. Frank and the girls are all the family I need."

"I smell cookies." The deep voice made both women jump in surprise. Frank came into the kitchen, lines of exhaustion tugging at his features.

Angela popped up from her chair and met him with a peck on the cheek. "Sit," she commanded and pushed him toward a chair at the table. "Did you eat dinner?"

"No time," Frank replied. He gave Haley a weary smile.

"I've got a plate warm for you in the oven."

As Angela began to bustle to serve her husband's immediate needs, Haley stood to leave. "Don't go," Frank said. "You might as well hear it from me as anyone else."

"Hear what?" Haley sank back down on the chair. Had they caught Monica's killer?

He raked a hand through his thick hair, his eyes haunted with darkness. "We had another one."

"Oh, Frank, no," Angela exclaimed. She set his plate in front of him, then placed her hands on his shoulders and gently kneaded with her fingers.

"Another one?" Haley frowned.

"Another murder." Frank picked up his fork but made no move to use it on his food. "Just like Monica's. No sign of forced entry, overkill with a knife." He set his fork down and shoved his plate aside. "What I'd really like is a drink."

Angela nodded, went to a cabinet and pulled down a bottle of Scotch. Frank remained silent until she'd placed the drink on the table. He wrapped his hands around the glass as Angela sat across from him.

"It was Sondra Jackson."

Haley wasn't sure whose gasp was louder, hers or Angela's. "My God," Angela exclaimed. "When did it happen?"

"We won't know for sure until the coroner's report, but we're assuming sometime late Friday night or early Saturday morning." He sipped the Scotch, his eyes still dark and troubled.

"So what does this mean? Is this some kind of a serial killer? Is it possible that Monica didn't know the person who killed her?" Haley's head reeled as she tried to make sense of this most recent tragedy and how it might relate to her sister's death.

"Officially, it's not a serial killer unless three people are killed by the same perpetrator," Frank said. "Right now we're investigating it as two connected murders."

"Connected how?" Haley's heart thumped an unsteady rhythm. "Molly's the connection, isn't she? Molly's mother and Molly's teacher are dead." Hysteria rose inside her, unexpected and unwelcome. "That's the connection, isn't it? Molly."

"Haley, calm down," Frank exclaimed. He picked up his drink and finished it in one large gulp, then pulled his dinner plate back in front of him. "We don't know yet what the connection might be. Yes, Molly is one, but there are others and we're exploring those."

"Like what?" Haley needed something, anything to take away the fear that made her half dizzy. What if this was all about Molly? She'd managed to convince herself so far that Molly wasn't in any danger, but now she wasn't so sure.

Frank picked up his fork once again and stabbed

it into the chicken breast on his plate. "Your sister worked a lot at the school, it's possible that's the connection."

"You mean the killer might work at the school also?" Angela asked, her tone appalled. "God, that's a terrifying thought."

"We don't know at this point. All we know is we have two pretty blond single women, one who worked at the school and one who spent a lot of time there. But needless to say this is just the beginning of the investigation."

"You look exhausted, honey," Angela said.

"Get used to it. In fact, I'm going to eat, then I need to head back to the station." He picked off a piece of the chicken and popped it into his mouth.

"I should get out of here," Haley said and stood once again. She felt bad. She felt bad because someplace deep inside her, in a very dark place, she was horribly relieved that there had been another murder. And that made her feel sick.

"You don't have to hurry off," Angela protested.

"No, really. You two need some time together and besides, it's time for me to start getting Molly ready for bed."

"I'll go get Molly." Angela got up and left the kitchen.

The minute she left the room Frank set his fork down again and stared at Haley with hollow eyes. "Maybe with this latest one we can figure out who killed Monica. We have two crime scenes to compare, two lives to pick through. Maybe this will break Monica's case."

"I hope you're right, although I'm sorry as hell about Sondra Jackson."

"Yeah. Me too."

She picked up her purse from the countertop, her head filled with thoughts of her meeting with the young, pretty teacher. "Frank, it might be nothing, but Friday night as I was leaving the school I was almost run down by a car racing out of the parking lot. I thought the driver was Grant Newton."

Frank straightened in his chair, the exhaustion that had tugged at his features momentarily gone. "Are you sure?"

"I . . . no, I can't be one hundred percent positive. But I remember thinking at the time that it was odd. Grant doesn't have any children in school, does he?"

"As far as I know Newton doesn't have any children at all."

Angela returned to the kitchen with Molly at her side. "Thanks for the cookies, Angela," Haley said, then forced a smile for her niece. "And now it's time for us to go home."

As they walked across the yard to their place, Haley suddenly realized it was up to her to tell Molly that Miss Jackson wouldn't be back to school.

She waited until Molly had taken her bath and was in bed before broaching the subject. Molly curled up on her side with her favorite stuffed lion tucked beneath her chin as Haley sat on the edge of her bed.

"Molly, I guess Miss Jackson wasn't in school today?" Molly's gaze darted in Haley's direction. "You had a substitute teacher?" Molly gave an almost imperceptible nod of her head.

How did you tell a child that her teacher had been murdered just like her mother? How much trauma could Molly take before she crawled so deep inside herself that nobody would ever be able to reach her?

"Molly, honey, I just want you to know that Miss Jackson won't be coming back to school for the rest of the year." Molly looked at her questioningly and Haley knew she wanted to know why.

For the life of her Haley couldn't tell her the truth. A fierce need to protect her made it impossible for Haley to tell her that Sondra Jackson was dead. Molly was only eight; there had already been too much death in her life.

"She moved away," Haley improvised. "I just wanted you to know that you'll probably have another teacher for the rest of the school year."

Molly squeezed her eyes closed and turned her head into the pillow. Haley sat on the edge of the bed for a long time, long after Molly had fallen asleep.

The silence of the room was broken only by the faint sound of Molly's childish snores. She'd turned over after she'd fallen asleep and now lay sprawled on her back, her rosebud lips slightly agape.

"Oh, Molly," Haley said softly. "If you'd just let me in." She reached out and gently swiped a strand of the baby-soft hair away from Molly's face.

Molly wouldn't have allowed the touch if she'd been awake. She never sought Haley's touch, never seemed to need a hug or a kiss. I need it, she thought suddenly. I need you, Molly.

Haley stood, stunned by this revelation. She'd spent all of her adult years priding herself on the fact that she didn't need anyone. After her father died she'd never asked for love from anyone.

But she needed this child of her sister's. She needed Molly not just to accept her, but to love her. The problem was Haley didn't know how to make that happen.

"So, I drove her to school this morning and spoke to the substitute about her talking issue," Haley told Grey the next day at lunch.

"You should have told her the truth, Haley. She's probably going to hear what happened to Sondra at school today, then she'll know you lied to her. That's not going to endear you to her."

Haley leaned back in the booth and sighed in frustration. "Okay, so I blew it. I looked at her face, looked into those innocent eyes of hers and I just couldn't tell her that her teacher had been murdered just like her mommy had." She tugged on a length of her hair. "Sondra Jackson's murder scared the hell out of me. I didn't want to scare the hell out of Molly."

Grey smiled sympathetically. "Your intentions were good."

"Yeah, but I just gave her another reason to hate me."

"Kids are wonderfully forgiving. Just tell her why you lied if it comes up." Grey stabbed a fry with his fork. "The police haven't called me in on this, I don't know anything about it. What are they telling you about this latest development?"

"Nothing. I called Tolliver this morning, but he said he had nothing new to tell me. If he can get free he's supposed to come by this afternoon to see if we can get Molly to write anything down, but with each day that passes I'm more and more convinced that Molly didn't see or hear anything that day."

"It's possible her trauma is from finding her mother's body, not necessarily from actually seeing or hearing the murder," he agreed.

She'd scarcely slept the night before, plagued by the same nightmare that had haunted her for so many nights in the past. She'd been beyond tense all morning, but the moment she'd stepped into the Salad Shoppe and had seen Grey, some of her inner demons had calmed.

But along with that calm came a swirl of excitement as well. It had been almost a year since she'd had a sexual relationship. Thankfully she'd discovered her last boyfriend, Tim, was a creep before she'd hopped into bed with him. And before Tim she'd gone through a dry spell where for a little over six months she'd sworn off men altogether.

As she sat across from Grey in the booth, surrounded by people, she was consumed with thoughts of sex and Grey. He had such nice lips; she wondered what they would taste like. Would his kisses be soft and teasing or harsh and demanding?

His hands were large and long-fingered, and it was easy to imagine them sliding down the length of her body, cupping her breasts with fevered heat. She let out a small gasp as her mind went even further and she imagined him naked lying next to her.

She stabbed a French fry into a pool of ketchup, wondering if she was finally completely and totally losing her mind.

"You okay?" Grey asked softly.

"Just stressed."

"How are you sleeping?"

"Terrible," she admitted. "You know, as far as I'm concerned the worst that could happen has happened. Somebody I loved was brutally murdered. The bad thing has already happened. It's done and over, but I can't seem to get rid of the feeling that something bad is still going to happen."

"That's pretty normal under the circumstances."

"It might be normal but it's damned irritating," she replied darkly, then sighed. "I'm not being very good company."

"It isn't your job to entertain me," he countered. "How are things going with your neighbor, the Stepford wife?"

"Angela? She's great. I don't know what I'd do without her, although I'll certainly never be like her. She's so amazingly perfect. Last night her husband came home late and she had dinner warming in the oven for him, she fixed him a drink and rubbed his shoulders."

"Sounds like heaven to me," Grey said, a teasing light in his gorgeous eyes.

She offered him a mock scowl. "She even has aprons. I didn't know there were still women who wore them, but Angela has them in every color." She dabbed her mouth with her napkin. "Angela is a very nice woman and she's been tons of help, but she's never going to be my best friend. She's never going to be somebody I can bare my heart to and tell all my secrets."

Grey looked at her intently. "Have you ever had somebody like that in your life?"

She considered the question thoughtfully. "Maybe my father when he was alive, but nobody since then."

"And why is that?"

She narrowed her eyes. "Are you analyzing me again?"

He grinned. "Stop being so defensive. Sometimes I just ask questions that are meant to get to know you better."

"Then the answer is that I don't really know. I've just never had a girlfriend or a boyfriend who I trusted enough to tell my secrets."

"What about Monica or your mother?"

Haley laughed. "No way. If I would have told Mom or Monica what kinds of thoughts were deep in my head, they would have had me committed by the time I was twelve." She rolled her eyes. "Guess that isn't the kind of thing you say to a psychologist. What about you? Did you tell all your secrets to your wife?"

Once again he leaned back against the booth and his eyes took on a distant look. "In the beginning of our marriage, yes. Sarah and I were college sweethearts. There was a time when we confided everything to each other."

"Then what happened?"

"I'm not sure. I guess we got busy with our separate lives. I was working hard to establish my practice. Sarah spent a lot of time volunteering and doing charity work." As always a deep darkness filled his eyes as he talked about his marriage, making Haley wonder what kind of unresolved issues the good doctor had about his own past.

Somehow she felt that Grey had demons of his own. What intrigued her was she'd never cared about anyone else's demons. She hadn't shared her inner thoughts and she'd never wanted anyone to share theirs with her. But she wanted his. She wanted to know everything there was to know about him. And that scared her more than a little bit.

"Anyway," he continued, "somehow in the rush of life, we drifted apart and stopped talking about the important things."

"If you had it to do over again, would you do things differently?"

She wouldn't have thought it possible but his eyes grew even darker. "Hindsight can be a wonderful gift, or a torturous curse," he said. "But to answer your question, yes, there are lots of things I would have done differently. What about you? You have regrets about how you've lived your life?"

"Absolutely," she replied without hesitation. "If I had it to do over again I would have never gotten those tattoos."

"That's it?" He quirked an eyebrow upward.

"That's all I'm willing to share at the moment," she replied with a grin.

"You don't trust easily, do you, Haley?"

"Most of the guys I've dated in the past weren't the type to deserve my trust." Funny, she'd never thought about it before, but she'd always chosen to date men who had more problems, more issues than she did. If she was a kite, then the men she'd involved herself with in the past had been missiles.

"I'll just have to see if I can change that," he said, a delicious flirting in his gaze.

"Shouldn't be too difficult. Isn't that what you therapists do? Inspire trust?" she said lightly.

"Haley, my desire to gain your trust has absolutely nothing to do with the fact that I'm a therapist and everything to do with the fact that I'm a man."

For just a moment Haley couldn't catch her breath. The heat of his gaze torched through her and once again she had the feeling that this man could be dangerous, in a decidedly delicious way.

"Why, Dr. Banes, I do believe you're trying to seduce me," she said half breathlessly.

"Ms. Lambert, I think you might be right," he agreed. "Although it's been a long time since I've tried my hand at seduction. I'm not sure if I'm doing it right."

"Oh, trust me, you're doing just fine." In fact, Haley couldn't remember the time she'd felt so utterly seduced. It surprised her: it was nothing he'd specifically said, and he'd scarcely touched her at all. It had everything to do with the look in his eyes.

He seduced by looking at her as if she were the sexiest, most beautiful woman in the world, by gazing at her so intently she felt as if for him there was nobody else in the room, nobody else in the world.

"Unfortunately, I've got to cut my seduction short as duty calls," he said with obvious regret.

"I hate when that happens," she replied.

They got up from the booth and as they walked toward the exit, Grey placed a hand on the small of her back. The touch sent electric currents shivering through her.

When they stepped outside on the sidewalk he dropped his hand, but remained so close she could smell the evocative scent of him, feel the heat of his breath on her face. "Sometime, when things are calmer in your life and Molly is better, I'd like to cook for you at my place."

"I'd love that," she replied. "Is that day going to come? When things are calmer and Molly is better?"

He reached out and placed his hand against her cheek in a gentle gesture that pierced through her. When was the last time she'd been touched with such gentleness by any man? She couldn't remember. "I promise you that day will come," he said softly.

He dropped his hand and stepped back from her. "And now I've got to get going. You'll call, if you need me?"

She smiled up at him. "You're number one on my speed dial."

Minutes later as she drove back to her house, she wondered if maybe what she felt for Grey Banes was some sort of weird patient-doctor transference. Hadn't she read somewhere that it wasn't uncommon for a patient to fall in love with her psychologist?

The only problem with that theory was she wasn't the patient and he wasn't her psychologist. Maybe it was nothing more than pure chemistry or hormone surges, or maybe it was simply the fact that she was alone in a dark and scary place, but Grey Banes drew her to him.

She knew she'd be wise to go slow where he was concerned, but she had a feeling she was going to do what she always did: dive in headfirst and deal with the consequences afterward.

NEED TO GET CONTROL.
NEED TO BREATHE. NEED TO THINK.
MUST BE SMARTER.
TOO MUCH, TOO FAST.
STUPID! STUPID!
NEED TO GET CONTROL.
BE SMART.
BE SLY.
GET RID OF HER.
GET RID OF THEM ALL!

Chapter 13

Haley knew she was in trouble the minute Molly got off the school bus. She held her princess book bag pressed tight against her chest and stomped past Haley without giving her a glance.

Haley hurried to catch up, entering the house in time to hear the thunderous slam of Molly's bedroom door. "You're in deep doo-doo," she muttered to herself as she knocked on Molly's door.

She supposed she should be grateful that Molly wasn't talking. At least she didn't yell "Go away, you lying bitch" through the door.

"Molly? Open the door, honey. I think we need to talk." The door didn't magically open, nor was there any indication that Molly wanted Haley anywhere near her.

"I'm coming in, Molly," she warned, then opened the door to see Molly seated on the edge of her bed. "I think maybe we need to talk." Haley sank down next to Molly.

Molly opened her book bag and pulled out a spiral notebook and a pencil. She opened the notebook and with the pencil carefully wrote something down, then held it up for Haley to see.

You lied. The words held the same accusation as that in Molly's eyes. She laid the notebook on the bed, then stood and ran out of the room.

"Molly!" Haley hurried after her. The kid was as fast as a Las Vegas dealer on a Saturday night. She was out the back door before Haley made it into the kitchen. "Molly, wait!"

Haley flew out the back door to see Molly running across the yard, then scampering up the wooden ladder that led to the tree house. By the time Haley got to the bottom of the tree Molly had disappeared into the neat little wooden box house with the blue curtains hanging on the tiny window.

"Molly, you need to come down from there," she called. "Look, I'm sorry, okay? Come down so we can talk about this."

She counted to ten, but there was no sign of Molly. You can do this, she told herself and grabbed hold of the sides of the ladder. She took one step up, tilted her head back to look at the tree house and instantly her breath caught painfully in her chest.

Oh God. She couldn't breathe. She couldn't get air into her lungs. Her legs wobbled as a wave of dizziness assaulted her. Panic attack. On some level of consciousness she recognized what it was but that didn't make it go away.

One minute she couldn't breathe and the next she was drawing quick, shallow breaths that rushed too much oxygen to her brain. She leaned against the ladder, her hands trembling as she fought for even breaths.

After several long moments she managed to release the wooden railing and fall back to the ground where she collapsed at the edge of the picnic table beneath the tree.

Way to go, sis. Monica's voice in her head held all the disgust that Haley felt for herself.

Molly sat in one corner of the small tree house, trying to ignore her aunt's voice. She was mad. She was so mad. Aunt Haley had told her a lie. Miss Jackson hadn't gone away. Miss Jackson had died. Their principal, Mr. Cookson, had told all the students that morning. Some of the kids had cried, but Molly hadn't. She'd been sad, but she'd gotten mad.

Her mommy had never lied to her about anything. Lying wasn't nice. "You'll never get in trouble if you just tell me the truth": That's what her mommy used to say. But Aunt Haley had told a big lie.

Her heart hurt so bad. She missed her mommy so much. Sometimes in the summer her mommy would pack a sack lunch for them and they'd eat it up here. They'd eat bologna sandwiches and talk about stuff.

Aunt Haley probably didn't even know how to make a good bologna sandwich. She didn't seem to know how to do much of anything. Except tell lies.

Molly frowned and watched the blue curtains shift a bit in the afternoon breeze. Her mommy had made those curtains from an old sheet. Molly had sat next to her while she'd sewn them.

A flash of blue.

A big sharp knife.

Molly sucked in her breath as the vision flashed in her mind. Her mommy on the floor. Blood. A flash of blue. A big sharp knife.

She squeezed her eyes tightly closed and shook her head as if to dislodge the images. She didn't want to remember. "I can't remember," she whispered to herself.

Sometimes at night she remembered everything in her dreams. Sometimes she woke up and thought she was hiding under her mommy's bed and she saw it happen all over again. But when she was awake, she wanted to forget. She tried real hard to forget.

"Molly? Please." Aunt Haley's voice drifted upward. "Please come down because I can't come up. Molly, can you hear me? I can't come up there because I'm afraid. I can't climb the ladder. I can't go into the tree house."

Molly frowned. Aunt Haley was afraid of the tree house? She scooted over to the window and looked out. Aunt Haley sat on the ground next to the wooden picnic table and she had her head down between her knees.

She scooted back to her corner, knowing eventually she'd have to come down out of the tree house. Sooner or later she'd have to potty or she'd get hungry. But she wasn't ready to climb down yet.

She needed to think about the fact that her Aunt Haley was afraid.

Sis, you're really messing this up.

It was Monica's voice that whispered in Haley's head, her voice filled with a profound sadness.

"Don't I know it," Haley muttered. She felt like throwing up and her niece was literally up a tree.

Tolliver found her there, on the ground with her head hung between her knees as the panic attack slowly faded. "I knocked on the front door, then heard your voice back here," he said. "Problems?"

Haley raised her head to look at the detective. "You have no idea." Slowly, still feeling a bit wobbly, she got to her feet only to sink down once again on the picnic bench. "Molly's up there." She pointed to the tree house. "She's mad at me. I can't get her to come down but maybe you can."

Tolliver sat across from her at the table. "What happened?"

"A mistake in judgment on my part." She told him about lying to Molly about Sondra Jackson. "I didn't realize she'd hear the truth in school."

"These days, a kid or a teacher dies and they announce it over the intercom, then provide counseling all day long for those kids who need it."

She'd thought the detective looked tired days ago, but today he looked almost ill with exhaustion. His skin had a gray pallor and bags hung beneath his eyes. "I don't suppose you've caught Sondra Jackson's murderer?"

"Don't I wish," he replied.

"From what Frank told me last night it's obvious Sondra was killed by the same person who killed my sister." She kept her voice low enough that Molly wouldn't be able to hear from her place in the tree.

"That's the theory we're working with." He pulled out a small bottle of antacids and popped two into his mouth, then continued. "It would have been easier for the investigation had your sister and Sondra Jackson been total strangers."

"Really? Why is that?" She would have thought just the opposite.

"Your sister and Sondra worked together at the school. They both were active in the PTA. They both were also on the board of the Pleasant Hill city council. The problem we have now is that there are too many people both women interacted with, too many connections. I've got a suspect list the length of my arm."

"You know, as awful as it sounds, I'm glad there are other connections," Haley said thoughtfully. "For a while last night after I spoke with Frank I worried that the only connection between the two was Molly."

They both looked up into the boughs of the tree where the late afternoon sunlight peeked through the leaves. Haley got up from the picnic table and walked to the ladder. "Molly, I know you're mad and don't want to talk to me. But Detective Tolliver is here and he needs to talk to you, so it's time to come down now."

To her surprise Molly peeked out of the window as if to make sure Haley wasn't lying about Tolliver's presence. A moment later she climbed down the ladder to the ground.

"Hi, Molly," Tolliver said. "I was wondering if we could go inside and I could talk to you for a few minutes."

Molly nodded and swept past Haley as if she were nothing more than a concrete birdbath standing in the yard. With a sigh of defeat, Haley followed the tall detective and the little girl into the house.

Tolliver sat at the kitchen table and motioned Molly into the chair next to his. "I've heard that you're a very smart girl and that you can write real well. Is that true?" Molly hesitated a moment, then nodded affirmatively. "So if I asked you some questions, you could write down the answers for me?"

Haley went to one of the drawers and withdrew a notepad and pencil, set them in front of her niece, then sat in the chair across from Molly. Nervous tension coiled in her stomach as she wondered what key Molly might hold to the murders.

"Maybe Dr. Tredwell should be here," Haley said. She suddenly worried about what Molly's reaction might be to the questions Tolliver intended to ask. Molly seemed to like Dr. Tredwell, to trust him. "What do you think, Molly? Should Detective Tolliver wait to ask you some questions until Dr. Tredwell is around?"

Molly gazed first at her, then at Tolliver, then shook her head to indicate it was okay for them to continue. Sometimes the strength of this kid astonished Haley, astonished her and made her proud.

"How do you feel today, Molly?" Tolliver asked. Despite his obvious exhaustion, his tone was gentle and filled with patience.

Molly picked up the pencil and twirled it between two fingers, then placed the lead end against the paper and wrote. *Sad and mad*. Her green eyes delivered a death ray in Haley's direction.

"I'm sorry you're feeling sad. I know you're mad at your aunt, but she was just trying to protect you. Sometimes when you love somebody you tell them little white lies so you don't make them upset."

Haley shot the detective a grateful glance, then looked back at Molly, who gazed at Tolliver expectantly.

"Molly, I want to talk to you about the morning that somebody hurt your mommy."

Molly's fingers tightened on the pencil, turning white with stress, and her eyes grew larger as she stared at Tolliver.

As much as Haley wanted answers, a fierce protectiveness surged up inside her as she saw the obvious tension that pinched Molly's features.

"Molly, honey, if you say or write 'stop,' then Detective Tolliver will stop asking you questions, okay?" She looked at Tolliver pointedly. He nodded to indicate that he agreed.

"Molly, that bad day, you stayed home from school because you were sick?"

Molly put pencil to paper. *Sore throat*.

"That's good, Molly. I can't believe how nice you write," Tolliver said. Molly seemed to relax a bit.

"So, you were home with a sore throat. Did you have breakfast?"

Molly nodded. *French toast*.

"You ate French toast, and then what did you do?" Tolliver asked.

Tension once again seemed to tighten Molly's features. Once again she wrote on the paper, then shoved it toward Tolliver so he could read what she'd written.

"Hide-and-seek. You and your mommy played hide-and-seek?" he asked. Molly nodded, her eyes huge and holding a sheen of imminent tears.

Emotion filled Haley as well. One of the last things her sister had done before her death was play hide-and-seek with her daughter. She could easily imagine Monica's laughter as she hid her eyes, counted to ten, then sought her daughter's hiding place.

"And where did you hide?" Tolliver asked.

Under the bed. Her handwriting wasn't as neat now. It showed tremendous stress.

"Now Molly, this is real important. When you hid under the bed did your mommy come looking for you?"

Molly stared at him for a long moment; then she wrote her answer, pressing the pencil so hard she broke the point. Haley got up and got her another one. "You're doing so well, honey. Your mommy would be so proud of you," she said as she handed the new sharp pencil to Molly.

Molly wrote, pressing so hard the pencil ripped the top sheet of paper. *Somebody came here.*

Tolliver sat up straighter and exchanged a meaningful glance with Haley. "You were hiding under the bed and somebody came. Did they ring the doorbell?" Molly shook her head. "Did they knock on the door?" She nodded, her breathing shallow and through her mouth. "Did you know who it was? Molly, do you know who came to the door that morning?"

Molly closed her eyes, her body trembling like a leaf in a wind-tossed tree. Haley wanted nothing more than to pull her into her arms, hold her until her trembling stopped. But before she could follow through on it, Molly opened her eyes and began to write.

Can't remember. A single tear trekked down her cheek.

"Did your mommy talk to the person who came to the door?" Tolliver asked. Molly jabbed her finger toward the words she'd just written, her breathing now rapid and uneven.

"Molly, did you hear or see the person who hurt your mommy?"

Molly shoved the notebook across the table at Tolliver, then jumped up and ran to her bedroom. Haley half stood to run after her, then sank back into her chair. She'd give Molly a little time alone, then go in and see if she could talk to her, comfort her.

"She's a dead end for us," Tolliver said, his disappointment obvious. "I think she probably has some knowledge that might be helpful, but she's too traumatized to access it and I'm not willing to push her any harder without Dr. Tredwell being present."

"Where do you go from here?" Haley asked.

The bags under Tolliver's eyes seemed to grow bigger. "Back to the drawing board," he said wearily. "We're looking into both your sister's life and Sondra Jackson's. We're comparing the crime scenes, looking for anything that might give us a lead."

"Did the killer leave behind prints or hairs or anything like that at the Jackson scene?" she asked.

"Just like your sister's, the Jackson scene was one of the cleanest I've ever seen."

"What does that tell you?" she asked curiously.

Tolliver ran a hand down his jaw where gray whiskers were beginning to show the length of his day. "It tells me that the killer is smart and that he has a good grasp of forensics."

"But it doesn't point a finger at anyone in particular," she said.

"Unfortunately, no." He got up from the table

and Haley walked him to the front door. He glanced down the hallway. "Will she be all right?"

"I hope so," Haley replied.

As soon as Tolliver left, Haley went down the hallway to Molly's room. As always when stressed, Molly sat on the bed, her stuffed lion in her lap.

"You okay?" Haley asked.

She didn't look at Haley, but instead drew her book bag toward her, withdrew her notebook and a pencil, then wrote something down. When she was finished she handed Haley the notebook.

Why are you afraid of the tree house?

Haley stared down at the words on the paper. Why indeed? She set the notebook aside and moved closer to Molly on the bed. "I'm not sure," she said. Molly looked at her in disgust.

"I'm not trying to get out of answering your question, Molly. Did you know my daddy, your grandpa, built that tree house? I was ten years old at the time and I helped him." Haley stared at the wall opposite the bed as her head filled with sweet memories.

The distinctive scent of sawdust, her father's strong, warm hand covering hers as she sanded a sheet of plywood. *That's it, Haley girl, sand it good and smooth.*

Along with the memories came the pain that always accompanied thoughts of her father. "Anyway, we got the tree house built, then for three days your grandpa and I spent time up there. We talked and we laughed and for those three days I thought my world couldn't get any better. Then one night my daddy went to sleep and he never woke up again."

She looked at Molly, who watched her as if she were a particularly interesting species of insect. "Anyway, after my dad was gone, I tried to go back up to the tree house, but I couldn't. I could get a step or two up the ladder, then I'd get so afraid I thought I might die. I couldn't breathe, my heart beat so fast I thought it was going to explode right out of my chest."

She closed her eyes and drew in a deep breath to calm the anxiety that seared through her just thinking about climbing that ladder. "Over the years I've tried to go back up there, but I can't. I don't know why, but I just can't."

Molly's little hand covered hers. Haley opened her eyes and looked at her. Their gazes held and in the depths of Molly's eyes Haley saw a child's compassion, an understanding of fear too great to name. It lasted only a moment; then Molly moved her hand and broke the gaze.

For the first time since arriving in Pleasant Hill, Haley felt hope buoy her heart. Maybe, just maybe she and Molly would make it after all. And for the first time since taking over the care of her niece, Haley didn't hear Monica's worried voice in her head.

"One step forward, two steps back," Haley said on Friday afternoon as once again she and Grey ate lunch at the Salad Shoppe. This was the third lunch they'd shared in as many days, and even though she tried not to always talk about Molly, the subject was never far from her mind.

She released a deep sigh and reached for the bottle of ketchup in the center of the table. "I thought maybe she was starting to accept me. Then this morning she wanted to wear a particular blouse to school and it was in the dirty clothes and she stormed to the bus stop like I was personally responsible for everything bad in the world."

Haley sighed again. Two weeks today. Two weeks ago on this morning Monica had answered her door and let a killer into her house.

"She'll survive a dirty blouse," Grey replied. "I've told you again and again, Haley, it's going to take time."

"I know, but patience has never been one of my strong suits," she said dryly. She squirted a pool of ketchup on her plate.

"I've noticed that," he returned with that teasing, flirting light in his eyes. The light faded. "Anything new on the case? I haven't been in to the station for the last week."

"Nothing. I'm beginning to think we'll never know who was responsible."

"Can you live with that?" he asked.

"I may not have any other choice."

"Do you miss your friends, your life back in Las Vegas?"

"I had bar acquaintances, not friends. And as far as missing my life, I haven't had time." She grabbed a French fry and dragged it through the tomato pool.

"And why is that, Haley?"

She frowned. "Why haven't I had time?"

He smiled. "No, why is it that you only had bar acquaintances in your life and no real friends?"

"Why do I get the feeling every time we talk that you're analyzing me?"

He grinned, that flash of humor that showed off his devastating dimples. "Maybe that's because I am."

"Then stop it," she said impatiently.

He laughed. "I can't help it. You fascinate me."

His words sent a rush of feminine pleasure sweeping through her. "I've always heard that therapists are half crazy themselves," she replied.

Laughter still rode his features, flashing his dimples and deepening the attractive lines around his eyes. She popped the fry in her mouth and chewed thoughtfully. "Why did you quit your private practice?" she asked.

He broke eye contact with her as a small frown pulled his dark brows closer to each other. "I was ready for a change, needed a change. I had a successful practice, but it required a lot of hours. I'd always wanted to teach and two years ago decided it was time to make some changes in my life."

"I'll bet you're a good teacher."

He raised a brow. "Why?"

She shoved her now empty plate to the side. "Because you're kind and you seem to have an endless supply of patience. At least you've been very patient with me. I imagine your students adore you."

He laughed. "I don't know about that. I wouldn't ask any of them right now how they feel about me. It's finals." As they got up to leave the restaurant he said, "You've got the weekend ahead. Any plans?"

"Nothing specific. I thought maybe I'd take Molly to the park or to a movie. Get us out of the house for a little while. Sometimes the quiet makes me feel as if I'm going a little crazy."

"Despite everything you've told me about yourself, I think you're one of the sanest people I know," Grey replied as they stepped out into the warm afternoon sunshine.

Haley laughed. "I'd hate to meet the other people you hang out with."

"Can I call you over the weekend?"

"I'd like that," she replied. She was hot for him, there was no question about it, but she was also a little afraid of yet another failure.

Driven by hormones, as usual, Monica's voice whispered in her head. Her voice held the loving indulgence it had often had when she'd chided Haley.

Minutes later in the car her thoughts remained filled with Grey Banes. Each time she saw him she experienced a euphoric high that was more pleasurable than a belt of the best Scotch on the shelf, more tantalizing than a piece of gourmet chocolate.

During the last two lunches they had shared, she had been surprised to learn that he was an avid motorcycle enthusiast, a passionate advocate for animal rights as well as children's rights, and that in the sixteen years of his marriage he'd never even thought about cheating on his wife.

What she hadn't yet learned was what caused the darkness that sometimes deepened the hue of his eyes, what he'd meant when he'd told her that grief had happened to his marriage.

With lunch behind her, Haley looked ahead to dinner. Maybe she'd see if Molly wanted to eat out. At least if they ate in a restaurant there would be noise. Other people would talk and maybe listening to them would ease the silence of their own meal.

Since the night that Haley had confessed her fear of the tree house, there had been no more moments of closeness between the two. However, Molly had begun not spending so much time in her bedroom and instead for the past two nights had sat in the living room with Haley to watch television until bedtime.

Instead of eating out that evening, Haley called for a pizza delivery. As they waited for the pizza Molly sat at the table doing homework and Haley stood staring out the window where dark clouds had begun to gather, portending a spring storm.

Monica had always hated storms. Haley loved them. There was something about the wild turbulence of nature's fury that spoke to something elemental and wild inside her.

She turned away from the window. "Looks like maybe it's going to rain." Molly looked up from her homework. "Are you afraid of lightning and thunder?" Haley asked. Molly shook her head.

At that moment the doorbell rang, signaling the arrival of the pizza. As Haley paid the pizza guy, she noticed Grant Newton standing outside on his front porch. He appeared to be looking directly at her.

There was no reason to believe Grant Newton felt any malevolence toward her, and yet that's what she felt radiating from him across the distance between their houses.

Maybe the police had told him that she'd mentioned seeing him at the school on the night of Sondra's murder. What other reason could he have for glaring at her? A chill danced up her spine.

She grabbed the pizza and went back inside, locking the door as thunder rumbled in the distance.

Bacon. The scent of bacon rode the air. It must be almost time to get up for school. Any moment now her father would come into her room. "Haley girl," he'd say. "Bacon and eggs in five minutes and I need to see your smiling face at the table."

Haley awakened with a start, opening her eyes to the complete darkness of the room. A dream. As the last of the bittersweet images faded, she sat up and frowned.

She was fully awake now, conscious enough to hear the wind blowing outside her bedroom window and feel the weight of the sheet against her bare legs. So why did she still smell bacon?

A terrible sense of something wrong rang alarms in her head. She swung her feet over the side of the bed and got up. When she reached her bedroom door the scent of something burning grew stronger.

"Molly?" A glance into Molly's bedroom assured her that Molly was in bed and appeared to be sound asleep.

She ran down the hallway, and as she came into the living room she could see a strange flickering light, tasted acrid smoke in the back of her throat and heard the distinctive crackle of fire coming from the direction of the kitchen.

A shriek escaped her as she flew into the kitchen and saw a skillet on the stovetop. The burner beneath was cherry red and flames danced up toward the ceiling.

For a moment she stood frozen in the doorway, her brain trying to make sense of what was happening. What the hell? The flames jumped to a dish towel next to the stove, and her inertia broke as she realized if she didn't do something fast the whole damn house was going to burn down.

Chapter 14

Panic torched through her as white-hot as the flames that leapt toward the ceiling. The smoke was thicker, making her cough as she ran to the sink to get water.

She stopped with her hand on the faucet, her mind racing frantically. Hadn't she heard somewhere not to use water on a grease fire?

Molly appeared in the kitchen doorway and released the scream that Haley had trapped inside her. "Molly, get out of here," Haley yelled. "Go outside . . . no, don't go outside. Go stand by the front door and if I tell you to run, then you run next door."

As Molly disappeared from the doorway, Haley left the sink and ran to the pantry where she grabbed a bag of flour, then hurried back to the stove and began to dump the flour on the skillet, the counter and anything else that looked as if it might at any moment burst into flames.

It took the entire bag, and by the time she was finished the stove, the nearby cabinet and she were all covered with the white powder, but the fire was out.

She tossed the empty flour bag on the floor and leaned against the counter, her legs trembling so badly she thought she might fall. What in the hell?

She finally managed to get to the window and open it to allow some of the smoke to dissipate as the night wind blew in.

"Molly? Honey, it's okay now. The fire is out."

Molly reappeared in the kitchen doorway and reached up to flick on the overhead light. With the flood of light, Haley saw the extent of the mess . . . and that a skillet she'd never seen before in her life was responsible for the mess.

Terror sizzled through her, a terror that she fought to hide from her niece. "Molly, we need to go next door." Molly looked at her in surprise. "I'm going to see if maybe you can spend the rest of the night at Angela's house so I can clean up this mess. Besides, I need to talk to Frank."

Haley glanced at the clock on the wall. Just after two. She didn't want to frighten Molly any more than she had already been frightened. She wanted Molly next door and she wanted Frank here now. She definitely didn't want Molly to hear what she had to tell Frank: that somebody had just tried to kill them.

It took only minutes for Molly to get her slippers on and grab her stuffed lion. Then she and Haley stepped outside the house into the thick, humid night air.

The storm that had been portended had apparently passed over without rain, but the night sky was filled with clouds, without moonlight or starshine. A perfect night for evil.

Haley held Molly close to her as they walked the

distance from their house to next door. Her heart banged unsteadily with the rhythm of fear as her gaze darted first in one direction, then in the other.

She felt surrounded by darkness: the darkness of night, the darkness of evil, the very darkness of her head trying to make sense of what had happened.

Her brain felt frozen, unable to process what had just occurred. When they reached the Marcelli front porch Haley rang the doorbell, hoping she didn't wake up the kids, but needing help.

She waited less than a minute, then rang the bell again. The porch light flicked on, half blinding her. She squinted as the door opened and Angela greeted them. "Haley? My God, what happened?" She opened the door and Haley guided Molly in before her. "What's going on? What time is it?" Angela swept her dark sleep-tousled hair from her face.

"It's after two. I'm sorry to bother you. Is Frank home?"

"He's in bed."

"Could you get him up? Please? And can Molly spend the rest of the night here?" Haley tightened her fingers on Molly's shoulders and prayed that Angela wouldn't ask any more questions.

Angela gazed at her for a long moment, then grabbed Molly by the hand. "Come on, sweetheart, let's get you tucked into bed." She looked at Haley once again. "I'll be right back. It might take a few minutes, Frank usually sleeps like the dead."

She disappeared with Molly down the hallway. Haley wrapped her arms around herself, trying to fight a shiver of terror that threatened to consume her.

Fire. Fire in her kitchen. In a skillet she'd never

WITHOUT A SOUND 185

seen. On a burner that shouldn't have been hot. Fire. In her kitchen.

It felt like an eternity before Frank came down the hallway, his hair askew and his eyes slightly swollen. He wore a pair of jeans and as he approached pulled a T-shirt over his head. Angela followed just behind him, her pink floor-length nightgown billowing with each step.

"Jesus, what happened to you?" he asked.

"There was a fire in my kitchen." She drew a deep breath in an attempt to steady herself. "I don't want to be overly dramatic here, but I think somebody tried to kill us, Frank."

"Let me get my gun." He turned and hurried down the hallway once again.

"My God, Haley, are you sure you're okay?" Angela reached out and took Haley's hand. She hadn't realized how cold her hand was until Angela's warm hand surrounded hers. "Listen, don't worry about Molly. She can spend the day here tomorrow. You take care of whatever needs to be taken care of."

"Thanks, Angela."

"Let's go see what we've got," Frank said as he returned. He had his gun in one hand, his police radio clipped to his jeans and a reassuring sharpness in his gaze.

"I smelled bacon," she said as they walked back across the yard. "I smelled bacon and when I went into the kitchen there was a skillet on the stove and it was on fire. I've never seen that skillet before in my life."

"You stay here," Frank commanded when they reached her front porch. "Let me clear the house, then you can come back in."

Don't leave me, Haley wanted to cry. She grabbed a piece of her hair and tugged, the slight pain of the pull momentarily stilling the hysteria that threatened to explode.

Lightning flashed in the distance, the remnants of the storm that hadn't released a single drop of rain. The wind whipped through her hair but she scarcely noticed it.

All she smelled on the wind was smoke. All she felt was the burn of fire against her skin. All she could think about was the fact that somebody had been in the house.

Somebody had gotten in and placed that skillet on a burner, then turned the burner on high and left it to catch on fire. That skillet had been filled with bacon grease. She knew it as certainly as she knew her own name.

"It's clear," Frank said from the front door. "I've called it in. Somebody should be here in a few minutes. You need to make an official report."

She followed him into the kitchen, where the smoke was almost gone out the open window, but the smell of fire still lingered. "Can't you just take my report?"

"I'd rather it be somebody else, somebody who isn't your next-door neighbor." Frank looked at the mess, then at her. "I didn't see any signs of a break-in. Was the front door locked when you and Molly left the house?"

"Yes, I unlocked it to leave."

"Was there a lot of smoke?" He looked up toward the ceiling. Haley followed his gaze to find him eyeing the smoke detector in one corner of the room.

"Enough that the smoke detector should have been screaming like a banshee," she replied.

She watched as Frank pulled a chair over to the wall, then stood on it and took the cover off the detector. From her vantage point she could see the battery in it.

"You got another battery?" he asked.

A drawer full of miscellaneous items yielded a fresh battery. She handed it to Frank and he replaced the old with the new. "Match or a lighter?"

She found a pack of matches in the same drawer and gave them to him. He lit one and held it just beneath the detector. It screamed its warning until he punched the button to shut it off.

"You might want to go clean up before the police arrive," he said as he got off the chair and placed it back into position at the table.

Haley suddenly realized she was clad only in the oversized T-shirt that served as her night attire. The shirt hit her midthigh and without a bra beneath was definitely more than a little bit risqué.

"I'll be right back." She left the kitchen and hurried back to her bedroom where she grabbed a pair of jeans, her bra and a T-shirt, then went into the bathroom to change.

She gasped as she saw her reflection in the mirror. Her face and hair held a dusting of flour. She looked like a skinny, frightened Pillsbury Doughboy.

As she scrubbed her face, then ran a brush through her hair to remove as much of the white powder as possible, she tried to keep her mind empty, but it refused to cooperate.

Somebody had been in her house. The words

reverberated over and over again in her head. Somebody had been in her house.

A person had crept in, in the middle of the night.

How had they gotten in? Had they opened a window and climbed through? She hadn't thought to check windows to make sure they were locked.

Or was it somebody who had a key to the house?

The thought chilled her, but no more than the entire incident did. It was insidious. It was evil. If Haley hadn't awakened, the house would have filled with smoke and it was possible she and Molly would have succumbed to smoke inhalation.

If she hadn't awakened, it was very possible that she and Molly would have been dead long before morning. The house would have burned down around them, and their deaths would have been written off as a tragic accident.

Her hand trembled violently as she pulled on her jeans. Had it been Monica's killer who had done this? Had it been an attempt to ensure that Molly stayed silent forever?

Who had keys to the house? Haley hadn't once considered the fact that the locks on the doors now were the locks on the door when her sister had been murdered. Maybe Monica hadn't opened the door and allowed her killer in. Maybe the killer had a key and had just come inside.

Who had the wickedness to even think of doing such a thing? Had the person who put the skillet on the stove and turned on the burner also made sure that the battery in the smoke detector was bad?

She pulled her T-shirt on over her head as a knock sounded on the front door. The police had arrived.

*   *   *

It was close to three thirty when the two officers who had arrived to take her statement left. "You going to be all right?" Frank asked as he walked to the door.

"They didn't believe me, did they?" Haley said flatly. Some of the fear that had clawed at her for the past hour had quieted, replaced by the frustration of talking to the officers who had responded to the call.

Frank raked a hand through his hair and released a tired sigh. "You made the report, that's what's important."

"You believe me, don't you, Frank?" She eyed him intently.

"Sure I do," he said after a moment of hesitation. But that hesitation let her know he wasn't quite sure.

"Go, get out of here and sleep for what's left of the night. And thanks for everything."

The minute Frank left, Haley's fear returned. The house felt alien, a landscape from a nightmare. The silence was deafening and the last thing she wanted was to be alone. She turned on every light in the house, but that didn't keep her fear at bay.

She wanted a shower to wash away the stink of smoke and the flour that was embedded in her hair, but she couldn't think of anything more terrifying than being beneath a spray of water and unable to hear or know who might be creeping back into the house. Visions of *Psycho* danced in her head, Janet Leigh slashed through a shower curtain.

She needed to talk to somebody. She wanted noise and another human presence. She wanted Grey.

She didn't take any time to talk herself out of it. She dug his home number out of her purse and picked up the phone.

He answered on the second ring. "Dr. Grey Banes." He sounded alert and awake, as if he'd just been sitting near the phone waiting for her call.

"Grey, it's me, Haley."

"What's happened? Are you all right? Is Molly?"

"Molly's fine. I need . . . could you come over here?"

"I'll be right there."

Haley hung up the phone, grateful that he hadn't wasted time asking questions. She knew he lived in an apartment complex about fifteen minutes away.

As she waited for him she made a pot of coffee. She used a pot holder to place the offending skillet into a plastic bag, then set the bag on the dryer in the utility room.

Her hands were steady, but the trembling hadn't disappeared altogether: it had just gone deep inside her.

Studiously ignoring the rest of the mess the fire had left behind, she carried a cup of the fresh brew to the table and sat, then wrapped her hands around the warmth of the cup. She was still having trouble processing what had happened. Even sitting there, staring at the aftermath on the stovetop, a sense of disbelief swept through her.

Who would have done such a thing? Who was responsible for such an evil act? Her gaze shot to the kitchen window, where cool night air drifted in. Was somebody out there now, watching her? Was somebody out there cursing the fact that she'd awakened and ruined their deadly plan?

She jumped up from the table and slammed the window, then locked it and pulled the curtains shut. It was beyond creepy. Had the person who had placed the skillet on the stove crept down the hallway and peeked into the bedroom to see Molly sleeping? To see her sleeping? If that person had wanted to kill them, then why not stab them in their sleep? Bludgeon them in their beds?

Because it was supposed to look like an accident. There was no other explanation. Somebody wanted either her, Molly or both of them dead, but hadn't wanted the crime to be investigated as a murder.

A knock sounded from the front door and she hurried to answer. She hadn't realized just how vulnerable she felt until Grey stepped into the entry and she launched herself at him before he could say a word.

He wrapped his arms around her as she burrowed her face into his chest. For the first time since awakening to the horror some of the chill was chased away by the warmth of his embrace.

"Hey, what's going on?" he asked softly.

"Somebody tried to kill us tonight."

He grabbed her by the upper arms and pushed her away from him so he could look into her face. "What are you talking about?"

She led him through the living room and into the kitchen, then explained what had happened. He stared at the stove, at the half-burned dish towel, then back at her. "Did you call the police?"

"I did. I took Molly next door to spend the rest of the night, then the police came and I made a report." She sighed gratefully as he pulled her back against his chest.

She closed her eyes and breathed in the scent of him, clean male coupled with a hint of spicy cologne. "They didn't believe me."

He led her to the table where she sat in one of the chairs and he took the seat opposite her. "What do you mean they didn't believe you?"

Frustration edged through her as she thought of the demeanor of the officers who had taken her report. "They thought I'd accidentally left the stove on and went to bed. They thought that it was just a careless mistake by a woman under stress."

She jumped up from the table, unable to sit while energy flooded her veins. "Heck, I wish that's what had happened. But when I was at the store I bought milk and forgot bread. I bought eggs but forgot bacon. It was bacon I smelled, bacon grease, but there wasn't a strip of bacon in this house."

Somewhere in the back of her mind she knew she was rambling, but he made no effort to stop her. It was as if he knew what she needed most at the time was to vent and somebody to listen to her vent.

"I was hoping they'd dust for fingerprints, take photographs and treat this like it was . . . like a crime scene," she continued. "It *is* a crime scene. Jesus, you're supposed to be safe in your own home. Then your sister opens the door and lets in a murderer and the next thing you know somebody has gotten inside in the middle of the night and tried to kill you."

"Is that fresh coffee over there?"

She froze and stared at him in stunned disbelief. She was having a complete and total meltdown, and he wanted to know if the coffee was fresh?

What an insensitive ass. She didn't know if she should pour it into a cup or pour it over his head.

It wasn't until she stalked over to the coffee machine that she realized what he'd done. By asking a simple question he'd effectively defused her, halted the rising hysteria that had threatened to explode.

She placed the cup of coffee in front of him, then plopped into the kitchen chair across from him. "You're obviously a very smart man and maybe just a little devious."

He nodded, as if to accept her character assessment. "How do you think they got inside?"

"I don't know." She frowned, troubled by the question. "It's possible there was a window unlocked. Either that or somebody has a key." She stared at the back door. "If they had a key it would have been pretty easy to come in through that door without me hearing anything."

"Who might your sister have given a key to?" he asked.

"I don't know. Yesterday I would have said that nobody had a key to this house. Monica had been alone a long time. She was always so careful. But now I'm not so sure. One thing is certain, first thing tomorrow morning I'm calling out a locksmith to change all the locks."

"Sounds like a smart thing," he replied. He lifted the coffee cup and took a swallow, eyeing her over the cup's rim. "Do you think this is about Molly? Maybe the killer returned to make sure she remains silent?"

"I don't know. In the last thirty minutes I've considered every possibility. If it isn't about Molly, then it has to be about me and I can't think of a single person I've pissed off so much since arriving here that they'd want me dead. Except maybe you, for waking you up in the middle of the night."

He smiled and placed his cup back on the table. "I'm glad you called me."

She held his gaze, wondering what it was about him that inspired confidence, encouraged trust. "I was scared," she admitted. "I was afraid to stay here alone for the rest of the night. I was afraid to get into the shower to clean up." Even now just thinking about what had happened, her throat threatened to close up with fear.

"Why don't you go take a shower now," he suggested.

She gazed at him hesitantly. "Are you sure you don't mind?" Although it made no sense, she felt dirty. It had nothing to do with the flour that itched at her scalp or the smoke that clung to her skin.

"Haley, I'm here for as long as you need me to be here. Go take a shower. I'll be right here when you're through."

Minutes later as she stood beneath water almost hot enough to raise blisters, she once again tried to make sense of the night's events. Had the motive been to kill Molly?

Somehow that didn't feel right. Monica's murder had occurred over two weeks before and if the killer was really afraid of what Molly knew, then wouldn't he have tried to silence her sooner? Why wait a week? Why wait two?

If it was about her, then who would want her dead? She hadn't made any enemies, at least none that she knew of. She suddenly thought of Grant Newton. Had he been the one who nearly ran her down in the school parking lot the night of the parent-teacher meetings? At the time she'd thought it was nothing but a close call with an unsuspecting driver, but now it took on more ominous undertones.

She remembered feeling as if he was looking at her earlier in the evening when she'd stepped outside to get the pizza from the delivery boy. His gaze had felt malevolent, as if he wished her ill.

Over the course of the past week there had been moments when she'd felt as if somebody was watching her, when the hairs on the nape of her neck rose in response to a chill walking up her spine. Was Grant Newton spying on her? Watching her coming and going from the house, watching as she and Molly went about their business?

But why would Grant Newton have any feelings, good or bad, toward her? He didn't even know her. But he knew Monica. And Monica knew Sondra Jackson. Was there something about her sister's life she hadn't known?

By the time she shut off the shower her head ached from all the questions attacking her brain. She dressed in a pair of sweats and a Las Vegas T-shirt, then returned to the kitchen to discover that Grey hadn't just been sitting at the table drinking coffee.

He stood at the stove, his shirtsleeves rolled up and a scouring pad in hand. "Grey, you shouldn't have," she protested.

He whirled around at the sound of her voice. "It actually looked much worse than it was," he said. "Once I got the flour cleaned up there wasn't as much damage as I thought there would be." His gaze held hers. "If you'd slept another five minutes it might have been a different story."

"Don't remind me. And please, don't scrub my stove anymore. You're making me feel horribly guilty."

He shrugged and tossed the scouring pad into the sink. It was at that moment that Haley realized she wanted this man. She didn't just want his company. She didn't just want his presence.

They hadn't even shared a kiss, had barely touched in any way other than casual, and yet she wanted to know him on an elemental level that had nothing to do with the way he laughed or how safe he made her feel.

She wanted to know the texture of his thick dark hair, trace the shape of his lips with her fingertips. She needed to know how he kissed, how well their bodies fit together, how skilled he might be in making her forget everything, including her own name, for at least a short period of time.

"Haley, what are you thinking?" he asked softly.

"I'm thinking that I'd like you to take me to bed and make love to me."

For the first time since she'd known him, he visibly lost his composure. His cheeks flushed and he leaned back against the stove as if momentarily knocked off balance. His jaw tensed. "Haley, believe me, there's nothing I'd like more, but I'm not sure you're thinking clearly right now and the last thing I'd want is for you to think, tomorrow or the next day, that I took advantage of you."

The fact that he hadn't jumped her bones before she could take a second breath only made her want him more. She walked to where he stood, stopping only when she was mere inches from him.

Although the odor of smoke still lingered in the

air, she could smell him, the distinctive scent of male that made a flurry of butterflies take flight in her stomach. "I would never, ever accuse you of taking advantage of me," she said. "And I would hope before this night is over you won't accuse me of taking advantage of you."

She reached up and placed her palm against his cheek, felt the bristle of whiskers against her skin. Someplace deep inside she knew her sister would judge this as just another self-destructive choice in a long line of such choices. But, it didn't feel self-destructive. It felt right.

"Why, Ms. Lambert, are you trying to seduce me?" His eyes held a teasing glint of heat.

"If you have to ask, then I must not be doing it right," she replied.

"Oh, trust me, you're doing just fine."

She saw the flash of his eyes just before he dipped his head to capture her lips with his. Tentative at first, his mouth was soft as it feathered against hers.

She leaned into him and closed her eyes. The simple, uncomplicated kiss worked magic on her frayed nerves and reached inside to heat the cold core she'd lived with for the past two weeks.

But the kiss didn't remain uncomplicated. With a throaty groan he deepened the kiss, touching his tongue first to her bottom lip, then to her tongue.

Haley felt electrified. Their tongues swirled together and he wrapped his arms around her, pulling her close, closer, until she was flush against the solid strength of his body.

His hands slid up her back, warming her through her T-shirt, and she couldn't help but notice how hard and masculine his chest felt against her own.

There was an intensity to his kiss that made her breathless. It was the same breathlessness she felt when he gazed at her so intently, as if he could see every secret, every thought in her head.

He finally broke the kiss, his midnight blue eyes staring into hers. "Haley, it's been almost two years since I've been with a woman." His cheeks took on a redder hue and he laughed softly. "If you're looking to make love until dawn, it's not going to happen with me. In fact, if I kiss you for too much longer, it's all going to be over before it even begins."

She smiled at his confession, feeling some of the nervous tension inside her begin to release. "It's been a year since I've been with anyone," she told him. "Grey, I want to be close to you."

He released his hold on her and traced the shape of her lips with his fingertip. "You know if we do this, nothing changes in your life. Your questions won't be answered, your stress won't go away and the danger doesn't disappear."

She smiled again. "Grey, I'm not delusional. I know what I'm doing here." In truth she didn't have a clue what she was doing, but that had never stopped her before.

She took his hand in hers and pulled him away from the stove and toward the kitchen door. Although she was realistic enough to know that going to bed with Grey wouldn't change anything in her life, she also knew that at least for a little while he could make her forget.

They didn't speak a word as they walked down the hallway and into Haley's bedroom. The room was a reflection of her life, disorganized and chaotic. She knew she should probably be embarrassed by the clothes on the chair, the clutter of cosmetics and perfume on the dresser, but she wasn't.

The chaos was as much a part of her as her blond hair, her deep green eyes and her inability from the time she was a child to adhere to the adage of "a place for everything and everything in its place."

Grey didn't seem to notice the mess. As they stepped into the room he kissed her once again. This time his kiss held voracious hunger and a powerful command that was compelling.

As he kissed her his hands smoothed down her back to cup her buttocks and pull her closer against him, close enough that she could feel his arousal.

She trusted him, trusted him more than she'd ever trusted any man in her past. She knew instinctively that he would take what she was willing to offer and ask for nothing more. He was probably the most well-adjusted man she'd ever been attracted to and that in itself held more than a little appeal.

It didn't take long for kissing not to be enough. She wanted him skin to skin. She broke the kiss long enough to step back.

It wasn't just his lips that spoke of his hunger for her: his desire smoked in his hot gaze as she pulled her T-shirt over her head.

His gaze lingered on her wispy bra, feeling like a caress that tautened her nipples and weakened her knees. His breathing was ragged as his fingers worked to unfasten the buttons of his shirt.

When his shirt came off his gorgeous, broad chest, something between them snapped. Haley managed to turn off the overhead light before the rest of their clothes came off and they fell together on the bed, a tangle of naked limbs and abandoned control.

Slow and languid, his hands learned her, sweeping over her breasts, down the flat of her stomach and down the length of her thighs. He touched her everywhere but where she needed him most, an exquisite form of pleasurable torture.

She too learned the lines and planes of his body, running her hands across his strong muscled chest, coiling her fingers in the springy dark hair there, then moving lower to his abdomen. The lower her hands moved, the more taut his muscles became, the more ragged his breathing.

She nipped at his neck with her lips and teeth, reveling in the throaty moans that escaped him. Thoughts of murder and mayhem melted away, tucked into the far recesses of her mind as she gave herself with abandon to the moment.

This was what she'd wanted, the falling into oblivion as her mind filled with Grey and her body ached with need. When she could stand it no longer, when she felt as if she might disintegrate from that need, she whispered to him to hurry.

"Now, Grey, please," she urged him, and she only had to say it once. He moved between her thighs and entered her, sliding into her moistness as if he belonged there.

Haley's senses spun with overwhelming sensations as he began to stroke in and out, his breath hot against her neck, every muscle in his body tense.

Thinking was impossible as she simply breathed in his scent, raked her hands down his broad back and felt the building of a climax. She gave herself to it, riding the waves as they crashed over her and through her.

He stiffened and released a deep moan as he found his own release. He collapsed on top of her and for a long moment remained there, as if too weak, too drained to move.

She didn't mind; rather she enjoyed the solid weight of him, his warmth that surrounded her and made her feel safe and secure.

After several long minutes, he rolled to the side of her, but instead of getting up as she thought he might do, he wrapped his arms around her and pulled her into a warm embrace.

That was the last thing Haley knew.

Grey knew the instant she fell asleep. Like a sated kitten she cuddled close, almost purring as she fell into the unconsciousness of slumber.

It was nearing dawn but Grey wasn't sleepy in the least. With Haley's warm, naked curves pressed against him, he found himself wondering once again what in the hell he was doing.

Almost two years ago his life had been exploded apart by a tragedy that would haunt him for the rest of his days. Six months after that his wife had walked out, effectively taking what little had been left of him with her. He'd vowed at that time that he would never again become emotionally involved with anyone.

And yet here he was, in bed with a beautiful woman who had somehow managed to get beneath his defenses. She was the strongest, most vulnerable woman he'd ever met. She was a bundle of contradictions, dealing effectively with situations that would bring others to their knees, and yet with a core of something that called to everything protective and masculine he had inside of him.

Haley Lambert had the potential to break his heart and there was nothing he could do about it. And somebody had tried to kill her tonight.

He tightened his arms around her and breathed in the scent of her, a touch of vanilla mingled with more exotic spices.

He believed her. He believed that she hadn't accidentally left a skillet on the stove. She hadn't been careless cooking.

He'd tried to keep up with the murder investigation that had brought Haley into his life, but for the last week he'd been busy with finals at the college. Besides, despite the fact that he was a familiar face at the police station, he wasn't a cop and often wasn't privy to everything the cops knew.

He closed his eyes, his head filling with a vision of Molly. He'd kept his distance from Jerry Tredwell, consciously not touching base to see how Molly was doing. He trusted his colleague was doing everything possible to try to reach Molly.

Still, the child haunted him. He'd never forget the terror in her eyes, the paleness of her face just after she'd been pulled out from beneath the bed.

She was the kind of patient he might have seen if he'd still been in private practice. Like Jerry Tredwell, his specialty had been children. And he'd been good: one of the best in the state.

It had taken only one failure to destroy him, a failure he would never forget, for it was etched painfully into his soul.

He'd told Haley to be patient when it came to

Molly's recovery, but it was difficult to be patient when he thought about what had happened tonight. Time might be running out for Molly and Haley.

His heart chilled. Haley had the potential to break his heart, unless somebody killed her before she got the opportunity.

Chapter 15

She smelled something cooking and shot out of bed, heart crashing against her ribs as she raced down the hall to the kitchen.

She nearly fell to her knees in relief as she saw Grey standing in front of the stove, flipping pancakes on a griddle. She must have made a noise for Grey looked up, obviously startled.

"I smelled something. I thought there was a fire."

"Pancakes. And if you plan to eat dressed the way you are right now, there *is* a possibility of a fire breaking out."

Heat leapt into her cheeks as she realized she was stark naked. "I'll be right back." She left the kitchen and headed to the bathroom, where she got into the tub and stood beneath a hot shower.

Things were going to be awkward. She hated mornings after. Most of the time she didn't indulge in them. In all of Haley's relationships, she'd rarely allowed men to spend the night with her nor had she spent the night at their places. It was easier to creep out in the middle of the night and not have to

endure sharing uncomfortable moments the next
morning.

Most of the time she rarely wanted more from her
lovers than an occasional night of pleasure. She
didn't want them controlling her life, insinuating
themselves into her emotions.

She was better than most men at loving them and
leaving them. Life was easier that way. She never
failed to live up to expectations. She never disappointed anyone.

She couldn't believe she'd just fallen asleep the
night before instead of getting up, thanking Grey
for being there when she needed him, then sending
him on his way.

By the time she was dressed and returned to the
kitchen Grey had the table set and coffee and a stack
of pancakes waiting. "This wasn't necessary," she
said as she slid into a chair at the table. "You could
have just gotten up and left."

He passed her the syrup bottle. "Is that what usually happens?"

She shrugged. "It's easier that way." She felt com-
pelled to say something about their night together.
"Grey, about last night . . ."

He held up a hand to silence her. "There's no
need to explain it or overanalyze it. You needed
somebody here with you, and I was here. Now eat
your pancakes before they get cold."

She nodded, relieved. At least he didn't want to
rehash it all or make things difficult between them.
A glance at the clock told her it was just after eight.
The sun was warm and bright as it drifted into the
kitchen windows. Through the pane the sounds of
birdsong came from the trees in the backyard.

It was difficult to believe that terror had occurred a mere six hours before in this room. Other than several scorched areas on the stovetop and a black area on the ceiling, there was no evidence of the crime. But seeing those places of destruction sent a chill through Haley once again.

"What are your plans for today?" Grey asked.

"The very first plan is to get the locks changed on the doors. The second is to contact Detective Tolliver. Even though those officers last night didn't really believe me, I want to make sure he understands that somebody tried to kill us."

"Don't you think Frank Marcelli will explain it all to Tolliver?" he asked.

"Sure, he probably will, but I want to make certain Tolliver knows it was no accident."

"Tolliver can't do any more than Frank did last night," he said.

"I know," she admitted with a sick feeling. She took a couple bites of her pancake, then shoved the plate aside and leaned back in her chair with a thoughtful frown. "None of this makes sense to me. It's pretty clear that Monica and Sondra were killed by the same person, but what does that have to do with me? I can't stand to think that Molly is the link, but I don't know the same people they did, I had absolutely no connection whatsoever with Sondra Jackson."

"Unfortunately whatever is going on doesn't have to make sense to us. It only has to make sense to the killer."

She stared at him thoughtfully. "Working with the police, you must get a glimpse into a lot of criminal minds. What do you think about all this?"

He added more syrup to his stack of pancakes. "I don't have enough information to make an assessment about it. I know the murder had all the appearances of a rage killing and yet the killer is obviously organized enough to carefully cover his tracks. As far as what happened here last night, it was incredibly devious."

"I'm just not convinced that last night was about Molly. Too much time has passed since Monica's death. If Monica's killer was worried about Molly, surely something would have happened sooner."

"I tend to agree with you." He took a sip of his coffee, ate a couple of bites, then continued. "And I'm not convinced Molly knows anything that can help identify her mother's killer." His gaze was troubled as it drifted toward the window. "Surely she understands by now how important it is to everyone that she tell what she knows. Maybe she just doesn't know anything." He directed his gaze back to Haley.

"I can't seem to get anything out of her but an occasional burst of anger," she replied.

"That's perfectly normal under the circumstances."

Haley stared down into her coffee mug. "It's never mattered much to me before if somebody loved me or not. Despite our differences, I knew my mother and my sister loved me. Before his death I knew my father loved me. But I've never worked very hard at getting anyone else to love me."

Unexpectedly, a surge of emotion welled up in her. She looked up at him. "I need her to love me, Grey. I've never needed anyone to love me like I need her to."

He reached across the table and covered her hand with his. "She's got to get to know you before she can trust you and she's got to trust you before she can love you."

"I know, I know, patience, right?"

He smiled. "You got it." He pulled his hand back and they finished their breakfast. He gestured to the dishes on the table, then glanced at the clock and stood. "I'm sorry, I need to go. I hate to eat and run, but I have a nine thirty class that I can't cancel."

Haley got up as well. "Please, don't apologize. I can't thank you enough for riding to the rescue."

"Haley, I didn't ride to your rescue. I was just here when you needed somebody to be here."

Was that what it had been for him? A nice gesture for a woman in need with a little sex thrown in on the side? That worked for her if it worked for him. Didn't it?

"Call me, Haley, if you need anything, if you just need to talk," he said as they reached the front door. To her surprise he leaned forward and kissed her on the cheek, a lingering kiss that reminded her of how good it had been with him the night before, good enough that she wanted him again.

He opened the door and stepped out, but turned back to look at her. "Haley, if you want Molly to love you unconditionally, then you need to figure out how to love yourself. You're going to have to learn to open yourself up, to be vulnerable, and I have a feeling you don't do that well."

He didn't wait for her reply, but instead turned and walked toward his car in the driveway. What does he know? she thought as she watched him back out and disappear down the street.

What did he know about her or her life? He'd only known her two weeks and already he was throwing Dr. Phil feel-good advice at her. Sleep with a man and he thought it gave him the right to give advice or point out flaws.

What did Grey Banes know about loving somebody and losing them? His father hadn't died when he was ten. His sister hadn't been brutally murdered.

Before she went back into her house she leaned out and looked at the house next door. Angela would already be up. Heck, she'd probably already baked bread, crafted a floral arrangement and color-coordinated her daughters in playclothes.

As she went back in the house she chided herself for her thoughts about her neighbor. Certainly she was grateful for Angela's calm and efficiency the night before. She'd handled a hysterical Haley and a frightened Molly on her doorstep at two in the morning with aplomb.

Haley had a feeling Angela was like her mother and Monica, and there wasn't much that life threw her that Angela couldn't handle with grace and competence.

The first thing Haley did when she got back into the house was pick up the phone and call Angela. Although her intention was to make sure Molly was up, then bring her home, Angela insisted Molly spend the day with them as she had planned a trip to the movies and dinner out with her girls.

"They'd love to have Molly as their guest," she assured Haley.

"I feel like I'm taking advantage of you," Haley protested.

"Trust me, you're not," Angela replied. "My girls always behave better when Molly is around. Besides, after what happened to you last night I'm sure you have things you need to take care of today."

It was true. The things Haley wanted to accomplish would be better taken care of with Molly not here. She didn't want the little girl to see a locksmith changing locks; she didn't want Molly to overhear the conversation she planned to have with Tolliver.

She hoped Molly thought that the fire last night was just a matter of her carelessness, that she'd been up late cooking something and things had gotten out of control. She didn't want Molly to know that somebody had come into the house, that somebody had tried to hurt them.

She called the first locksmith she found in the phone book. A man at Able Locksmith promised to have somebody at her home within an hour.

As she waited she cleaned up the breakfast dishes and found herself thinking about Grey. It was funny: she'd been oddly disappointed that he'd left without asking when he might see her again, when they could make love again.

Although she'd always been determined not to need anyone, not to want anyone so much that she might be disappointed if they didn't want her, something about Grey made her feel a little bit vulnerable, a little bit afraid.

She shoved thoughts of him away as she finished cleaning the kitchen, then went into the laundry room to throw in a load of clothes. In her life in Las Vegas, she only did laundry when she ran out of things to wear. But here she had Molly to think about, and Molly had favorite clothes she liked to wear over and over again.

As she picked up the little pink T-shirt with the words "Princess Lollipop" across the chest, she suddenly remembered that Monica had often called her daughter Lollipop, or Lolly for short.

"Lolly." She whispered the nickname as an ache of sadness pierced through her. She would never hear her sister's voice again, never again see the sweetness of Monica's smile, hear her chiding with wise advice. Molly would never again know the loving touch of her mother's hand or hear her mother's laughter.

Haley started the washing machine, then moved into the living room to sit and wait for the locksmith. As she sank down on the sofa, she stared at the Fenton glass collection on the shelves. Tradition. That's what Monica had started. She was sure there were other traditions that she didn't know about, but at least this one she could continue.

She moved from the sofa, crouched in front of the shelves and stared at the various pieces. The first discovery of Molly's existence, first smile, first step, first fart and first day of school, each piece as beautiful as the next in the marking of Molly's time on earth.

She frowned as she saw a piece she'd never seen before, one that Monica had never told her about. A heart. A small blue heart. It sat just off to the side of the others. She picked it up off the shelf and turned it around in her hands, wondering when Monica had bought it and for what occasion.

The doorbell rang and she quickly replaced the heart on the shelf to let in the man who was going to change her locks and hopefully return a sense of safety to her home.

It took Bob the locksmith two hours to complete his task. Then he wrote up his invoice, received a check and handed her the keys to her brand-new locks.

Fifteen minutes after he left the doorbell rang again. Haley answered to see the man from the parent-teacher meeting standing on her porch. She remembered he was the president of the association, but she couldn't remember his name.

He must have seen the blankness in her eyes. "Haley, Jay Middleton. Remember we met last Friday night?"

"Yes, of course." She didn't allow him inside the house but rather stepped outside on the porch to speak to him. Monica had invited her killer inside. Haley didn't intend to make the same mistake.

She noticed he carried a large tote bag. "What can I do for you, Jay?"

"The Parent's Association has a little office in the school building. I was there this morning going through some things and realized there were some personal items of Monica's there. I thought you'd want them." He held out the tote bag to her.

"Thanks, that was very thoughtful of you." Haley took the bag.

He made no move to leave. "I'm sure you've heard this before, but you look a lot like your sister," he said. "She was a beautiful woman."

"Yes, she was," Haley replied, distinctly uncomfortable with the turn of the conversation.

The sun glinted off his blond hair as he remained

standing on the porch. His brown eyes gazed off in the distance; then he focused on her once again.

"I still can't believe she's gone," he continued. "I keep expecting to walk into the office and hear her laughter, see her smiling face as she talks about her latest fund-raising idea."

"I can't believe she's gone either," Haley replied and took a step back from him.

"Are you getting settled in okay?"

"Fine, thanks. The neighbors have been wonderful."

His gaze swept the length of her, the quick, assessing gaze of a man on the make. "Look, if you need somebody to show you around town, just give me a call."

"Thanks, that would be great. Maybe you and your wife could meet me for a drink one evening," Haley said brightly. "I've heard she's a wonderful woman."

It was obviously not the answer he was looking for. Murmuring "That would be nice," he finally backed off the porch and left.

Haley carried the tote bag into her bedroom and set it on the bed, then went back to the kitchen, grabbed her purse and car keys and left to go to the police station for a talk with Detective Tolliver.

As she drove, she thought about Jay Middleton. He was a good-looking man and it was obvious he and Monica had spent a lot of time together. Had they simply been co-workers or had their relationship been something more?

Ridiculous, she thought. It was absolutely ridiculous for her to even consider that Monica might have had an affair with a married man. Even Haley didn't go there, and Monica's standards and morals were much higher than Haley's.

But Haley knew a player when she met one, and Jay Middleton was definitely a player. Had he tried to initiate a relationship with Monica and Monica had spurned his advances? Had she maybe threatened to tell his wife?

It was hard to believe that once upon a time Haley had thought Pleasant Hill boring and provincial. A vicious murder, an angry teenager and a peeping tom . . . and all of them in a quiet little cul-de-sac.

The president of the Parents' Association was a slimeball, the neighbor down the street was a weird little man with sweaty hands and somebody had crept into her kitchen the night before and tried to kill her and Molly.

Boring? Provincial? No way.

Were all the people she'd met and interacted with exactly what they appeared and nothing more? Or was one of them hiding an evil that would only be sated when she and Molly were dead?

Chapter 16

Detective Tolliver took her back to the interrogation room where they'd sat for past meetings and gestured her to a chair. He didn't say a word to her until they were both seated and she'd set the plastic sack she'd carried in on the table before them.

"Haley, I know how much you want us to catch your sister's killer, but coming here almost every day for updates isn't going to work. When I have something to tell you, I'll call you."

"That's fine, but that's not why I'm here. Have you heard what happened at my house last night?"

Tolliver frowned, the lines on his face deeper than they had been when she'd first met him. "I heard something about a stove fire."

"It wasn't a stove fire, it was attempted murder," Haley said, irritated that the incident had been written off so easily. That was exactly why she'd wanted to come here and talk to Tolliver in person. "I knew this was what would happen. I knew those officers last night didn't take me seriously or believe me."

She fought a healthy dose of irritation. "I thought at least Frank believed me."

"Look, I've been kind of busy with two murder investigations. Forgive me if I'm not up to speed about what happened last night and what officers did or didn't believe. I haven't read the report. Frank just mentioned it to me in passing earlier this morning. I've hardly had a chance to talk to him."

Haley's irritation grew hotter, flirting dangerously with anger. "You don't need to read the report. I'm here to tell you exactly what happened." And she did, beginning from the time she'd awakened to the moment when the responding police officers had left.

When she was finished, the lines on Tolliver's face were even deeper, looking like barely healed wounds. "We had pizza for dinner last night," she said. "You can check with Pizza Hut, I had it delivered. I didn't go near that stove before I went to bed." She placed a hand on the plastic bag she'd brought with her. "This is the skillet that was on the stove last night. I don't know where it came from, but maybe there's some fingerprints on it or something."

"If everything you've told me is true and somebody really did sneak into your kitchen and start a fire, then they were probably smart enough not to leave any prints behind." He leaned back in his chair and released a deep sigh but said nothing.

As always, when a silence stretched too long Haley jumped right into the middle of it. "I don't think it was about making sure Molly doesn't talk. If that was the case, something would have happened long before last night."

He nodded in agreement and wiped a hand over his gleaming head. "But it certainly isn't the signature of the killer we're hunting. Is there anyone you've had words with, pissed off since you've arrived in town?"

"Nobody." She frowned thoughtfully, remembering the way Grant Newton had looked at her the night before. "Grant Newton . . . have you fully investigated him concerning my sister's murder?"

"Why? Do you know something that we should know?" Tolliver sat up straighter in his chair.

"Not really. He just seems weird."

"If we could arrest people for being weird, half the town of Pleasant Hill would be behind bars."

"Did Frank tell you that I thought I saw Grant leaving the school parking lot the night of Sondra's murder?"

"He told me and we checked it out. You were right. Newton was at the school that night. Apparently he had a late date with one of the fifth-grade teachers. When he got there she told him she was too tired to go out after the meeting. We checked it out and the teacher confirmed his story."

Haley remembered the brief conversation she'd had with Newton on the day of Monica's funeral. "That man seems to invite rejection. I would guess if you get enough of that you might be filled with rage."

"Yeah, I would guess the same thing, but there is absolutely no evidence to point to Grant Newton as our killer." He leaned forward, resting his elbows on the table. "Look, Haley, it sounds like whatever happened last night might not be related to these murders. My recommendation to you is to be smart.

If somebody is trying to hurt you, then take precautions when you go out, make sure your doors and windows are locked when you're at home. You might even want to consider installing an alarm system."

He leaned back and placed a hand over his stomach, as if that part of his body ached. "We're a small police department dealing with two murders. The best I can offer you right now is to double up on the patrols in your area."

"I had the locks changed this morning and nobody is getting a key other than me, but the extra patrols might help." The anger that had threatened to erupt was gone.

He sighed. "I don't want you to think that I'm not taking what happened to you last night seriously. I am. I do. I intend to talk to the officers who responded, but I'm not sure what else can be done at this point."

She nodded, satisfied. She stood, knowing she'd taken up enough of his time. "I just wanted you to know exactly what happened. I have a feeling it was written up as a careless accident. I'm stressed. I'm overwhelmed by everything. But I know what I did and what I didn't do last night, and I didn't go near that stove."

Tolliver stood as well and together they walked out of the interrogation room. He walked with her to the entrance of the police station and didn't say anything until she started to push open the door to leave.

"Haley," he said, stopping her progress. She turned to look at him. He gazed upward, as if contemplating whether to tell her what was on his mind or not. When he looked at her once again his gaze was troubled.

"There are a lot of connections between your sister and Sondra Jackson and we're checking out those connections, but there's one nobody has mentioned to you."

"And what's that?"

"Both of them were blondes. Attractive, single blondes. There's no way of knowing at this point if it means anything. It's just an obvious connection that we're considering along with everything else. I just thought I should mention it, you know, because you're an attractive single blonde."

Haley stared at him for a long moment, a new chill raising the blond hairs on the nape of her neck as the full impact of his words washed through her. "If you're trying to make me feel better, it isn't working," she said, forcing a small laugh.

"Look, it's possible that has nothing to do with anything, but I just want you to be careful. If what you told me about last night is true, then one way or another somebody doesn't like you very much. I'll order the extra patrols by your house, and Frank is right next door if anything else happens."

In other words, she was on her own, as she had been for most of her life. As she drove home from the station she found herself thinking about the possibility that there was a crazed killer running the streets of Pleasant Hill killing all the blond single females in town.

Surely if the police really thought that was the case they would make an announcement. But hadn't Frank said they wouldn't consider this the work of a serial killer unless he killed again? Damned if she wanted to be the third victim.

It was still possible the deaths had nothing to do with the color of their hair or their marital status. Unfortunately, as Grey had reminded her that morning, there just didn't seem to be enough information to know why the two women had been brutally murdered.

Haley rarely allowed herself to indulge in depression, but that was the emotion that sat on her shoulders as she returned to the house.

Angela's van wasn't in the driveway so she assumed they were all still gone to the movies. Maybe it would be a good time to go through the boxes in Monica's bedroom and clean out the master bathroom.

It was a job that needed to be done while Molly wasn't around and now seemed as good a time as any. She locked the door and threw the dead bolt, then dropped her purse on the sofa and headed for Monica's bedroom.

The boxes in the closet were stacked from floor to ceiling and contained everything that had been in Monica's dresser and nightstands.

The first several boxes yielded clothing, which Haley set aside to go to charity. Even if she and Monica had shared a similar style or size, Haley couldn't imagine wearing her sister's things. As unsettling as Haley found the idea, she was sure Molly would be even more disturbed by it. Two boxes held personal items she needed to sort through. She sat on the new carpeting in the bare room to go carefully through them. She pulled the smaller box next to her and opened the top.

The first thing she saw inside was a silver frame containing a photo. She didn't know who had taken the picture, but it was obviously a snapshot of Monica and Molly in an embrace, faces close together and filled with happiness.

A lump the size of Nevada jumped into Haley's throat. She touched her index finger to the image of her sister, then slid her fingertip over to touch Molly's smiling face.

The killer hadn't just stolen Monica from her; he'd also stolen Molly's smile, the sparkle in her eyes, her very innocence.

Haley stared at the picture until she could no longer see it through her tears, tears that had waited two long weeks to be shed.

The tears didn't fall alone: they came with horrendous sobs that ripped her guts, tore her bones and stabbed her heart. She threw herself facedown on the carpet and let the grief consume her.

She cried for every loss she had suffered beginning with her father, a painful loss that she'd never really gotten over. She cried for her father, her mother, her sister: then finally her tears were for herself and for Molly, who were left behind to pick up the pieces and go on.

Finally she was finished, all the tears shed, the burst of emotion spent. She remained lying on the carpet, completely empty.

She stared up at the white ceiling and heard Grey's words echoing in her head. *If you want Molly to love you unconditionally, then you need to figure out how to love yourself. You're going to have to learn to open yourself up, to be vulnerable, and I have a feeling you don't do that well.*

"What does he know," she said aloud. She swiped her eyes with the back of her hands, knowing she'd hopelessly smeared her mascara.

She'd been open once, she'd been vulnerable once, when she'd been young and had adored her daddy. She'd learned when she was ten that being vulnerable only made you hurt. Opening yourself up only led to disappointing others and being disappointed.

Been there, done that. And Grey might have slept with her, but he didn't know anything about her at all.

"That's what I get for sleeping with a therapist," she muttered as she pulled the box back toward her to finish what she'd started.

A novel. A box of tissues. A wooden jewelry box that held a variety of cheap necklaces and bracelets and the wedding band Monica had finally stopped wearing when Molly was three. Haley set the jewelry box aside to pack away for Molly.

The ring of the doorbell interrupted her task. She got up from the floor and found Dean on her doorstep. "Wow, I didn't know you were into goth," he said.

"What?" She realized he was talking about her eyes, which were probably ringed with her mascara. "I'm not. What do you want, Dean?"

"I heard you had a fire last night. I just thought I'd stop by and see if you needed any cleanup work done."

Haley narrowed her eyes. "How did you hear about my fire?"

Dean snorted a laugh. "There's not much that goes on in this little cul-de-sac that everyone doesn't eventually know about. Somebody must have said something, because my mom told me this morning as she was racing out the door to the job that is more important than anything on the face of the earth."

In those two sentences Haley realized two things about Dean Brown. The first was that the teenager was far more intelligent than he looked or acted, and the second was that he was just another latchkey kid who probably had too much stuff and not enough parental attention.

"Dean, don't you have something better to do than scrub my stove or cut my lawn? You're not a bad-looking kid. What about a girlfriend?"

"The girls at school are dumb. I'm more into older women." Although he said the words seriously, the tips of his ears turned red.

"You'd better be nice to those girls at school. One of these days they will be older women. And thanks for asking, but I've already gotten the mess cleaned up."

He shrugged, shoved his hands into his jeans pockets and stepped away from the door. "Another couple of days and your grass will need to be cut again."

"Check back with me in a couple of days." She watched as he walked up the street toward his house. It was only when she was back inside that she remembered Dean had been at the school the night Sondra Jackson had been murdered.

Dean liked older women. Sondra had been older. Monica had been older. Was it possible the teenager had suffered a major crush on them and when they didn't reciprocate his feelings, he killed them?

She started to close her door, then reopened it as

she saw Angela's van pull into the Marcelli driveway. She ran to the bathroom and washed away her goth mascara, feeling better as the water cooled her dry eyes.

By the time she stepped outside, the van in Angela's driveway was empty. As she walked the short distance between the houses she saw a flash of white streak around the corner of Angela's house. A cat, she thought. Well, at least it hadn't been a black cat.

Angela answered her knock. "Oh, I was just going to call you to tell you we're home. Come on in, the girls are playing back in Adrianna's bedroom."

"Do you guys have a cat?" Haley asked as she trailed behind Angela to the kitchen.

"Heavens no, why?"

"I thought I saw a big white cat skirt around the side of your house."

"It belongs to the people in the next block, the Mallerys. I sometimes throw scraps outside for him, so he hangs out here pretty regularly." She gestured Haley into a chair at the table. "So, tell me how you're doing today." She kept her voice low. "You must have been terrified."

"I still am," Haley admitted. "But I got the locks changed and I think first thing Monday morning I'm going to call and get a security system installed."

"Sounds like a good plan. Is there anything I can do for you?"

Haley smiled. "You've already done it by not freaking out when I rang your doorbell at two in the morning and by letting Molly stay here. I can't thank you enough."

Angela waved her hand as if to dismiss Haley's gratitude. "That's what neighbors are for."

Haley shook her head. "You went above and beyond the call of a neighbor."

"Okay, then that's what friends are for," Angela said.

I don't have friends, Haley thought. I have close encounters with strangers and bar talk with acquaintances. I have superficial relationships, not friendships. *And why is that, Haley?* Grey's voice rang in her head. Damn the man anyway.

"Frank said he wasn't sure the officers who responded believed your story," Angela said, jarring the disturbing thoughts out of Haley's head.

She grimaced, remembering the doubt that had lingered in the eyes of the policemen as Haley had insisted somebody had come into her house and left the skillet on the stove. "No, they didn't believe me."

"It is the strangest thing I've ever heard."

"It was more than strange. It was evil." Haley leaned back in the chair and frowned thoughtfully. "What do you know about Jay Middleton?"

"You mean other than the fact that he's a sleazeball?"

"A sleazeball? What do you mean?" Haley asked, although she'd suspected the same about the man.

"His wife works as a flight attendant for some major airline and is gone most of the time. I think Jay has slept with half the single women in Pleasant Hill and probably an equal amount of married women. Why are you asking about him?"

"He stopped by earlier and brought me some of

Monica's things. I got the feeling he might be a player. He mentioned taking me out for a drink."

Angela wrinkled her nose. "Personally, I can't stand the man."

"You think he and Monica had something going between them?" The question left her lips with dread. Even though she couldn't imagine her sister sleeping with a sleazeball, especially a married one, she had to ask the question.

"I think your sister was too smart to get involved with a man like Jay Middleton," Angela said. "But," she added, "I suppose anything is possible."

Haley nodded, then got up from the table. "And now it's time for me and Molly to head home."

"Hang tight, I'll go get Molly." Angela got up from the table. "Oh, before I forget it, Adrianna's birthday is next Saturday and she's having a slumber party. I told her she could invite five friends and naturally we want Molly to be one of the five."

"Sounds like fun," Haley said.

Angela laughed. "Sounds like I've lost my mind." She left the kitchen to get Molly.

Haley worked to put on a happy face for her niece, the happy expression she always tried to wear when she was around Molly. Happy and in control, that's what Molly needed.

"Hi, honey," she said as Angela returned to the kitchen with Molly in tow. "Did you have a good time at the movies?"

Molly nodded. She was dressed in a pair of jeans and a T-shirt Haley didn't recognize and assumed belonged to Adrianna. "I'll get these clothes back to you as soon as I wash them," she told Angela.

"No hurry."

"Thanks for everything, Angela."

Angela grinned and shook a finger at her. "I told you thanks aren't necessary. I'm sure you'd do the same for me."

Moments later Haley and Molly made the silent walk from the Marcelli house back into their own. Molly flopped down on the sofa and turned on the television and Haley stood at the window, staring out at the backyard and the tree house.

It was just a place of plywood and two-by-fours, a miniature building that shouldn't haunt her, that shouldn't fill her with dread . . . but it did.

She turned and looked at Molly. "Did your mommy play with you in the tree house?" Molly nodded. Of course she did, Haley thought. Well-adjusted Monica wouldn't sense the ghost of their father haunting the tree house, wouldn't feel the wretched grief that Haley did whenever she looked up into the branches of that tree.

Molly returned her attention to the cartoons on the television and Haley sighed, wondering how long Molly's silence would last.

The afternoon and evening passed the same way all the others had, with the television making the only noise in the house. Dinner was Salisbury steaks and a can of green beans; then it was bedtime for Molly.

While deciding on what to fix for dinner and rummaging around in the pantry, Haley had discovered a bottle of wine. Once Molly was asleep, Haley poured herself a tall glass and carried it and the bottle to the coffee table in the living room.

She curled up on the sofa and took a deep drink of the ruby red wine, hoping it would work some magic on the tension that had been building inside her all day.

"Here's to new locks on the doors," she said aloud and raised the glass to her lips once again. She should be feeling safe and secure, comforted by the fact that whoever had crept into the house the night before would find it more difficult tonight.

But even though there were shiny new locks and she'd made certain every window in the house was locked, she still had a feeling of overwhelming dread. She'd thought nothing could be worse than Monica's murder, but she had the terrible feeling that the worst was yet to come.

By the time she'd finished two big glasses of wine, the bottle was over half empty and the sharp edge of fear and worry had been shaved away by the anesthetic magic of the alcohol.

In truth, she was more than a little drunk. She'd never had much tolerance for wine and knew she'd probably have a wicked hangover in the morning, but at the moment she didn't care.

All she cared about was that the house was too quiet, that she felt as if her life had been put in the spin cycle in a washing machine and she couldn't quite get her feet firmly on the ground.

All she knew was that if it weren't for her responsibility to Molly, she would have already picked up and run, left Pleasant Hill and Grey Banes far behind her.

She frowned and poured herself another glass of the wine, wondering why she'd thought of running away from Grey. Because he'd already gotten closer to her than she allowed most men? Because he had the ability to see things inside her that nobody else had taken the time or the trouble to see?

She thought of what he'd said to her that morning when he'd left. A free dose of analysis. She'd told him time and time again to stay out of her head.

The more she thought about it, the angrier she got. She picked up the cordless phone on the end table next to the sofa and punched in Grey's number, vaguely wondering when she had memorized it.

He answered on the second ring, his voice that low, sexy bass that shot a flutter of heat through her stomach. "Grey, it's me," she said.

"Haley, I was just thinking about you. Is everything all right?"

"Yes and no. Nobody has tried to kill us again, but I've been sitting here drinking a little wine and thinking about things, and I've decided you pissed me off this morning when you gave me your free analysis of me."

"And just how much wine is a little?" he asked, his voice holding a touch of amusement.

She looked at the bottle, surprised to see it held just a swallow in the very bottom. "Maybe a little more than a little," she admitted.

"Did the locksmith come?"

"Locks have been changed, Molly is asleep, I'm half drunk, all is well with the world at this moment, except I'm mad at you."

"You don't sound too mad," he countered.

She took one last swallow of her wine, then placed the glass on the coffee table and tried to summon up the self-righteous indignation she'd felt moments ago.

But all she could think of was how good it had

felt to be in his arms, how much she wanted to be in his arms once again. "Molly has a slumber party this Saturday night. She's going to spend the night next door."

"And what is Molly's aunt going to do that night?" Grey asked, his voice taking on a husky undertone that increased the fluttering heat in her stomach.

"I think she's going to be lonely . . . and hungry," she added as an afterthought, remembering that he'd said when things calmed down he'd love to cook for her.

He laughed, that marvelous earthy sound she loved to hear. "I can't let you go hungry, now can I? How about steaks at my place on Saturday night? Oh yeah, and I'll try to keep you from getting too lonely as well."

"I'm beginning to forget why I was mad at you," she said.

"That's good, because I don't want you mad at me."

They spoke for several more minutes. By the time they hung up the wine had fully hit Haley and she was ready to fall asleep. But the idea of getting up off the sofa certainly didn't appeal. She pulled the afghan off the back of the sofa and covered herself, deciding that the light being on didn't bother her at all.

She'd just about drifted off to sleep when the phone rang. She swung her hand out to grab the receiver, in the process hitting the bottle and knocking it off the coffee table. "Damn," she exclaimed as she grabbed up the phone. "This better be good, Dr. Grey."

"Whore."

The ugliness of the word rang across the phone line, making Haley feel as if the caller had just spit in her face. "Who is this?" Haley demanded and sat up so quickly her head spun dizzily.

"Leave town, whore. Leave now before it's too late." The voice was androgynous, a deep low moan of malevolence. A click told Haley that the caller had hung up. But Haley remained on the line, gripping the receiver against her ear and listening to the hiss of emptiness.

Stone-cold sober. Nine words had effectively banished anything the bottle of wine might have done to dull her senses. *Leave town, whore. Leave now before it's too late.*

Until this moment she'd forgotten about the other call she'd received on the day of Monica's funeral. In all the activity that day had brought, the strange phone call had somehow been lost.

Now it came back to haunt her. It had been the same voice. A devil's voice, calling to her from someplace dark and frightening.

This wasn't about Molly. Whoever had made those two calls had made them to Haley. Somebody didn't like Haley. Just like somebody hadn't liked Monica.

Chapter 17

"I know you're getting sick of seeing my face every other day or so," Haley said to Owen Tolliver the next morning. Once again Tolliver didn't look particularly pleased to see her when she arrived at the station, but Haley didn't care.

She'd already had a bad morning. It had taken her forever to fall asleep the night before following the horrid phone call. Then, because she'd finally gone to sleep on the sofa, she'd overslept without the aid of her alarm clock to wake her up.

She'd awakened with a sickening wine hangover headache and with just enough time to get Molly up and dressed and out the door with a granola bar to eat on the bus. No time for a real breakfast, no time for small talk, only time to once again feel like she was screwing things up. She'd put Molly on the school bus, then had driven directly to the police station to talk to the detective.

"You want coffee?" he asked. "I've been living on coffee and antacids for what seems like months now."

"No, thanks, I'm fine," she replied. "Look, I'm

not trying to be a pain in your ass, but when something happens I just think it's important I let you know."

"What's happened?" He looked at her, his eyes bloodshot and not quite as sharp as they had been on the first day she'd met him.

"I'm getting weird phone calls."

"Weird how?"

"I can't tell if the caller is male or female, but the first call came on the day of Monica's funeral. I picked up the phone and somebody said 'whore,' then hung up. Then last night I got another call."

"Same voice?"

She nodded. "The caller was a bit more chatty. The voice called me a whore, then told me to leave town before it was too late."

"Too late for what?"

"Heck if I know." Even though she was seated in a room in the police station, probably the safest place in the entire city, as she remembered that voice, those words, a whisper of fear edged through her once again. "All I can tell you is that the voice sounded evil."

"What did your caller ID indicate?" Tolliver asked.

Haley frowned. "My sister was probably the last person in the world who just had basic phone service. No caller ID, no call forwarding, no bells or whistles at all. But when I get home I intend to get hooked up with caller ID."

"Look, I know anonymous phone calls are disconcerting, but there's really nothing we can do about them. You're doing the right thing getting caller ID, and if you don't find out who is calling you, then you might want to contact the phone company and explain the situation to them."

"I didn't expect you to be able to do anything," Haley replied. "I just want you to be aware of everything that's going on. I mean, after everything that has happened it's more than disconcerting."

"I'm sure it is. It's possible that it's some creep who knows what happened to your sister and is getting some kick out of tormenting you. It happens more frequently than you know. A widow gets a call from the grave from her recently deceased husband, a parent gets a call of a baby crying after a SIDS death, and some sick bastard laughs his ass off from his phone in his bedroom."

Tolliver's voice rang with his disgust, but oddly enough his words made her feel better. Probably somebody had read about Monica's death in the paper and was now having fun tormenting her survivors.

"I don't suppose you have an idea if either Monica or Sondra were getting strange phone calls before their deaths?"

"There's been nothing to indicate that either one of the women received any threatening calls before their deaths." The interrogation room opened and Frank Marcelli came in.

"Haley, what's going on?"

Tolliver quickly filled his partner in on what had brought Haley to the station. "Have you checked out Jay Middleton?" Haley asked on impulse.

"I interviewed him after Sondra's death," Frank said. "Why?"

"I don't know, something about him makes my skin crawl. Did he have an alibi for the murders?"

"I don't remember exactly what he told me about your sister's murder, but if memory serves me, after the parent-teacher thing at the school he went to Trader's, the sports bar over on Main, and was there until closing, then went right home."

"Have you confirmed that?" she asked.

Frank eyed her suspiciously. "Are you sure you don't know something you aren't telling us?"

The headache she'd awakened with suddenly returned with a vengeance, pounding at the center of her forehead with near nauseating intensity. "No, nothing in particular. It's just that I've heard that Middleton is a real ladies' man, and that has made me wonder if maybe he was having a relationship with my sister and Sondra and maybe they found out and threatened to bust him to his wife." She was rambling, grasping at straws in an attempt to make sense of the senseless.

Tolliver rubbed his stomach and Frank frowned thoughtfully. "I have to confess, I haven't had a chance to check his alibi. I'll do that today," Frank promised.

Haley sighed wearily. "And would you do me a favor? Would you see if you can find out if either Monica or Sondra was receiving threatening phone calls before her death?"

"We've already pulled their phone records," Tolliver said. "I can tell you that at first glance we didn't see anything on those records that raised a red flag."

"Maybe the calls you're getting have nothing to do with the murders." Frank eyed her sympathetically.

"So it's possible somebody just thinks I'm a

whore. Gee, that makes me feel a lot better," she said dryly.

"It could be they're nothing but prank phone calls," he countered, reiterating what Tolliver had told her only moments before.

A few minutes later as Haley drove home, she thought about the possibility of the phone calls being nothing but a prank. Was Dean having some fun with her?

If it hadn't been for the fire danger in the middle of the night, she could have easily written off the phone calls as nothing but the silly prank of a teenager. But taking everything altogether, it was impossible for her to dismiss the calls so easily.

There was no way she could describe to the two detectives the venom that had been in the caller's voice. There were no words adequate in the English language to convey the depth of malignancy that had oozed over the phone.

Despite the fact that she'd been locked inside her home, with the curtains drawn tight, the call had shaken any sense of security she might have momentarily entertained.

Illogical, yes. A voice on the phone couldn't reach through the line and grab her by the throat. A voice on the phone couldn't harm her, but it could certainly play with her head and make her question who might want to hurt her in some way.

There were no more phone calls for the rest of the week. While nothing bad happened, nothing particularly good happened either. Molly stayed silent and distant. Haley continued to force a happy face with an air of confidence whenever with her niece.

She often felt Molly's gaze lingering on her, as if

the child expected something, needed something from her, but for the life of her Haley couldn't figure out what she wanted or needed, and Molly wasn't talking.

By the time Saturday evening arrived, Haley was more than ready for her time alone with Grey. She'd seen him twice that week for lunch but had longed for some alone time with him.

At four o'clock she walked Molly next door for the slumber party. Angela answered the door, looking as cool and calm as the Madonna despite the fact that little girls squealed and giggled at the volume of a rock concert from the direction of Adrianna's bedroom.

"The girls are waiting for you, Molly," she said. As Molly ran down the hallway to join the fracas, Angela smiled at Haley. "I'm giving them one hour of playtime, then I have planned activities for the rest of the night."

"What time should I come and get her in the morning?"

"Not until afternoon. I'm taking all of them to church, then we're going to Polly's Pizza for lunch, so we probably won't be back here much before two or so."

"Wow, that's how long slumber parties last?" Haley shook her head. "I have so much to learn."

Angela laughed. "Go enjoy your evening and don't worry about learning anything tonight."

"Before I leave, is Frank home?"

Angela's smile instantly fell a notch. "No, I was hoping he'd be here this evening to enjoy the fun, but he's working. Do you want me to pass along a message when he gets home?"

"No, that's all right. I'll just talk to him tomorrow." With a wave of her fingers, Haley left the Marcelli house and headed back to her own place to get ready for her date.

If Frank had been home she'd been planning to ask him if he'd followed up on Jay Middleton's alibi, but the question could wait.

She knew she was probably irritating both Frank and Tolliver with her frequent trips to the police station, but she didn't want them to forget her. She didn't want them to forget Monica.

But tonight she didn't want to think about murders or detectives. She didn't want to think about slumber parties or silent little girls with accusing eyes, little girls with needs Haley didn't know how to fill.

Tonight she didn't want to think about all the things she was probably doing wrong. She didn't want to hear her sister's voice whispering in her head that she was screwing things up.

She took a long, leisurely bubble bath, then pulled on the only dress she'd brought with her when she'd left Las Vegas. She'd seen the short red dress in the gift shop at the Golden Nugget, and although she hadn't known when she'd ever wear it, wasn't even sure she would ever wear it, she'd had to have it.

As she looked at her reflection in the mirror, she nodded with satisfaction. The bright color complemented her blond hair and pulled color into her cheeks. The silky material felt marvelous against her skin and for the first time since Monica's death she felt vibrantly alive and more than a little bit sexy.

If she'd felt a little bit sexy standing in front of her mirror, Grey's appreciative gaze when he arrived at six thirty to pick her up made her feel like she might combust at any moment.

"You look amazing," he said.

"You clean up pretty nice yourself, Dr. Grey," she replied. Rather than his usual jeans, tonight he wore navy slacks that seemed tailor-made for his long legs and slim hips. A light blue shirt made his eyes look impossibly blue and reminded her of how firm, how solid his chest was beneath the material.

"Good day?" he asked once they were in his car and headed to his apartment.

"It was all right if you take away the fact that I had an awful phone call last night, woke up with a raging hangover this morning and spent part of my morning at the police station."

"Tell me about the phone call."

As she explained what had happened, she couldn't help but notice that the interior of the car smelled like him. She wondered when the scent had become so familiar, so comforting.

"Anyway, I contacted the phone company and by Monday I should have caller ID working."

"You have any idea who it might be?"

"Throughout the day I've had about a million thoughts on who it might be, starting with the creepy neighbor down the street, then wondering about the teenage boy who cut my grass. What do you know about teenage boys?"

His hands tightened on the steering wheel and the muscle in his jawline tightened. "What do you want to know?"

What she wanted to know at the moment was

why her question had made him tense. And he was tense. She felt the swell of energy that filled the car and she wanted to know what he was thinking, what was going on in his head, but she didn't.

"Is it possible that a teenage boy could viciously kill Monica, then come over and offer to mow my lawn and do odd jobs as if nothing was wrong?"

His fingers relaxed their death grip on the steering wheel. "Sure, anything is possible. Teenage boys are filled with testosterone. Unpredictable rage is possible, as are bouts of depression. You've seen the news, Haley. Teenage killers used to be relatively uncommon, but not anymore. Kids are not only killing other kids, but they're killing their parents, their grandparents and themselves."

"I think he might have a little crush on me," she said, remembering the last conversation she'd had with Dean.

"Stay away from him, Haley. I can't tell you if he's dangerous or not just by what little you've told me, but I can tell you that teenage boys can be volatile, they can easily confuse love and hate and often they don't have the control to manage their raging hormones."

He turned into an attractive apartment complex and parked in front of one of the units. "Did you live here with your wife?" Haley asked curiously.

"No, I got this place after the divorce." He turned the key to shut off the car engine. "When my private practice began to really take off, Sarah and I bought a big house in Kansas City." He unfastened his seat belt but made no move to get out of the car.

"Sarah liked things. She loved living in a big house in an affluent neighborhood. She joined the neighborhood association and spent most of her time decorating the house. It was an ongoing project. She was something of a perfectionist."

"Do you miss the house? That kind of lifestyle?" she asked.

"Not a bit. I was never home to enjoy it. I was working ten and twelve hours a day to pay for it all. There's more to life than things, but I have a feeling you already know that." He opened the car door and got out. Haley did the same and together they walked to the front door of his apartment. He unlocked the door and pushed it open, then motioned her to precede him inside.

She'd been curious about where he lived, how he lived. The apartment definitely held a masculine aura. The overstuffed sofa was black and brown with smoked glass end tables on either side. A heavy dark wood entertainment center took up one wall, the shelves on either side of the television stuffed with books.

"This is nice," she said.

"Come on, I'll give you the full tour."

He took her down the hall, showing her a nice-sized guest bath. The first bedroom was set up as a home office with a desk and file cabinets.

The second bedroom held a king-sized bed covered in a navy spread with white and navy accent pillows. Once again the furniture was masculine, oversized and dark. There was a bath off the master bedroom, also decorated in navy blue.

"And now I'll take you into the kitchen, where I plan to dazzle you with my culinary skills."

And he did. He made strip steaks perfectly marinated and broiled, with twice-baked potatoes and a salad that had ingredients Haley didn't know existed.

They flirted shamelessly over dinner and when the meal had ended she helped with the cleanup. The tension between them heightened with each brush of their hands, every glance he shot her way.

When the table had been cleared and the dishes were in the dishwasher, he stepped close to her, so close she could feel the heat radiating from his body, so close she imagined she could hear the beat of his heart. "So, dessert?" he asked softly.

"Well, you've already thrilled me with your culinary skills, but I was thinking maybe you had some other talent you'd like to show off for me," she teased.

"Great minds think alike," he murmured, just before he took her in his arms and kissed her. The man definitely knew how to kiss, his lips nibbling on hers before his tongue dipped into her mouth. Fire shot through her veins, weakening her knees as pleasure eddied through her.

"That dress looks great on you," he said when he broke the kiss, his lips trailing to the sensitive skin just beneath her ear. "But all I've been able to think about all evening is how great it would look off of you."

"The zipper's in the back."

His hands warmed the silky material as they slid up her back to the top. As he slid the zipper down his mouth found hers again, nipping, teasing, tormenting, until finally the back of her dress was open.

She shrugged, allowing the garment to fall from her shoulders and pool at her feet. "Maybe we should take this into the bedroom." His voice was husky as he stepped away from her, his gaze hot and hungry.

The walk from the kitchen to the bedroom took a long time as they paused with each step to kiss and shed another article of clothing. By the time they reached the bedroom they were both naked and had left a trail of clothing throughout the apartment.

Pulling covers and pillows off the bed, Grey turned out the light and they slid between the sheets.

His breath was ragged as he gathered her against him. His hands seemed to be everywhere, first stroking down her back, then greedily cupping her breasts.

She was greedy too, wanting to touch, to taste every inch of his skin. She loved the way her name sounded when it whispered from his lips. She loved the sound of his moans when she touched him, the way he trembled when she stroked the hard length of him.

And he made her moan and tremble, his caresses alternating between sweet tenderness and hungry desperation.

"I think I could be with you day after day for a hundred years and never get enough of you," he whispered as he was poised to enter her.

As he slid into her, she closed her eyes and drew him into her body not only on a physical level, but also on an emotional one. He filled her, her body, her mind, her heart.

No man she'd ever been with had managed to invade her on so many levels before. He stimulated her not only physically, but intellectually as well.

He made her laugh and she suspected that if she let him all the way inside, he might be the one man who could make her cry.

That was her last conscious thought before she gave herself to the mindless pleasure and over-whelming sensations of Grey's lovemaking.

She was running. Running as fast as she could, terror causing her heart to beat so fast she feared she might die. She was afraid to look back, afraid to see what chased her. She only knew that if she were caught her life would be over.

Haley shot straight up, a small cry escaping her.

"Haley?" Grey's deep voice came out of the darkness, banishing the nightmare as she found herself wrapped in his arms. "You okay?"

She nodded, then, realizing he couldn't see her response, whispered a soft "yes." "Bad dream," she added. "It's the same one I have a lot."

He released his hold on her and turned on the lamp on the nightstand. She closed her eyes, momentarily blinded by the sudden light. When she opened them again Grey was looking at her worriedly.

His dark hair was sleep-tousled and a line from the edge of the pillow creased one cheek. He looked sexy as hell. "Tell me about it," he said. Once again he wrapped her in his warm arms and pulled her back against the mattress.

"There's not a lot to tell." She tried to relax into his embrace, but found herself needing some distance, finding the cocoon of his arms almost too pleasurable. He dropped his arms from around her, as if he sensed her need.

She sat up, raked a hand through her hair and captured one of the strands, then tugged on it thoughtfully. "It's always the same. I'm running as fast as I can, running away from something, but I don't know what. All I know is that if I stop, if whatever it is catches me, my life will be over."

"Sounds scary."

"It is, but it's just a stupid dream." She frowned. "I didn't mean to fall asleep. What time is it?"

Escape. She felt the need rushing through her. This was too cozy, too intimate. Dammit, she'd fallen asleep again, slept in his arms.

"It's almost midnight."

"I know it's a lot to ask, but would you mind taking me home?"

He sat up, his frown of concern growing deeper. "If you really want to go, then of course I'll take you home. But why?"

Why? There was no way to explain what she wasn't sure she understood herself. "I just have a rule never to spend the night with a man. It's better if I wake up alone in my own bed."

She wished she hadn't shed her clothes before getting to the bedroom. Now she was going to have to stalk naked through the house to get dressed once again.

"So break your rule," he said. "The night is already half over, we're both in bed." He paused a moment, his eyes narrowing slightly. "Is this what you do, Haley? When you feel like somebody is getting too close. You run?"

"I asked you not to analyze me." Her voice held a touch of irritation.

He held her gaze for a long moment. "I'm not. I'm falling in love with you."

His words horrified her. "That's crazy. Believe me, you don't want to do that, so stop it right now." She slid out of the bed and found her underpants just inside the bedroom door. She grabbed them and stepped into them, her heart pounding as if she were back in her dream.

She had to get out of here. She had to get away from him. She'd stayed too long.

As she left the bedroom to search for her other clothing, she was conscious of Grey getting out of bed. *I'm falling in love with you.* His words echoed in her head as she pulled on her bra, then hurried into the kitchen for her dress.

I'm falling in love with you. What was he thinking? He was a smart man, smart enough to know better than to fall in love with a woman like her.

She'd just pulled on her dress when he appeared in the kitchen doorway. He'd put on a pair of jeans and a T-shirt, and he walked over and indicated she should turn around so he could zip her dress.

When she was zipped, he spun her back, his fingers on her shoulders as he faced her. "Now I'm going to give you a little free analysis, whether you want it or not. I think the day you lost your father, you decided it hurt too much to love anyone or to let anyone too close. I think you've spent your life since then running from love, determined to keep your grief embraced so tightly nothing good can get inside you. You haven't cornered the market on grief, Haley."

She pulled away from him and stepped back. "He was my rock, the only person who understood me, who loved me." She had begun to cry and wasn't sure why. "You can't know what it's like, to love somebody, then have them die. You don't know what it's like to be a little girl and lose the father you loved."

"No, but I know what it's like to be a father and lose the only son I loved." His eyes darkened with the haunting shadows she'd seen before. "I know what it's like to walk into your son's bedroom and smell the scent of gunpowder, see his brains splashed on the wall and try to breathe life back into his dead body." His nostrils flared with an anger of his own. "Don't tell me that I don't know what it's like to love somebody and lose them. Don't get into a pissing match with me."

He turned on his heel and left the kitchen, leaving Haley to stare after him.

Chapter 18

A yawning dark sadness threatened to consume her. This was why she didn't get close to people. She had too much pain of her own to want to share the pain of others. And yet his words echoed in her head, in her heart, in the depths of her very soul.

A son. Grey had once had a son and something awful had happened. Haley stood for a long moment in the kitchen, her eyes closed as she tried to digest what little he'd just shared.

The pain that had ripped through his voice still lingered in the room, seeking purchase in her head, trying to weave in her heart. She knew if she accepted his pain inside her, then a piece of him would be forever with her.

But she had no choice except to go to him, to wrap her arms around him and try to ease some of the pain. He was already more than a little bit in her heart. As frightening as it was at this moment, she needed to be there for Grey more than she needed to escape all that he represented.

He stood at the windows in the living room, his back rigid and filled with tension. He must have sensed her presence in the room, although he didn't turn around to look at her.

"His name was Danny and he was fourteen years old and on March twenty-third two years ago he put a gun to his head and killed himself."

She gasped softly, then placed a hand on his back, felt the taut muscles beneath her palm. "Why? Why would he do something like that?" She moved to the side of him. The brilliant moonlight pouring through the windows illuminated his face, a study in torture and pain.

"Depression. Despair. Believe me, I've asked myself that same question a million times." He sighed, the sound like that of a mournful wind through barren trees.

She took his hand. "Come sit with me." She guided him to the sofa, then leaned over and turned on the lamp next to where they sat. "Talk to me, Grey. Talk to me about what happened."

He drew a hand down his face. "There isn't a lot to tell. I had no idea Danny was in trouble. He'd always been a quiet kid, rarely gave us any problems. Sarah had mentioned to me that he'd seemed quieter than usual and I tried to talk to him, but he assured me everything was fine."

He leaned forward and buried his face in his hands, as if the memories were too painful to endure. Haley's heart broke. She felt his pain in every inch of her body and the worst part of all was she knew that there was nothing she could say, nothing she could do to make it better, to help him escape from those horrible memories.

He reared back and looked at her with his dark, haunting eyes. "That day I got home from work

early. Sarah was at a luncheon and the minute I unlocked the front door, I knew something was terribly wrong. I smelled the gunpowder. I didn't own a
gun. It didn't make sense to me. I heard music coming from Danny's room and raced up the stairs."

He shed no tears. It was as if his grief was too big,
too profound for normal human emotion. "I found
him on the floor. He was already dead, but I called
911, then tried to administer CPR." He released another bone-weary sigh. "Later we found that he'd
left a note. He and a friend of his were being bullied
at school. They both felt isolated and alone and had
made a suicide pact."

"And the other boy?"

"Thank God he chickened out at the last minute.
What might have been two tragedies was only one."

"Grey, I'm so sorry. I don't even have the words to
tell you how sorry I am." She placed her hand on his
knee and squeezed, wishing she could reach inside
him and hug his wounded heart. After a moment his
hand reached out and clasped hers.

They sat for a long time in silence, his hand gripping hers tightly. Finally he released his grip and
leaned back. "Danny's death was the end of my
marriage. I was so filled with grief that I didn't realize at first how filled with rage Sarah was. And all
her rage was directed at me."

"At you?" Haley looked at him in surprise.

He nodded. "It took almost six months for her to
explode, but when she did I knew our marriage was
over. She told me she hated me because I could help
everyone else's sons, but hadn't been able to help
my own. I was trained to see warning signs, edu-

cated to save children, but when it all came down, I hadn't been able to save her son."

"But that wasn't fair," Haley protested.

He smiled for the first time since they'd awakened. "Maybe not, but it crystallized for me just how distant Sarah and I had become from each other over the years. We'd both been alone when we buried our son and it never occurred to her to reach for me to share the grief. We grieved alone, separately, at a time when we should have found some comfort in each other. When she finally told me she was leaving me, it was almost a relief."

He stood suddenly, his features calmer now, without the tension that had ridden them before. "You know, it is safer never to love, never to let anyone get close. You don't get hurt that way, but it's not the way I want to live. Even knowing the tragic outcome of Danny's life, I wouldn't give back one day of loving him. Put your shoes on, I'll take you home."

He was only doing what she'd requested of him, but she wasn't at all sure she wanted to leave. She wasn't at all sure that if she left now it wouldn't be something she'd regret for the rest of her life.

"I could stay."

"Not this way. Not now." There was a distance in his eyes that made her get her shoes, a distance that told her it was too late. He was forcing her to do what she'd always done in the past, escape.

It was the longest fifteen-minute ride she'd ever endured. The silence echoed in the confines of the car. Haley couldn't remember a time she'd ever been lost for words, but she was now.

He seemed disinclined to talk as well, as if

spilling the memories of the darkest days of his life had depleted him mentally and physically.

He'd been her rock. From the moment she'd met him he'd grounded her with his quiet competence and support. He'd offered her a soft place to fall when the madness around her became too much to bear. For the first time in her life, she wanted to be a rock, but she wasn't sure she knew how.

He pulled into her driveway but didn't cut the engine. Instead he turned his lights to high beam, then looked at her. "I'll wait here until you get inside."

"You could come in with me."

"I could, but I'm not going to." He directed his attention out the front window. "I told you I'm falling in love with you, but I don't want to be just another man that you have to run from. Maybe it's best if we don't see each other for a while."

Her heart skipped a beat and her throat went dry. She should be relieved that there wouldn't be an ugly ending to whatever relationship they might have briefly had, that they could end it now as adults making what was probably the best decision for both of them.

"Okay, if that's what you think is best." She started to open her door but stopped as he placed a hand on her arm. She turned back to look at him.

"Haley, that dream you're having?" His features were barely visible in the light from the dashboard. "Have you ever considered that maybe what is chasing you is life? Love? And until you stop running and turn around to face it, you're never going to know true happiness."

She had no reply. Instead she opened the car door and got out. As she walked to her front door she wondered how the night had gone from dinner and lovemaking to tragedy and a final ending that hurt far more than it should have.

She refused to look back as she unlocked her door. She went inside, punched in the security code to stop the alarm from sounding, then stood in the entry and fought the unexpected burn of tears.

Walking into the living room she jumped in surprise as the telephone rang. She eyed it warily. Was it possible Grey was using his cell phone to call her from his car?

She raced across the living room to pick up.

"You've been warned."

The thick, guttural voice seemed to ooze through the line, reaching out invisible fingers to close off her throat and steal away her breath.

"Who is this?" she asked. "Dammit, who are you?"

"Death, Haley. And I'm coming for you soon."

Click, and the line was empty.

SHE'D BEEN WARNED.

SHE'D BEEN WARNED.

SHE'D BEEN WARNED.

SHE'D BEEN WARNED.

SHE'D BEEN WARNED!

THEY MUST DIE.

HALEY AND MOLLY.

MOLLY AND HALEY.

HALEY AND MOLLY MUST DIE.

Chapter 19

Somebody was watching her. Somebody named Death.

Haley hung up the phone and stared around the room. The curtains were drawn but she felt no comfort from that fact. The phone had rung moments after she'd stepped inside the house. She went again to the front door and checked the locks, then went to the back door to assure herself that it was locked as well.

Somebody was watching her.

Somebody had seen her get out of Grey's car, unlock the front door and come inside. She knew it was true. She felt it in the chill of her bones.

But who? One of the neighbors? Or someone else, watching her house from a car, from a secret hiding place nearby?

She was being systematically terrorized and it was hard to protect herself from mental assault from an unknown source.

She'd been somewhat mollified by Tolliver explaining to her that these kinds of things happened all the time, grieving people being tormented by sick twists. But the idea of somebody watching her from the shadows lent a new dimension to the terror.

On Monday she'd have the caller ID service working, and hopefully if the calls continued either the phone company or the police would do something about it.

You've been warned.

She left the lights on in the living room and went into her bedroom. *Death, Haley. And I'm coming for you soon.*

Death knew her by name. There was no way to believe that the calls were random pranks. They were intended for her and her alone.

If the call had come yesterday she wouldn't have hesitated to pick up the phone and call Grey: just to hear his strong, deep voice, just to know that he was in her corner.

But she couldn't call him now. It wouldn't be fair. She couldn't push him away with one hand and pull him closer with the other.

I'm falling in love with you. Had he really said those words? As she undressed and changed into her nightshirt, she tried to dismiss them.

He was mistaking love for lust. She'd been the first woman he'd connected with since the terrible tragedy that had pulled his world apart. It was only natural he'd fancy himself in love with her.

So how did she dismiss the fact that she was falling in love with him? Her sister had been murdered, she was receiving threatening phone calls and had a niece who refused to speak. Grey had been the sanity in all of the insanity. Was it any wonder she wanted to cling to him? Was it any wonder she might think herself in love with him?

She got into bed but kept the nightstand lamp on, for the first time in her life afraid of the dark, afraid of what might happen in the shadows of the night.

Staring up at the ceiling overhead, she thought of everything that Grey had said to her. He'd said that even knowing the eventual outcome would be tremendous pain and loss, he wouldn't have given back a day he'd spent loving his son.

She wouldn't have given up one day spent with her father either: even knowing that she'd lose him, even knowing that the pain of that loss would resonate inside her forever.

She wanted to dismiss Grey's free analysis, she wanted to believe he was full of it and didn't know anything about her at all. But she suspected he was right. She'd been running for most of her life, running away from any relationship that might have the capacity to hurt her.

And she'd pretty well screwed things up with Grey, hadn't she? She'd run from him and he'd let her go. But this was the first time in her life she'd wanted to turn around and run back into a man's arms. She had a feeling that tonight she'd made the biggest mistake in her life.

You blew it, sister. Monica's voice whispered in her head. *He was a good man, just the kind you need in your life. A rock. And you blew it big-time.*

She sighed and stared up at the ceiling, trying to avoid thinking about the fact that somebody named Death was coming for her and she was as alone as she had ever been in her life.

*   *   *

Over the next couple of days Haley found her feeling of aloneness intensified. She hadn't realized how much support, how much comfort Grey gave her until she didn't have that anymore.

Each time the phone rang she found herself scared that the caller would be another threat, and hoping that the caller might be Grey. She now had caller ID, so if another frightening phone call came she hoped the ID would show her where the calls were originating.

But she knew there were ways to circumvent caller ID. If the calls were coming from a prepaid cell phone, they would be nearly impossible to trace. By punching in a particular code, the call could be made anonymously.

By Thursday, she'd begun to hope that whoever had been making the horrible calls had moved or dropped dead or decided to torment somebody else.

She'd seen Grey once during the course of the week. They'd run into each other at the police station. She'd gone there for yet another update from Tolliver and Grey was obviously there working.

He'd been friendly but distant, as if they hadn't shared anything of consequence between them. It had been awkward and she'd returned home depressed, both by the no-news report from Tolliver and by her encounter with Grey.

That evening she and Molly had eaten another silent meal, then had gone into the living room for yet another couple of hours of quiet television time.

Night had just fallen, the purple shadows outside the windows transforming to complete darkness.

"Would you like me to make some popcorn?" She forced her usual note of cheerfulness into her voice.

Molly shook her head and focused her attention back on the television. Haley sighed dispiritedly and glanced toward the window. Every nerve in her body tensed as she saw the unmistakable gleam of eyes looking in.

Her initial impulse was to scream, to jump up and twirl the wand on the blinds to keep those eyes out. Instead she stared back at the television, the hairs on the nape of her neck standing out.

"I think I'll go make me a snack," she said to Molly and as calmly as possible got up and headed into the kitchen. She didn't turn on the kitchen light, but picked up the telephone and punched in the Marcelli number.

Frank answered. "Frank, somebody is looking into my back window. Could you meet me outside?"

Haley didn't give herself time to think about her actions. All she knew was that she was tired of feeling victimized by an unknown person. She was enraged by the fact that somebody was calling with threats, peeping into her windows for whatever kicks they could get.

As quietly as possible she unlocked the back door, then slid into the night shadows. In the faint light spilling down from the moon, she saw somebody standing at the back of the house, looking into the window of the room where Molly sat watching television.

She launched herself and tackled him. She screamed as they both tumbled to the ground. He grunted in surprise, then struggled to get free, but she held on to him. It was too dark for her to know who it was, but she was determined not to let him up.

He punched at her, the blow catching her square in the chest, but she didn't release her death hold on him.

"Freeze!" Frank Marcelli pointed a bright flashlight with one hand and his gun with the other.

"Get this crazy bitch off me."

Haley recognized the voice. She got up from the ground and glared at Grant Newton. "I'm a crazy bitch? You're a sick pervert." She watched as Frank put away his gun, then grabbed Newton by the collar and yanked him to his feet.

"You okay?" Frank asked her.

"Why are you asking her? I'm going to sue the crazy bitch for assault." Grant's face was a twisted mask of rage.

"Fine, but I want him arrested," she exclaimed.

"I'll take her for every dime she has."

"Shut up, Newton," Frank said. "You're going to have a tough time convincing anyone that you're the victim here."

"I want him arrested for trespassing and window peeping. He's probably the one who's been making phone calls to me. He's probably the one who killed my sister!" Her voice rose with wild rage.

She'd known the guy was a creep and now her suspicions had been justified.

"I didn't kill anybody," Grant protested as Frank cuffed him. "And I didn't make any phone calls to you either."

"Then what were you doing in my backyard? Looking into my windows?"

He clamped his mouth shut and refused to say

another word. "I'll take him down to the station and book him," Frank said.

Within minutes Frank and Grant were gone and Haley was back in the house. Thankfully Molly appeared to have heard nothing of the drama. Her attention was transfixed by the Disney movie playing from the DVD.

Haley returned to her seat in the chair opposite the sofa and stared at the television, but her mind raced with thoughts. Was Grant Newton not only a window peeper but a murderer as well?

He'd admitted he'd asked Monica out several times and she'd turned him down. Had he also asked out the pretty Sondra Jackson? He lived down the street from Monica, and had been at the school on the night Sondra had been murdered.

So many coincidences. Too many.

At eight thirty she put Molly to bed and at ten a soft knock sounded on her door. She answered to see Frank. She motioned him inside.

"He was out before I finished the paperwork," he said.

"What?" Haley stared at him in disbelief. "What do you mean he was out?"

"Posted bond and left. We could only charge him with a couple of misdemeanors. Look, Haley, the man is obviously a creep, but that doesn't necessarily make him a killer."

"But he's still under investigation for Monica's death, isn't he?"

"This little stunt today moved him up the list as far as I'm concerned, but so far there is no real hard evidence to tie him to the murders. It doesn't matter what you or I believe, we have to have evidence to make a case for murder."

Haley sighed in frustration. "Did he say anything? Did he say why he was peeping in my window?"

Frank hesitated, then shoved his hands in his pockets, his gaze brooding. "He confessed that he'd had a thing for Monica, that he thought she was the prettiest woman he'd ever seen." He stared at some point over her head, his eyes darkening with each word. "He was obsessed with her and admitted that he sometimes looked in her windows to watch her."

"Then why was he looking in at me?"

Frank directed his gaze back on her. "Because you look so much like her." He pulled his hands from his pockets. "Listen, Haley, if Grant Newton killed Monica, I'll make sure he spends the rest of his life behind bars. I know you want her killer caught, but believe me, no more than I do."

He turned and opened her front door. "Newton has been warned to stay away from you and Molly, but I'd advise you to be careful and make sure you stay away from him. We don't know what he might be capable of or if he figures into Monica's and Sondra's deaths."

Frank left to return home and Haley locked up the house, armed the security system and went into her bedroom to prepare for bed.

She supposed she should feel better that at least the police had Grant Newton in their sights, that he'd probably be investigated inside out and upside down to see if it was possible that he was the killer.

But it was hard to feel better knowing that even though Grant was obviously some kind of voyeuristic pervert, the police hadn't yet been able to tie him to the murders.

What was it he had said to her after Monica's funeral? Something about if he killed every woman who rejected him, then he'd leave a trail of victims to rival Ted Bundy? At the time she'd thought it an odd thing to say. Now the memory of his words sent chills up her spine.

And he was still free to walk the streets, to possibly hunt for another victim, an unsuspecting woman who might decline the offer of a date, who might be rude to him.

No, Haley didn't feel better about capturing Grant Newton peeping through her window. If anything she was more afraid. The monster now had a face and a name and he lived right down the street.

The scream tore through Haley, yanking her from her sleep. She shot straight up, heart thudding frantically. Early morning sunshine drifted through the curtains and a glance at the clock indicated it was just after seven. Her alarm was set to go off in fifteen minutes.

The scream came again, a horrifying, bone-chilling sound. Molly! Haley jumped out of bed, her feet hitting the floor at a run.

She ran down the hallway and stopped in the doorway of Molly's room. The bed was empty and her niece was nowhere to be seen.

The kitchen. "Molly!" Haley screamed as she ran through the living room and into the kitchen.

Molly stood at the back door, her face as pale as paper, her little fingers gripping the open door so tight it looked as if they might snap.

"Molly? Honey, what is it?" Haley stepped behind her and looked out the door. She gasped in
horror. On the stoop just outside was the white cat
she'd seen skirting around the Marcelli house.

It was obvious the cat was dead. A knife pro-
truded from the bloody fur and a note was tucked
under the hindquarters.

YOU'RE ONE DEAD WHORE. JUST LIKE
YOUR SISTER.

"Oh my God!" Haley took Molly by the shoulders and pulled her away from the door. "Sit down,
honey." She pointed Molly to the table. "I need to
call the police."

She didn't call Frank, but instead called Tolliver,
who told her he'd be at her house as soon as possible. When the call had been made, Haley sat at the
table next to Molly. "I'm so sorry you had to see
that," she said.

"His name was Snowflake."

For a moment Haley thought she was hallucinat-
ing the little voice. Molly had talked. A thrill of eu-
phoria momentarily swept away the horror of the
dead cat and the terrifying note. She drew a deep
breath to calm herself, not wanting to startle Molly
with her reaction. "Snowflake is a nice name," she
replied.

"He was a nice kitty." Molly's lower lip trembled.
"Why would somebody do that to him? He never
did anything wrong."

"Whoever did that to Snowflake was a sick, evil
person. The same kind of person who hurt your
mommy." Haley leaned closer to Molly, unable to

stop the edge of excitement that whirled inside her. "Molly, tell me what you saw the morning that your mommy was hurt. Tell me what you heard."

Molly shook her head, but Haley wasn't taking no for an answer. She grabbed Molly's hand. "Molly, whatever you can tell me about that morning will help us find the bad person who hurt your mom. You can talk now, you have to tell me what you remember."

Molly jerked her hand away from Haley's grip. "I can't. I don't want to remember."

"You have to!" Haley replied with a sense of urgency.

"No, I don't." Tears appeared in Molly's eyes, making them shine with an unnatural gleam. "I don't want to talk about that."

"Dammit, Molly," Haley exploded in frustration. She drew another deep breath to steady herself and reached for Molly's hand once again but the little girl whirled out of her chair and ran to the back door.

"Molly, stop!"

She didn't stop. She jumped over the dead cat and raced for the tree. Haley jerked up from the table and followed, cursing herself for losing control, for pushing the child.

By the time Haley reached the bottom of the tree, Molly was in the tree house, the only sign of her presence there little sobs that drifted down on the morning air.

Jesus, what was she doing? She'd lost all control, pushed way too hard. "Molly? Come down here. I'm sorry, honey." Haley grabbed the wooden railing of the ladder that led up the tree, a wealth of

emotion nearly overwhelming her. "I didn't mean
to yell at you."

Molly didn't answer but her sobs became louder.

Her cries ripped through Haley, who wanted
nothing more than to hold her, to cry with her. The
calls, the notes, the dead cat and now this. It was too
much. It was all too much. "Molly, please come
down."

Tears of frustration burned at Haley's eyes. *Can't
you do anything right?* Monica's voice whispered
through her brain.

Haley gripped the railing more tightly and stared
up into the tree house. She had a feeling this moment, more than any other she would ever have,
would forever define her relationship with Molly.

It was obvious Molly wasn't going to come
down. Haley needed to go up. She stepped on the
first rung, her heart beating fast and her chest tight-
ening painfully.

The tree house held her memories of her father,
and just as Grey had said, she'd spent a lifetime running from those memories. But it was time to stop
running, time to put her little-girl hurts away so she
could deal with Molly's little-girl hurts.

She moved to the second rung and her tears came
faster, splashing onto her cheeks as a roar of pain
rushed through her. It wasn't the pain of losing the
people she loved; rather it was the heartbreak of realizing she and Molly still hadn't connected on any
real level.

As she moved up to the third, then fourth rung,
she realized Grey had been right about so many
things. There was a part of her that even now
wanted to run away, a part of her that feared she

would never be enough, never manage to do the right thing for Molly. But for the first time in her life a bigger part of her wanted to fix things, wanted to stand and see it all through.

By the time she reached the tree house every muscle in her body trembled from the effort. She pulled herself through the opening and moved to sit on the opposite side of the little house from Molly, who was curled in a corner just under one of the windows.

Molly didn't look at her, but kept her face hidden in her hands. Suddenly, Haley's emotions spun out of control. Monica was dead. Molly hated her. She'd shoved Grey away. She'd screwed up everything in her life.

Sobs ripped through her as she buried her face in her hands. How could she teach Molly to make good decisions when she made such poor ones for herself? How could she teach Molly to love when she was afraid to love?

"I just wanted you to love me," she cried, her face still buried. "But I'm screwing it all up. I don't know how to cook and I forget to wash your favorite clothes. I'm so scared that I'm messing you up."

Gasping sobs shook her shoulders. "Sometimes I don't remember to set the alarm clock and I don't know anything about what you like and don't like. I want to do right, but I don't know what you need from me."

Once again a torrent of sobs escaped her. She caught her breath as Molly's little hand grabbed hers. She opened her eyes to see Molly's shiny, adultlike gaze. "All I really need for you to do is to love me," Molly said.

"Oh, honey, I do." Haley wrapped her arms around Molly and pulled her into a tight embrace. "You'll never know how much I love you, how much I want to do right by you."

For several long moments they remained in the embrace and silent tears trekked down Haley's face, tears of gratitude. Somehow, someway she knew this was a breakthrough, that her relationship with Molly would be forever transformed by these moments here in the tree house.

"You told me you couldn't come up here." Molly finally broke the silence. "You said you were afraid to climb up here."

"I guess my fear of coming up here wasn't as big as my need to be with you." Haley stroked Molly's soft, baby-fine hair, comforted by the weight of the child leaning so trustingly into her arms. "I'm sorry I yelled at you. I didn't mean to."

"I miss her," Molly said softly.

Haley tightened her arms around her. "I miss her too."

"Sometimes I want to talk about her."

"You can talk about her whenever you want to. She was a terrific sister and I know she was a terrific mom."

"Sometimes you're too happy. It's like you don't care that she's gone."

Once again Molly's words pierced through Haley. "I've been trying to be cheerful and happy to make you feel better, but inside I've been crying."

Molly nodded, as if satisfied. She drew a deep, tremulous breath. "I saw something blue."

Haley froze. Don't blow it, she commanded herself. "Something blue?"

"I was hiding under the bed when the bad person came into the house. Mommy fell on the floor beside the bed and she saw me. She told me to shush, to not make a sound. Then I saw something blue and a knife." Every muscle in Molly's little body tightened. "Then there was blood everywhere and I squeezed my eyes closed."

She sat up and looked at Haley with tears once again sparkling in her eyes. "I should have saved my mommy. I should have crawled out and saved her."

"Your mommy wouldn't have wanted you to do anything differently, Lolly. You were right to mind your mommy and stay quiet and hidden. You couldn't save her, sweetheart." She pulled Molly back into her arms and stroked her hair once again.

A breeze lifted the curtains, bringing with it the scent of grass and flowers in bloom. Haley leaned her head back against the plywood and could almost hear her father's laughter echoing off the walls.

She'd feared this place would make her sad, that all she'd be able to remember if she came up here was her father's loss. But that wasn't the case. Good memories were contained within the four walls of this miniature house: sweet memories that she wouldn't trade to mitigate the pain of her father's death.

"Hello? Haley? Molly? Anybody home?" The familiar deep voice came from the backyard.

Molly sat up and Haley scooted over to the window and looked down to see Tolliver. "We'll be right down," she yelled. "Come on, Molly. We need to talk to Detective Tolliver. Maybe he can find out who hurt Snowflake."

As they climbed down to meet the detective, for the first time since she'd arrived in Pleasant Hill hope filled Haley's heart.

Chapter 20

"Heard you had some more excitement yester-day." Dean stood on Haley's front porch on Wednesday morning. "Nothing like a dead cat to freak you out."

"You seem to know everything that's going on in this neighborhood. Why don't you know who killed my sister?" Haley asked the teenager.

He shrugged. "The neighborhood was pretty boring before your sister was killed and you moved in. I wasn't paying much attention to things then." He shoved his hands into his jeans pockets. "If I was a betting man, I'd put money on Grant Newton. He's a real creep."

Haley agreed. In fact, she'd made the case to Tolliver the day before that Newton had killed Snowflake and left her the threatening note. It was too coincidental that he'd been caught and arrested for window peeping and the next morning a dead cat was on her porch.

She was ninety-nine percent certain that Grant Newton wasn't just a voyeuristic pervert, but a murderer as well. And he was still walking the streets. Tolliver had taken the cat and the note away with him and promised to investigate, but Haley wasn't holding her breath.

"What do you want, Dean?"

He pulled his hands from his pockets and gestured toward the yard. "You're past due for some yard work."

She was surprised to realize it was true. So much had been happening the last two weeks that she hadn't paid much attention to the fact that the grass was too tall. "You're right. Go ahead and mow."

"Same price as last time?"

"Fine," Haley replied.

A few minutes later she stood at the front window and watched as Dean cut a swath with his lawn mower through the tall grass. There had been times when she'd wondered about Dean, when she'd worried that maybe he had killed Monica.

She didn't think so anymore. She suspected he was just a teenager dealing with the horrors of adolescence. Too many raging hormones and not enough parental support.

She turned away from the window and headed toward the master bathroom off Monica's bedroom. She had decided to clean out those cabinets today while Molly was in school.

Immediately after school they had an appointment with Dr. Tredwell. She'd called him yesterday to tell him there had been a breakthrough with Molly, that she'd finally found her voice. She hadn't spoken to him, but instead had left a message on his machine. He'd called back last night and had set up the appointment for this afternoon.

She wanted to call Grey and tell him the news.

He'd been through almost every difficult moment she'd had since Monica's death. It seemed unfair for her not to share the good news with him. But it also seemed unfair for her to call him when she wasn't sure what she wanted, what she needed from him.

The night before, she and Molly had cuddled up together on the sofa and talked about Monica and what she would have wanted for them. It had been a wonderful night, filled with sweet memories and promises for their life together.

When Haley had tucked Molly into bed, it had been Molly who had reached to give Haley a kiss, Molly who had whispered an "I love you" that had etched a permanent mark on Haley's heart.

Hope. It was an amazing emotion. It filled her up, stealing away some of the grief that had been with her since Monica's death. It made her feel strong and capable of dealing with whatever life might throw her way.

She and Molly were finally talking, connecting with each other on a soul level. They were going to be all right. All they really needed was for Grant Newton to be arrested and put away for the rest of his life.

Monica's master bathroom was large and airy and decorated in shades of white and pink. Just seeing her sister's toothbrush lying on the edge of the sink, her facial cream nearby, caused a swell of emotion to push against Haley's chest.

This would be the final goodbye. These were the last of the personal items that had belonged to Monica. She began in the cabinet beneath the sink, sorting through makeup and cotton swabs, talcum powder and bath salts.

Items that needed to be tossed were thrown away and those she was keeping she put in a cardboard box. When she'd finished with the things beneath the sink, she moved to the overhead medicine cabinet.

A bottle of aspirins nestled next to a box of Band-Aids. Vitamins shared a shelf with Neosporin cream. But it was a familiar pink pill case that shocked Haley with its very presence in the cabinet.

She grabbed the plastic case and opened it to see the tiny pills inside. Birth control pills. Haley certainly recognized what they were because she took the same kind herself.

She sat on the edge of the tub, the case of pills in her hand. There were eight pills missing, but no prescription sticker to indicate whether this was an ongoing prescription or a first-month supply.

In any case, it didn't matter. What mattered was that her sister was apparently taking birth control pills. Why would a woman who wasn't even dating be on birth control pills?

Because she either intended to have sex or was having sex at the time of her death. With whom? Haley gripped the pill container tightly in her hand. Might this have something to do with Monica's murder?

In all their conversations Monica had never mentioned any man. But what if she was having an affair? A secret affair? What if the man she was having the affair with was married? A man who might have a lot to lose if word of an affair got out?

Even as she allowed her thoughts free rein, she shook her head ruefully. Monica would never have an affair with a married man. Monica always played by the rules, did the right thing.

Although she tossed the pills in the garbage, she couldn't get them out of her mind. She had assured Tolliver from the very beginning of the investigation that Monica wasn't seeing anyone. Now she wondered if she'd been instrumental in steering the investigation in the wrong direction.

Just before noon she got in her car to drive to the station and tell Tolliver about her discovery. Was it possible that Grant Newton wasn't just a pervert and a creep, but had been Monica's lover and when she'd tried to call it off he'd killed her? How did Sondra Jackson figure into that scenario?

Tolliver was not happy to see her. He led her back to his desk and gestured her into the seat in front of it. Frank sat at the desk next to him and he nodded a greeting at her.

"I found birth control pills in Monica's bathroom," Haley said without preamble. "I think maybe she was having a relationship with somebody."

"Just because she was taking the pill doesn't necessarily mean she was having sex with anyone," Frank said. "Don't women take those pills for other reasons?"

"To regulate their periods, but Monica was always regular as clockwork. As much as the thought of it makes my skin crawl, maybe she slept with Grant Newton and when she tried to end the relationship, he killed her. Or you might check out Jay Middleton again. He's a player, and Monica would have probably been susceptible to his charm."

Owen leaned back in his chair and eyed her

sadly. "You've got to let it go, Haley. You've got to let our investigation proceed and you need to work on getting on with your life."

She flushed warmly. "I am working on getting on with my life, but I want Monica's killer behind bars. I want the person who's making threatening phone calls to me and leaving dead cats on my porch put in jail. It's hard to get on with my life when my sister has been brutally murdered and somebody tried to start my kitchen on fire and each day that passes I know the odds of you finding the killer get worse."

"Haley, we're doing the best we can," Frank said. "We can only work with the evidence we have. We can't deal in speculation." He leaned over and placed a hand on Haley's arm. "Believe me, I want her killer behind bars as badly as you do."

She sighed as Frank removed his hand from her arm. "I'm just scared. The dead cat along with that note definitely freaked me out." With the breakthrough with Molly and her suddenly talking, Haley had scarcely had time to process the horror of the brutally stabbed cat.

"If it's any consolation, we've found nothing to indicate that Monica or Sondra were receiving threatening notes and phone calls before their deaths," Frank said.

"We don't believe the person who is messing with you is our killer," Tolliver added. "You know we've doubled the patrols going by your house and we have an ongoing investigation into the note and the dead cat. Let us do our job, Haley." His words were a definite dismissal.

Later as she drove home from the police station

she found herself thinking about the cat. She'd never understood the kind of people who could hurt an animal. It took a particular kind of evil to stab an innocent creature. And that particular evil had her in its sights.

A sense of foreboding rode her shoulders as she got home and went into the kitchen to make herself a late lunch. The same person who had been making the threatening calls to her had obviously left the cat. A definite escalation of the horror. So what happened next? What came after a dead cat?

She'd just made herself a peanut butter and jelly sandwich and sat down at the table when somebody knocked on her front door.

"Hey, girl." Angela greeted her bearing a tin of fudge brownies in one hand. "I did some baking this morning and thought you and Molly might like a little chocolate."

"Chocolate is always a good thing. Come on in, I was just having a sandwich."

Angela followed her into the kitchen and sat at the table. "Frank told me Molly has started talking again."

"Did he also tell you about Snowflake?"

"Yeah, how creepy is that?" Angela frowned. "I've never been nervous in the house before, but with all this going on and Frank gone so much, I told him that maybe it was time we get an alarm system in our house. So, tell me about Molly."

"It was rather anticlimactic after all this time. She's the one who found the dead cat. She screamed and I pulled her away from the back door. She sat down at the kitchen table and told me the cat's name was Snowflake. I was so stunned. But as simple as that she started talking again."

"Has she said anything about the morning of Monica's death?"

"A little. She told me she saw something blue and a big knife and blood."

"Something blue? Like a shirt?"

"She didn't get more specific and I didn't push her too hard." Haley picked at the crust of her sandwich. "I think maybe she knows more than what she's telling, but doesn't want to remember any more. I'm taking her to see Dr. Tredwell this afternoon and I'm hoping he'll have a little better luck with her."

"But you'd think if she saw who killed her mother, she would have told you," Angela said. "She's old enough to realize that the police need her help."

Haley sighed dispiritedly. "I don't think she knows who the person was, but I'm hoping she'll have enough memories that the police can piece together a suspect. Are you sure Monica never mentioned having an interest in some man?"

Angela looked at her in surprise. "I thought you were fairly certain that she wasn't seeing anyone."

"I was until I found birth control pills in Monica's medicine cabinet."

"Maybe she was having period problems?"

Haley shook her head. "I don't think so. I talked to Monica on the phone at least once a week. We talked about everything. If she had been having any kind of problems, she would have mentioned it to me."

"So you think she was taking the pills because she was sleeping with somebody?"

"I don't know what else to think. You think it's possible she slept with Grant Newton?"

"No way." Angela released a sharp burst of laughter. "She thought Grant was a creep. She was always nice to him because that's the type of person she was, but the only way she'd have sex with him was if she was tied up, blindfolded and too drunk to know what she was doing."

Haley shoved her sandwich aside. "It's just so frustrating. The one thing we know for sure is that Monica knew her attacker. She knew and trusted the person enough to open up her front door and let him in."

"Haley, honey." Angela reached over and placed her hand on Haley's forearm. "Let the police do their jobs. Owen and Frank are working overtime on this. They're good cops. They'll figure it out."

Haley nodded. "Frank is the best. I don't know what I would have done without him these last couple of weeks."

Angela removed her hand. "He's great and he's a good cop. Unfortunately, he called me just a few minutes ago to say there was a drive-by shooting on the other side of town and he won't be home until the wee hours of the morning."

"I guess that's one of the drawbacks to being married to a cop, the long hours."

Angela nodded and stood. "I've got to get out of here. I've got tons of things on my agenda this afternoon."

Haley stood to walk with her to the front door. "You always stay so busy."

"You know the saying about a woman's work never being done. This afternoon I'm taking my girls to stay at Frank's parents' home so I can spend the evening doing some heavy-duty spring cleaning."

"That doesn't sound like fun."

Angela smiled. "I don't mind. There's nothing I love more than having the house perfect for Frank and the girls."

"I didn't realize Frank had parents here in town."

She wrinkled her nose. "Yes, he does, but I really don't get along with them. I don't have much to do with them but I do let them see the girls pretty regularly. In-laws can be real pains. Remember that if you ever get married."

Marriage certainly didn't look like it was in her future anytime soon, she thought after Angela had left. Thoughts of Grey filled her head as she returned to the kitchen.

She pulled her sandwich back in front of her and took a bite, tasting only the bitter regrets that filled her heart. They had been building something, she and Grey.

Over those lunches they had shared thoughts and feelings and information about each other to create an intimacy between them. Their lovemaking had been wonderful and she'd felt safe and secure in his arms, so safe and secure that she'd run from it, run from him.

It had been the biggest mistake she'd made in her life.

In the last couple of days Haley had realized that her feelings for Grey had nothing to do with the fact that she didn't know many people in town. It had nothing to do with the fact that she'd been thrust into unfamiliar territory, both as a guardian to

Molly and with frightening threats directed at herself.

Grey had touched her in places where she hadn't been touched before, he'd found parts of her she hadn't known needed and he'd filled those needs. And she'd screwed it up. She'd allowed him in just far enough to scare her, then had backed away.

And what exactly was it she was afraid of? She was scared of people who left dead cats on her porch. People who made phone calls that promised death frightened her. As she thought of everything that had happened in her life over the last month, she was amazed to think that loving somebody and being loved by that person might have frightened her.

It didn't now. And now it was too late. "A day late and a dollar short," she muttered as she took a bite of her sandwich.

Men had come and gone through her life since she'd been a teenager and she'd always survived. But this was the first time she'd allowed her heart to get involved and she was surprised by how much it hurt.

He'd sneaked in so quickly, so completely beneath her defenses, and now she was left with another feeling of bereavement.

When she'd finished lunch she sat on the sofa and stared at her sister's glass collection. Each and every piece held a particular meaning, bought for a specific purpose, except that blue heart. Like the birth control pills in the medicine cabinet, the blue heart didn't seem to belong.

And yet it did. So why had Monica bought it and

for what reason? Haley asked Molly that very question when she got home from school that afternoon.

"I don't know, Aunt Haley," Molly said. "Mommy bought it one day but she didn't tell me why." Molly reached up and tugged on a strand of her hair. "I guess we won't get any more pretty blue things since Mommy's gone."

"Of course we will," Haley replied. She bent down on one knee in front of her niece. "I intend to buy a pretty blue piece of glass for all kinds of wonderful things that you're going to do in the future."

"Like what?" Molly gazed at her curiously.

"Oh, I don't know exactly. Maybe we should buy one because you started talking once again. Then we'll get one when you start junior high school and when you have your first date. Your mommy started a tradition with the glass collection and you and I are going to continue the tradition. And stop pulling on your hair or you're going to be bald before you're thirty."

"Then I'll buy a wig." Molly dropped her hand from her hair. "A purple wig. I think it would be cool to have purple hair."

Haley stood and stared at Molly. "I just sounded like your grandmother, and you just sounded like me when I was younger."

Molly grinned, an impish smile that sweetened her features. "Mommy always told me I was just like my aunt Haley." She tilted her head to one side and gazed at Haley curiously. "Did you want purple hair when you were eight?"

"Pink. I was definitely into pink when I was eight. Now we need to get out of here. We have an appointment with Dr. Tredwell."

Minutes later as they drove toward downtown Kansas City and the appointment with Tredwell, Haley considered Molly's words.

So Monica had told her daughter she was just like Aunt Haley. Haley glanced over at her niece, a wealth of warmth filling her heart.

Her love for Molly had always been an abstract kind of thing. Before Monica's death Haley had loved Molly because Molly was her niece and people were supposed to love their relatives. But now she was learning to love Molly simply because she was Molly. It was a tremendous feeling, to love a child.

The fact that Molly was a lot like Haley could only make things easier. Haley knew what it was like to not quite conform, to want purple hair and to be strong-willed.

She had no illusions about raising Molly. She knew the years they would share ahead would be filled with frustrations, fights and failures. But they would also be filled with triumphs, laughter and love.

"We're going to be all right, Molly," she now said. "I'm going to make a ton of mistakes and probably so are you. But if we love each other, we'll get through it all just fine."

"But maybe could you learn to cook better?" Molly asked.

Haley laughed. "I promise over the next couple of days I'll spend some time reading your mom's cookbooks."

"Okay." Molly's gaze remained on her. "And sometimes can we just be sad about Mommy?"

The question ripped out a piece of Haley's heart.

She reached out and touched Molly's hand. "Whenever you feel sad about your mommy, all you have to do is tell me and we can be sad together for a little while." She put her hand back on the steering wheel. "But you know, Molly, it's okay for us to be happy. Your mom would have wanted us to be happy too."

Haley parked the car and together she and Molly got out. A half an hour later as Haley sat in the chair outside the glass room watching Dr. Tredwell and Molly talk, her thoughts returned to Grey.

He'd lost a child. A child he'd loved for fourteen years. She'd only been with Molly a few weeks and already she couldn't imagine losing her.

He'd shared his grief with her and she'd run. He'd shared the scars on his soul and she hadn't protested him taking her home. She hadn't insisted she stay, she hadn't wrapped her arms around him and shared his grief.

She'd been strong enough to barrel out her back door and tackle a man who had been peeping in her window, but a coward when it came to opening herself up to loving Grey.

She didn't realize she'd become a cliché of a lovesick woman until she sat outside the glass enclosure and suffered her heartache. Thinking about Grey made her want to weep. There had been so many losses in her life and she had only herself to blame for this particular one.

As she watched Molly with Dr. Tredwell she suddenly realized that Molly had spent most of her life so far without a father figure.

You haven't cornered the market on grief, Haley.

Grey's words haunted her. He was right. People

suffered grief every day and still had the strength, the courage to reach out and love once again. She wanted to be one of those people. She was so tired of running.

When they arrived home after the appointment Angela invited Molly over to play with her girls for a while before dinner. Haley walked her next door, then returned to the house and sat at the table with the phone in her hand.

Call him. Monica's voice whispered in her ear. *Come on, sis. At least call him to tell him that Molly found her voice. You owe him that much.*

She dialed the first three digits of his number, then hung up, her heart twisted into a pretzel of tension. What if he didn't want to hear anything she had to say? What if he told her to permanently lose his number?

She'd never know unless she tried. Haley frowned, drew a deep breath and punched in the number. He answered on the second ring and his deep, familiar voice filled her with both apprehension and a sweet rush of heat.

"Grey, it's me."

"Haley." The sound of her name on his lips, so gentle, so nonjudgmental, forced emotion to swell inside her.

"Molly is talking." The words blurted out of her. "There was a dead cat named Snowflake and he was left on the doorstep along with a horrible threatening note for me and Molly started talking. It just happened. She talked." She was rambling and she knew it, but she couldn't seem to stop herself.

"She started talking and I tried to make her tell me about what she saw and she ran up into the tree house and I was so scared, but I managed to climb up after her. I told her I loved her more than I feared the tree house and we cried and we hugged."

"Haley." His soft voice broke into her monologue. "Take a breath."

She leaned back in the chair and pressed the phone more tightly against her ear. She drew a deep steadying breath and imagined the humor sparkling in his eyes and the way his dimples danced when he smiled.

"I promised her I'd learn how to cook. I'm going to study Monica's cookbooks and figure out how to cook real food."

"I'd say you've made tremendous progress over the past couple of days."

"I have a good therapist," she replied with forced lightness.

"I'm not your therapist, Haley," Grey said. "I'm your friend." He paused. "So, how are you feeling about things?"

She was surprised to feel tears burning in her eyes. "I'm hoping the police will be able to figure out who killed the cat and has been threatening me. I hope they're getting closer to identifying Monica's killer. I think Molly and I are going to be fine. And I'm absolutely miserable." She swiped at the tears that suddenly leaked down her cheeks. "Do you believe in second chances, Grey?"

"Generally speaking I do." His tone was slightly wary, a bit cautious.

Surely he knew what she was trying to say to him. Surely he could feel the emotion that oozed from her very pores right through the phone line.

"You were right about me," she said. "Everything

you said about me was right. I took my grief over my father's death and wrapped it around me like a protective shield. I've spent every moment of my life since then keeping people out."

She sighed tremulously. "But you got in. You got into my heart, Grey. It scared me so much I wanted to run. But I don't want to run anymore. I want you in my life, but I need to know if it's too late."

"Let me tell you something about me, Haley. Maybe you haven't noticed, but I'm not given to flights of fancy. I plan everything in my life as much as I can and I'm not very spontaneous."

It was his turn to release a sigh. "Haley, I'll never be a kite. I'll always be a rock, and when rocks fall in love they fall hard. Rocks don't fall out of love in a week or two. I'm in love with you, Haley. Even if you don't love me back, I'm going to stay in love with you for a long time to come."

His words, spoken so earnestly in his beautiful deep voice, forced more tears from her and she swallowed against a half-strangled sob. "I do love you, Grey. I love you like I've never loved anyone in my life."

"If I was there right now you'd be in my arms and I'd be kissing you like you've never been kissed before. I knew you were trouble the first time I saw you. The first time I laid eyes on you something came alive inside me. I know this sounds crazy, but I'd been in a dark place for a long time, then you came in and suddenly the darkness was gone."

Haley wanted to crawl through the phone and into his arms. "I felt the same way. I've spent so much time being afraid of relationships, but I'm not afraid anymore. Grey, I'm so sorry about your son. And I'm sorry about everything."

"You have nothing to be sorry for."

She reached up and tugged a strand of her hair, gazing absently across the room. "Grey, this isn't just about sex, is it? I mean, it had been a while for both of us and I just wondered if . . ." She trailed off, half embarrassed.

"Haley, I love making love to you. There's no denying that the sex between us is fantastic. But I also love that you pull your hair when you're nervous. I love that you can't cook but you're willing to learn. I love the way you laugh and how easily you can make me laugh. I love that you're a kite and even have one tattooed on the cheek of your very sexy bottom. But most of all I love the courage and strength you've shown by stepping into this life you didn't plan for."

His words, coupled with the emotion that vibrated in his voice, vanquished any doubt she might entertain. "Haley, I'm in this relationship for the long term, but you're the one who is in control. You decide how fast or slow we go, how far we take this."

"We have to take it slow, for Molly's sake," she said thoughtfully. "But, Grey, I'm in this for the long term as well."

"So, lunch tomorrow?"

She laughed, the first uninhibited burst of soul laughter she could remember enjoying for a long time. "I'll do you better than that. Why don't we plan dinner here tomorrow night? I'll cook and it will be a perfect opportunity for Molly to get to know you better."

"You sure you really want to cook?"

"I'm sure. I have twenty-four hours to figure it out. Why don't we say around six thirty? And be prepared to be amazed."

She felt his smile even though she couldn't see it. "You've amazed me from the moment I met you. I'll call you this evening."

Haley danced on air as she hung up the phone. He loved her. He wanted a future with her and Molly and his love resonated in every fiber of her being.

Finally you're getting things right, Monica's voice whispered softly. Yes, she was getting things right, except she'd just agreed to cook.

The evening passed quickly. Molly and Haley spent much of the time seated at the kitchen table poring over Monica's cookbooks and trying to decide the menu for the next evening.

"This looks good." Molly pointed to a picture of beef Wellington.

"It looks real good," Haley agreed. "But I think it's pretty ambitious for a beginner cook."

It was just after eight and the sunshine outside the window had begun to fade, transforming from golden yellow to the purple shadows of coming night.

"You don't mind Dr. Grey coming to dinner tomorrow night, do you?" Haley asked Molly.

"No, I think it will be fun. He's nice and he has pretty blue eyes."

"Yes, he does."

Molly looked at her and giggled. "You like him like a boyfriend, don't you?"

"How do you know that?"

She giggled again. " 'Cause your voice gets all mushy when you say his name."

"Mushy? I'll give you mushy!" Haley tickled Molly, who broke into peals of laughter.

When the laughter had died the two once again thumbed through cookbooks. Molly pointed to another picture. "I like meat loaf."

Haley scanned the recipe. "It sounds pretty easy. Okay, meat loaf it is. Now we need to think of a vegetable."

"Corn. Mommy always had corn with meat loaf."

"Then corn it is." Haley closed the cookbook. "And now it's time for bath and bedtime."

Half an hour later Haley sat on the edge of Molly's bed. "Just think, in another week you'll be out of school for the summer. Won't that be nice?" Molly nodded. "Is there anything you'd like to do during the summer?"

Molly yawned. "Swim and play with Adrianna. And maybe sometimes we could have a picnic up in the tree house."

"We could do that," Haley agreed.

Molly's eyes drifted shut. "Mostly I just want to spend time with you."

Haley leaned forward and kissed her on the forehead, love swelling up inside her so intensely it brought tears to her eyes. "And I want to spend time with you," she replied softly, but she knew Molly was already asleep.

She left Molly's bedroom and went around the house, closing blinds and checking to make sure all the windows and doors were securely locked. She armed the alarm system, then went directly back to the kitchen where she took a package of hamburger from the freezer and placed it in the refrigerator. She wasn't about to screw up dinner by not having the meat thawed in time.

It was too early for her to go to bed, but she went into her bedroom, changed into her nightclothes, then curled up on the sofa for an hour or two of television.

But the sitcom playing on the screen couldn't hold her interest. The last couple of days had been filled with so much, she found her mind racing backward, touching here and there on the events that had finally brought her and Molly together and her and Grey together.

It amazed her that out of the horror of Monica's death, at least something good had come. When Haley looked back on her life in Las Vegas, she recognized it now for what it had truly been, a life of emptiness.

She'd vicariously lived through her customers' triumphs and failures, raising a glass to honor a dead relative, a promotion, the birth of a new baby. She'd listened to their happiness, commiserated their failures, but had kept herself distant from any emotional involvement.

True, the way she'd lived she hadn't suffered any emotional pain, but she hadn't known any real happiness either.

Her gaze fell on the blue glass heart and she frowned thoughtfully. *Why did you buy it, Monica? What does it mean? Does it have something to do with Molly? Or did you buy it for something else . . . someone else?*

She sighed in frustration. Her sister had been talking in her head since the day she'd arrived in

Pleasant Hill, but there was no whispering answer now.

The phone rang and she quickly grabbed it up, smiling as she heard Grey's deep voice. "How's your evening?"

"Nice. Molly and I spent most of the time going through cookbooks. There are some recipes we looked at that I'm pretty sure you need a degree in engineering to make."

His deep laughter filled the line. "Anything you cook will be fine with me, and if you change your mind about cooking, then the three of us could always go out for dinner."

"No way. One of the things I promised Molly was that I was going to learn how to cook. I now have a plan, a recipe and the will to succeed."

"Have I told you lately that I love you?"

She squeezed the receiver closer to her ear. "Not since this afternoon and that was far too long ago."

"I love you, Haley."

She allowed the words to whisper through her like a warm shaft of sunshine on a chilly day. "I've just been sitting here thinking about life and love."

"Pretty deep subjects for a Wednesday night."

"Maybe, but what I've realized is that life is filled with both pain and joy and you can't have a life and not have both of those." She settled deeper into the sofa cushions, enjoying the intimacy of the dim lighting and the voice of the man she loved filling her head. "I don't think I'll have my nightmare anymore. I don't think I'll ever wake up again gasping for breath, afraid of what is chasing me."

"That's because you now have the strength to turn around and face whatever is chasing you."

"One of the things Molly told me yesterday was that sometimes she wanted it to be okay to talk about her mommy. I want you to know that if you ever want to, if you ever need to talk about your son, I'll be here to listen."

There was a long moment of silence and when he spoke again his voice was deeper, lower than it had been moments before. "He's still in my heart, just like Monica and your parents will always be in yours."

"We take the bad with the good, right?"

"It's called life, Haley, and we're going to have a wonderful life together."

They spoke for a few more minutes and then said good night. Haley hung up the phone and snuggled back against the cushions, a sense of well-being cascading through her, a well-being she hadn't felt since the moment the officers had appeared on her doorstep in Las Vegas.

Death occurs and life goes on.

She watched television for another thirty minutes and was finally getting sleepy when a soft knock sounded on the front door.

She glanced at the clock. Just after ten. Who on earth might that be? She pulled herself off the sofa and hurried to the front door. She turned on the porch light, peeked out the little peephole and relaxed.

Haley punched in the code to shut off the alarm system, then unlocked the door and pulled it open. "Hey, what's up?"

The knife caught her in her upper right shoulder.

Deep.

Agonizing.

Pain seared through her as she stumbled backward.

What happened? What in the hell was happening?

The pain. Oh God, the pain. She couldn't think. She had no time to figure out why this was happening, for even as she stumbled backward she realized the knife was poised to strike again.

Chapter 21

Owen Tolliver sat in the break room alone, sip-
ping from a tall carton of milk and trying to remember why in the hell he ever wanted to be a
detective in the first place.

Rarely did Owen have the kind of bad feeling
that he had been entertaining the past couple of
days. It was a sick feeling, one that alternated between confusion, suspicion and guilt.

He leaned back in his chair, tipped the milk carton up to his lips and took a long drink, his thoughts
on the one man he'd trusted like a brother.

Frank Marcelli had been his partner for the past
two years, since the young, handsome detective had
transferred from the St. Louis metro to the Pleasant
Hill department.

Owen had liked Frank from the first day they'd
met. Marcelli was a good cop, methodical and hard-
working. He was smart, and Owen had never
doubted that Frank had his back no matter what the
situation.

All that made it even more difficult for Owen to

now entertain the kinds of thoughts he was having about Frank Marcelli.

When had the dark thoughts begun? Had it been the day that Frank had confessed that he hadn't followed up on Jay Middleton's alibi? No, it had to have been before that. Owen could have easily chalked the unchecked alibi up to a careless oversight if he hadn't already felt something odd wafting off Frank.

He set the carton on the table and leaned back in the chair, closing his eyes in weariness despite the fact that his mind raced over everything that had happened from the moment they had gotten the call to check out Monica Ridge's home.

Frank had been horrified when they'd discovered Monica's body, but so had Owen. No matter how long you'd been on this job, no matter how inured you thought you had become, seeing the result of brutal death still had the ability to grab you by the throat and momentarily squeeze off your air.

By the book. They had processed the crime scene by the book. Nothing out of the ordinary except Frank had seemed unusually upset.

Owen had figured it was because the terrible murder had taken place next door to where he lived. But now that Owen really thought about it, he remembered something. It was a fleeting memory of that scene that hadn't taken real form in his brain until this moment.

Frank, bagging Monica's hands. But before he'd put the bag on one of her hands he'd held it, stroked it. It had happened quickly, so quickly it hadn't really registered in Owen's mind until now.

He rubbed a hand across his jaw. Had the gesture

simply been that of a man saying goodbye to a neighbor? Or had it been something more?

Frank, quick to say that just because a woman was on birth control pills didn't mean she was having sex.

He leaned forward and reached for the milk carton once again, hating himself for the direction of his thoughts, yet too good a cop not to follow that direction.

He hadn't thought about it before this moment, but there was another connection between the two murdered victims, and that connection was Frank.

Owen knew Frank liked to flirt, and he'd always assumed his partner was indulging in a little harmless fun. But was it possible he hadn't stopped with harmless flirting with Monica? With Sondra? Was it possible he'd been sleeping with both of them and they had gotten wise and threatened to go to Angela?

Frank might like to flirt but that didn't mean he was ready to have his wife walk out on him. That didn't mean he was prepared to have his children taken away by an angry, betrayed wife.

Owen wondered if he was grasping at straws in an effort to solve two cases whose investigations had stalled.

Too bad Grey Banes wasn't around the station tonight. He wouldn't have minded bouncing his thoughts off somebody who could be objective, somebody who had studied human behavior and the darkness of the mind.

Maybe it was time he had a heart-to-heart talk with his partner. He finished the milk and tossed the carton into a nearby trash can, then stood.

Dread swept through him as he thought of the conversation he was about to have. If his dark thoughts were right, then it was possible the man he liked, the cop he respected, might be a murderer. If he was wrong, then the relationship he'd enjoyed with his partner would be forever changed.

Now all he had to do was find Frank.

Chapter 22

Pain and blood.

The pain in her bleeding shoulder made it difficult to think, but Haley didn't need to think to know that she was in trouble.

"What in the hell are you doing?" she cried as she backed into the living room, fear whipping her heart into a frenzied rhythm. The back of her legs bumped into the coffee table and she nearly fell over backward, but managed to steady herself. If she fell, she wouldn't have a chance of escaping the knife.

"Whore." Angela, clad in a pair of shorts, a T-shirt and a cheerful yellow apron, stared at her with hate-filled eyes.

Haley gasped at the familiar sound of that word. Angela. It had been Angela who had made the calls to her. "Angela, for God's sake, what's wrong with you?"

Angela advanced toward her, the knife ready to strike again. "Nothing is wrong with me. I'm just protecting myself. Protecting my family."

"What are you talking about?" Haley allowed her

gaze to dart around the room, looking for something, anything she could use as a weapon.

"Whores. You blond-haired whores who can't stay away from my husband. I've seen the way you look at him. I've seen the way you lust for him, but he's mine." Angela leapt forward.

Haley jumped sideways and the knife plunged into one of the sofa cushions. She picked up the floral centerpiece off the coffee table and threw it at Angela. It bounced harmlessly off her chest.

Angela, Stepford perfect in a yellow apron. *I have them in every color,* she'd told Haley.

Did you have a blue apron? Where is it now, Angela? Where is your blue apron? Haley's head reeled with fragments of thoughts.

I saw something blue, Molly had said.

Angela would have had a key to the house. She'd made those phone calls. She'd set the fire and killed the cat. Angela had done it all. Oh God, she'd killed Monica.

Angela pulled the knife from the sofa cushion with a roar of rage and once again launched herself toward Haley. All Haley could think about was Molly. Molly, sleeping in her bedroom. Molly, unaware that death had once again entered the house.

Haley ran for the kitchen, Angela coming after her.

Pain and blood.

If she allowed herself to think too much, to feel too much, the pain in her shoulder would bring her to her knees. Then Angela would kill her. And when she finished killing Haley she'd go after Molly.

Molly, who had hidden under the bed when her mommy had been killed. Molly, who had seen something blue. Molly, who would be the only person left after Haley who could tell the police about Angela. Angela would go after Molly.

Haley couldn't let that happen.

In the kitchen the two women wound up on either side of the round oak table. The room was illuminated with only the light from the living room drifting in.

Haley gripped the edge of the table and panted as Angela stared at her across the wooden surface. Her face was a mask of rage-twisted features, the bloodied knife gripped in a taut hand.

"I tried to warn you," Angela said. "I tried to tell you to go away, to leave. I like you, Haley. I didn't want it to come to this."

"Angela, please. I don't know why you're doing this. I don't want your husband."

"Shut up, you lying whore. You all want him, all you blond-haired whores. I see the way you look at him . . . just like your sister. Just like Sondra. You want him, but you can't have him. He's mine. He belongs to me."

She's mad, Haley realized. She's absolutely certifiable. "I'll move," Haley said. "I'll move away."

"Too late. It has to be finished my way now." She tilted her head slightly, as if she were listening to something only she could hear. "You hear that? The buzzing. There's only one way to make it stop. I have to make it stop."

She moved to the left and Haley did the same, keeping the table between them. This was how it happened to Monica. She'd opened the door to let in the next-door neighbor, the woman she trusted, the woman she considered a friend.

Haley bit back a burst of hysterical laughter. They'd all been looking for a man. Detective Tolliver, Frank and she had never considered that the killer might be a woman.

Angela moved around the table again and so did Haley, wondering when this impasse would break. Haley now stood between Angela and the kitchen doorway, but she refused to consider leaving the kitchen.

She didn't want to take the deadly battle back into the living room. She absolutely couldn't carry it down the hallway. She didn't want Angela to remember that Molly was here.

"Angela, put the knife down and we can talk. It's not too late to get help," Haley babbled, trying to ignore the blood that splattered on the top of the table from her shoulder wound.

"I don't need help. I have everything under control. I always have everything under control."

At that moment Molly appeared in the doorway to the kitchen.

As she saw the knife in Angela's hand she screamed, a piercing shriek of terror.

"Run! Run, Lolly!" Haley screamed.

"Molly, stay there. You stay right there," Angela demanded.

Molly turned and disappeared from the doorway. Haley nearly sobbed in relief, but the relief lasted only a second as Angela stepped out from behind the table and began to head for the kitchen doorway.

With a cry of outrage, Haley threw herself in front of Angela. The two women fell to the floor and

Haley managed to grab the wrist of the hand that held the knife.

Pain and blood.

Haley sobbed as she fought the ever-growing weakness that suffused her muscles. She knew if she let go of Angela's wrist she'd be dead. Molly would be dead.

You can't let that happen! You have to protect my baby! Monica's voice screamed in Haley's head.

Angela grabbed a handful of hair and pulled, the pain shooting tears in her eyes, but Haley refused to let go. Blood decorated the front of Angela's apron. My blood, Haley thought. Too much blood.

Somebody's going to have to hire that cleaning service again.

I'm supposed to make meat loaf tomorrow night for Grey.

Crazy thoughts drifted through Haley's head as she saw the bloodlust in Angela's eyes and felt her own strength waning.

Hold on, she told herself. Don't let go of the knife. Yet even as she said those words to herself she felt her grip slipping, her strength leaving her.

Angela roared with rage and yanked her arm upward so violently Haley lost her grip. She slammed a fist into the side of Haley's face, the blow causing stars to dance in her head.

Pain and blood. Darkness rushed up to meet Haley.

She remembered!

Molly slid out the front door and raced around the house to the backyard. She remembered. Mrs. Marcelli. It had been Mrs. Marcelli who had come into the house on the morning her mommy had been killed. She'd been wearing a blue apron. She'd killed her mommy and now she was killing Aunt Haley.

Molly cried as she ran to the tree house, the only place she knew to go. It was like that morning all over again, that awful morning, only this time she wasn't hiding under the bed.

She climbed up and got inside the little house, then curled up in the corner and squeezed her eyes tightly closed. She didn't know what else to do but sit here and wait and pray that Mrs. Marcelli didn't kill her too.

Chapter 23

*G*et up. Wake up, Haley.

The familiar voice cut through the darkness and pulled Haley back into the world, back into the pain.

You have to get up and help Molly.

Help Molly? I can't help Molly. I hurt too much. I just want to go back to sleep. She felt as if her brain were wrapped in cotton.

"Molly? Honey, it's okay. You can come out now." A singsong voice called from somewhere in the distance. "Molly, I need to talk to you. Everything is all right now."

That voice.

Not Monica's.

Who was calling out to Molly?

Angela!

The name rocked through Haley's brain, ripping the cotton away. Angela with the knife. Angela who was looking for Molly.

Had to help Molly! Haley sat up, her head reeling.

"Molly, come on now. I'll take you home and you

can play with Adrianna and Mary. We'll make brownies and you girls can have a tea party."

Haley got to her feet just as she heard the sound of the front door opening. Angela had apparently decided Molly wasn't in the house and had gone outside looking for her.

Haley knew where Molly would be, where she always went when she was frightened or sad. The tree house. Haley headed for the back door, hoping, praying she could get there before Angela did.

As she slid into the darkness of the night with only the moon to guide her way, she heard Angela softly calling for Molly at the side of the house.

Haley pushed past the pain and ran to the ladder. There was no hesitation as she pulled herself up each rung. She had no time to entertain a panic attack. She was focused only on protecting the niece she loved.

Although the moonlight barely made it into the little window, there was enough illumination for Haley to see Molly curled up in one corner, her face buried in the knees that were pulled up to her chest.

"Lolly," she whispered.

Molly released a strangled sob and threw herself into Haley's arms. "Shh, we have to be quiet," Haley whispered as she held Molly tight.

Molly nodded and buried her face in Haley's nightshirt as Haley tried not to feel the pain of Molly's pressure against her.

This was the worst possible place for them to be. Trapped in a little house in the boughs of a tree with a knife-wielding crazy woman hunting them down. But there was nothing she could do about it now.

"Molly?" The faint whisper was close, letting

Haley know Angela was searching the backyard. Molly stiffened in Haley's arms.

"Shhh," Haley whispered.

"Come on, Molly. I promise you everything is going to be just fine. We'll go to my house and put a movie on the DVD. You like *Sleeping Beauty*. We'll all watch it together and make popcorn." Angela's voice held a singsong rhythm that sent chills up and down Haley's spine.

Promising an eight-year-old movies and popcorn, brownies and tea parties when your real intention was to stab her to death, took a particular kind of evil that Haley couldn't even comprehend.

Maybe Angela wouldn't think about the tree house. Maybe she'd never find them up here. One advantage Haley and Molly had was that Angela didn't seem to realize Haley was gone from the floor in the kitchen.

If she did come up here, she wouldn't know Haley was here to make certain that nothing happened to Molly. And as Haley held tight to Molly, her sister's child, the love of Haley's heart, she knew she'd do whatever it took to make sure Molly survived this night.

She'd scream for help, but she didn't want to do anything that might draw Angela to their hiding place. For now, it was important to stay quiet.

It had been Angela who had put the skillet of grease on the stove with the intention of starting a deadly fire. Angela. The perfect neighbor.

"Molly?"

The voice drifted up the ladder and Molly stiffened once again, clinging to Haley with a death grip around her neck. As Haley heard the sound of Angela coming up the ladder, she pulled Molly's hands from around her neck.

"Get behind me, Lollipop." She quickly shoved Molly behind her, then raised herself to a crouch. There was no way in hell Angela was going to hurt Molly.

The ladder creaked beneath Angela's weight and Haley drew herself up, summoning every ounce of strength she'd ever possessed both mentally and physically.

She shoved past the pain in her shoulder, beyond the horror of the night, and readied herself for the fight of her life.

She'd hoped to get a punch in before Angela got completely up into the tree house, but Angela led with the knife, slashing the air as she stepped up inside.

"Well, well," she said in surprise as she saw Haley. "I should have finished you off instead of going after Molly."

Haley knew there was a big chance that she was going to get hurt . . . badly hurt. But her single goal was to make sure that Molly survive, that Molly go to junior high and to her first dance. That Molly get married and have children of her own.

Haley wanted all of that for her. She needed to know that no matter what happened to her, Molly would be okay. She tensed and felt her sister's strength joining her own, and without thinking of consequences she launched herself toward Angela.

She barely felt the knife that delivered a glancing slice to her side as she plowed Angela into the side of the tree house. The knife clattered to the ground and nails squealed a protest as the side of the old, weatherworn tree house shuddered and crackled beneath the hit.

Molly screamed. And screamed. And screamed. And Haley slammed Angela against the side again and again and again. With a scream of her own, Haley backed up and once again hit Angela, the two women crashing into the side. A loud splintering noise joined Molly's scream.

Suddenly the side of the tree house was gone, crashing to the ground below, and Angela and Haley were in midair.

A kite, Haley thought. I'm a kite flying through the night. It was the last thought she had before darkness slammed into her and she knew no more.

Chapter 24

She was running. Pumping her legs as fast as she could, running away from something. Stop, she told herself. Remember, you weren't going to run anymore. Stop and turn around. No more running, Haley.

She slowed the movement of her legs until she stopped. She drew a deep breath, then turned around. Nothing. There was nothing behind her.

A bubble of laughter escaped her. She'd spent her life running away from nothing. As she turned back around to walk away from nothing, she left the dream and became aware of pain.

There didn't seem to be a place on her body that didn't hurt. She kept her eyes closed and sought to find the dream again, wanting to go back to running, needing to escape the pain.

Always taking the easy way out, Monica said in her head. *It's time to wake up, to get on with your life. Honestly, Haley, take the pain because it means you're alive.*

She cracked open an eye and squinted against a shaft of sunshine that poured in through a nearby window. She was in bed. Why was she in bed in the middle of the afternoon? Had she gotten Molly up for school or had she overslept again?

It took her only a moment to realize she wasn't in her own bed in her house, but rather in a hospital bed.

Angela.

A knife.

Pain and blood.

Molly.

"Molly?" She sat up, heart pounding, and gazed frantically around the room.

"Haley." Grey got up from a chair nearby and hurried to her side.

"Molly?" She grabbed his hand and clutched it tight.

"She's fine," he replied. "She's down the hall right now with a nurse who's showing her how to give shots to a stuffed lion." He squeezed her hand tightly, lines of strain cut deep in his handsome face and deep shadows pooled beneath his beautiful eyes. "Jesus, Haley, I thought I'd lost you before we'd even had a chance."

She laid her head back on the pillow and winced. "I feel like I've been run over by a truck."

"You took twelve stitches to the shoulder, you broke your left leg and have enough bumps and bruises to keep you moving slow for some time."

He reached out and touched her cheek, an infinitely gentle touch that momentarily soothed any pain she might feel. He grinned then, that sexy wonderful smile. "I guess this just shows one thing."

"What's that?"

"That you'll do anything to get out of cooking a meal."

She laughed. He pressed his lips to her forehead, finding the only place on her body that didn't hurt; then she closed her eyes and drifted back into dreams.

Over the next couple of hours she was vaguely aware of nurses coming and going, taking her vital signs, checking her IV and asking her if she needed something for pain.

By the time she came fully conscious again the light at the windows was waning, indicating early evening. Owen Tolliver sat in the chair that Grey had sat in earlier.

"Hey there," he said as he realized she was awake. "Feel like talking?"

"Okay." The fogginess that had been in her head earlier seemed to be gone. She pushed the button that raised the head of her bed.

"I'd like to ask you some questions."

"Before I answer yours, I'd like you to answer some of mine. Like how I got here to the hospital. Where's Molly and what happened to Angela?"

"Angela is in a room on another floor here in the hospital. She broke both her legs when she hit the ground. When she's healed she'll go directly to jail to face a number of charges. Molly is with Dr. Banes."

A wave of relief swept through her. Molly would be safe with Grey, and it warmed her to know that the two people she loved most in the world were together. "And how did I get here? My last memory is of pushing Angela out of the tree house and flying through the air."

Tolliver pulled his chair closer to the side of her bed. "Apparently a teenage boy who lives down the block, Dean Brown, heard Molly screaming. When he arrived in your backyard he found you and Angela unconscious on the ground and called 911. He then went up and got Molly out of what was left of the tree house and got her safely to the ground. By that time we'd arrived on the scene."

"She killed them, Tolliver. She killed my sister and she killed Sondra Jackson. She's crazy. She made the phone calls to me, killed that cat, all because she thought I had something going on with her husband."

"I know. Despite the fact that she's got broken bones, she's been quite chatty this afternoon. She told me about not only Sondra Jackson and your sister, but also a woman she'd killed in St. Louis, although in her mind none of them were murders, they were all self-defense."

"Protecting her family, that's what she told me." It was beyond comprehension. "Poor Frank, I guess he had no idea."

Tolliver frowned. "He's half destroyed by it all."

"She seemed so normal, so nice."

"And she almost got away with the perfect murders."

Haley nodded and touched the bandage on her shoulder. "If this had been the killing blow I think she intended it to be, then she probably would have gotten away with it." She frowned thoughtfully. "What I don't understand is why she didn't kill Molly when she found out Molly was under Monica's bed. I mean, I let Molly spend the night there.

Angela had any number of opportunities to hurt Molly."

"There was no reason for her to. Molly saw her after the murder and didn't react in any negative way. Even when Molly started talking again, she didn't point a finger at Angela." He frowned. "I owe you an apology."

She eyed him curiously, noting the weariness that rode his features, the bloodshot eyes that held regret. "Why do you think you owe me an apology?"

"For not taking the threats against you seriously enough." He rubbed a hand across his lined brow. "I dropped the ball."

"Don't beat yourself up over it." Haley fought unsuccessfully to stifle a yawn. "All's well that ends well."

Tolliver stood. "I'll leave you alone for now, but in the next day or two I'll need to get a complete statement from you."

Haley nodded, already exhausted. Before Tolliver left the room, she was once again asleep.

The next time she opened her eyes the room was in semidarkness. The windows displayed the black of night and if it hadn't been for the heavy cast on her leg that had bumped against the bed railing, she probably wouldn't have awakened at all.

She jumped in surprise as she realized somebody was seated on the chair in the shadows of the room. She squinted and recognized her visitor.

"Frank?" she said softly.

He looked up, his dark eyes filled with more pain than any man should feel. "I wanted to talk to you. I needed to tell you how sorry I am. You must hate my guts." He looked back down at his hands in his lap, the torture in his voice so thick Haley felt it resonating deep inside her.

"I don't hate you, Frank. You didn't kill my sister," she said gently. This was a man who'd just had his life destroyed. His children had virtually lost their mother and he'd lost his wife. "We're both victims, Frank."

He was silent for a long moment. "I loved her." The words held the bittersweet longing of a broken heart.

"Of course you do . . . did. She's your wife."

He looked up, his eyes filled with the shine of tears. "Not her. Not Angela. Monica. I loved your sister, Haley. I loved your sister so much." A single sob escaped him, but he stifled it with a deep inward breath.

Haley stared at him. Frank and Monica? It would have never entered her mind. "You're the blue glass heart?"

Frank gave a barely perceptible nod of his head. "She bought that on the day I told her I intended to leave Angela. We were planning a future together. We were going to be so happy."

Haley was stunned by the revelation. Monica had fallen in love with Frank?

"We didn't mean for it to happen," he continued. "It just happened. I wasn't happy at home and your sister, she was some special woman. When she died, a piece of me died with her." Tears trekked down his face.

"Did Angela know?" Haley asked, tears burning at her eyes as well.

He sucked in a deep breath. "I don't know.

Yesterday I would have told you there was no way she knew, but today I don't know for sure. Even if she knew about me and Monica, that doesn't explain Sondra's death because there was absolutely nothing between me and Sondra Jackson."

He stood abruptly, as if he needed to get out as soon as possible. "I just wanted to tell you I'm sorry . . . for everything."

"What are you going to do, Frank? What are you going to do now?"

He shrugged and raked a hand through his thick, dark hair. "I don't know. Take some time off, think about my options and take care of my girls." He started for the door but before he got there he turned back to look at her. "Monica would have been so proud of you, Haley. You saved Molly's life last night. She talked about you all the time. She thought you were the smartest, strongest and most courageous woman she'd ever known."

Haley didn't see him leave the room: her tears were too thick. Oh, Monica, I'm going to miss you so much, she thought.

She cried for Frank Marcelli, who would never be the same again, and she wept for her sister, who had always done everything right in her life but had fallen in love with a married man who had an insane wife.

And finally the horror of the night she had endured filtered through her and she wept the tears of fear and pain that she hadn't been able to weep until this moment.

When she was finished, a calm peace swept over her. For the first time since she'd heard about Monica's death there was no terror threatening to steal her breath, no self-doubts yammering in her head.

Monica had told Frank that Haley was a smart, strong and courageous woman, and although she'd never believed those words about herself before, she did now.

She would raise Molly with all the love she held in her heart; she would build a relationship with Grey and never again be afraid of the intimacy of loving.

And sooner or later, she would learn how to cook.

Epilogue

The Pleasant Hill cemetery was small but filled with large, leafy trees and flower gardens flush with color despite a month of hot July sun.

As Haley and Molly walked the path that would take them to Monica's grave, Molly cradled a blue glass angel in her arms. "Am I going too fast?" she asked, turning to look at her aunt.

"No, sweetie, I'm doing just fine." Haley tapped the cast on her left leg. "Another week or so and we won't have to worry about this darn thing anymore, and then you and I are going to have a dance party in the living room."

Molly giggled, a wondrous sound that had been a frequent one over the last month, a month of transformation and healing.

This was their second visit to Monica's grave. The first time they had come had been two weeks ago. On that visit they had brought flowers. They'd sat near her headstone and had talked about the woman who had been taken from their lives before her time.

It had been Molly's idea to return here today and

bring the angel. They had bought two, one to bring here and one to add to their collection at home.

Dean had offered to rebuild the tree house and after some consideration Haley had agreed to have it rebuilt. She thought it was important not only for Molly but for herself to know that although something bad had happened there once, it could also once again be a place of happiness and joy.

When they reached Monica's grave site, they eased down in the lush grass just off the path and for a long few minutes neither of them spoke.

Finally Molly reached out and set the angel directly in front of the marble stone. Then she sat back and reached for Haley's hand. "I think Mommy would like the angel," Molly finally said.

Haley squeezed her hand. "I know she'd love it."

Molly leaned back against Haley. "I'm going to miss Adrianna and Mary."

"I know, honey." Haley reached up and stroked Molly's hair. "But it's nice that they're going to live with their grandparents."

A moving van had taken away the last of the Marcelli belongings the day before. Haley and Frank had watched as the three little girls had exchanged tearful goodbyes.

He'd told her he'd gone to see Angela, who was back in the hospital for another surgery on one of her legs. He'd gone to tell her he'd be seeking a divorce.

"It was like she didn't even hear me," he told Haley. "All she talked about was how she couldn't wait to get back home, that she was going to make my favorite supper and everything was going to be just fine." He'd shaken his head with the look of a man whose very world had been turned upside down.

Haley had watched him drive away, her heart aching as she thought of the demons that must haunt him. He had been a cop, and he hadn't had a clue that he was living with a killer.

The Marcelli home wasn't the only one in the cul-de-sac sporting a For Sale sign in the yard. Grant Newton was getting out of town and had put his house on the market two weeks before.

Dean, who always seemed to have his ear to the ground when it came to neighborhood gossip, had told her that Newton had transferred to Chicago.

That night in the tree house had forever changed Molly and Haley's relationship. Whatever doubts Molly had about her, whatever reservations she'd had about trusting and loving Haley had vanished.

That night a bond had been forged, a bond of love that Haley knew nothing and nobody would ever be able to break. Although Haley might never have any children of her own, Molly was the daughter of her heart.

"I'm ready to go now," Molly finally said. She stood, then held out a hand to help Haley up.

As Molly ran up the path to where the car awaited, Haley looked one last time at her sister's headstone. MONICA RIDGE. BELOVED MOTHER AND SISTER.

"We're going to be okay, sis," she said softly, then turned and began the trek back to the car.

As the car came into sight, a burst of warmth filled Haley. Grey leaned against the side of the vehicle awaiting their return. His lips curved into a tremendous smile as he caught sight of them.

Molly reached him and he scooped her up in his arms, kissed her on the cheek, then set her back down on the ground. By the time Haley reached the car Molly was buckled in the backseat.

Grey reached for Haley's hand as she got to the car. "You doing okay?"

"I'm fine." As always her heart swelled with joy as she gazed into his beautiful blue eyes, saw the loving concern that lingered there.

"I know this must be hard on you, coming here."

"Actually, it wasn't so hard today, and as long as Molly needs to come here, I'll come."

He leaned forward and kissed her, a lingering kiss that half stole her breath away.

"Hey, save it for after the wedding," Molly said from inside the car.

Grey and Haley laughed and they got into the car. The wedding was planned for the first of September. Nothing elaborate, just a small ceremony to bind with a legal piece of paper what had already been bound with love.

"I was thinking about making my famous tuna surprise tonight for supper," Haley announced once they left the cemetery. There was a moment of utter silence.

"Actually, I thought it might be nice if we went out for pizza tonight," Grey countered. "What do you think, Molly? Tuna surprise or pizza?"

"I think it would be nice if Aunt Haley made her tuna surprise another time." There was a moment of hesitation, then she added, "Like maybe when I get old and move out of the house."

Haley and Grey laughed and Molly giggled, and in the joyous sound Haley heard her future, a future she knew would be filled with lots of laughter and some tears.

Life and love. Haley was embracing them with open arms, no longer guarding herself. She was ready to accept all the joy and the heartbreak of life. She'd be fine with Molly and Grey at her side.

You finally get it, Haley. I'm so proud of you. I love you. Monica's voice whispered through her head and Haley had a feeling that it would be the last time she'd hear it. Monica was finally at peace.

Angela lay in the hospital bed, the buzzing in her head coming and going like an irritating fly circling around her ears.

She couldn't believe that she was going to have surgery again and nobody had sent her flowers. It was as if everyone had forgotten about her. Her family. Her friends. The people she'd worked with on committees and as a volunteer. The minute she'd fallen out of the tree house, she'd fallen out of their thoughts.

But things would get back to normal. As soon as her leg healed and she had her day in court, she'd be back in the arms of her loving family. She'd be back at her volunteer work and taking care of things like she always had. There was no doubt in her mind that any jury would find her not guilty. She'd only done what she'd had to do.

I'm filing for divorce. That's what Frank had told her when he'd come to see her. But she knew he was just confused. And she knew why he was confused.

The buzzing began again, deep inside her brain. That nurse. That blond whore. She'd seen the way she looked at Frank when he'd been here. She'd seen the want in her eyes.

Protect the family. That's what Angela had to do. Frank was hers and she wasn't about to let him go. But that blond whore was trying to screw things up for her.

Angela snuggled back against her pillow. She'd take care of that nurse. Before she left this hospital, she'd make sure that bitch was dead. Then Frank would want her again.

The buzzing was back. She smiled. But she knew how to stop it.

Read on for a preview of Carla Cassidy's
next thrilling romantic suspense

Paint It Red

Coming from Signet Eclipse in August 2007

The dream awakened her just before dawn. Vanessa Abbott woke with a gasp, her heart thundering an unnatural rhythm. Her bedroom was dark except for the night-light that burned in a socket near the door.

She sat up, worried a hand through her tangle of long dark hair and glanced at the clock on her nightstand. Almost six. She reached over and shut off the alarm that would ring in half an hour, then got out of bed.

There was no point in trying to go back to sleep, not with her heart still racing and the taste of fear in the back of her throat.

She slid out of bed and grabbed the robe on the end. She pulled it around her shoulders as she left the room, hoping that the terry cloth material would absorb some of the chill the dream had left behind.

She went only a short distance down the hallway, then turned in to another bedroom that was lit by the faint illumination of a night-light.

Johnny was curled up on his side, a half smile on his face as if his dreams were happy ones. All ten-year-olds should have happy dreams. There had been a time when she hadn't been sure her son would ever have a happy dream again.

She fought the impulse to lean over and kiss him, to feel the reassuring warmth of his forehead beneath her lips. He still had an hour to sleep and she didn't want to wake him up by indulging in her motherly need.

Instead she left his bedroom and made her way down the stairs to the kitchen. There, she turned on the small light over the stove and made a pot of coffee.

As she waited for the brew to finish, she sat at the kitchen table, staring out the window where the eastern sky was transforming from the black of night to the gray of predawn.

She pulled the robe more tightly around her, telling herself her chill came from the drafts in the old three-story house rather than from the fact that she'd had the dream again.

It wasn't until she had a cup of coffee in front of her that she allowed herself to think about the visions that had awakened her.

It was always the same. In her dream she stood on a deck and Canadian geese flew overhead. At first there were just a few, silently winging to the south. Then more appeared, their thick bodies and large wings blocking out the sun, turning day into night. And they were no longer silent, but honking so loudly, so discordantly she thought she'd go mad.

It was always then, when the sky was black with them, when she thought she'd go crazy with the noise that she awakened, heart pumping with fight-or-flight adrenaline.

She wrapped her hands around the warmth of the coffee mug and stared out the window. She'd only had the dream three times that she could remember. The first had been when she'd been ten, the day her parents had died in a car accident.

The second time had been in college, and she'd received a phone call that her grandfather, the man who'd raised her after her parents' death, had suffered a heart attack and died.

The last time she'd had the dream had been two years ago. She'd awakened just after dawn to find her husband gone from their bed, and she'd known something terrible had happened.

The "something terrible" had been worse than she could have imagined. It wasn't until the police officers had appeared at her door that she knew the horror the dream had portended.

They'd found Jim's car parked on the Broadway Bridge. There had been a note on the driver seat and an eyewitness who had seen a man jump from the bridge into the cold, murky waters of the Missouri River below. The note had simply said, *Forgive me. I can't go on.* As if that somehow explained everything. As if that somehow made it all okay.

His body had never been found. It was as if the river had swallowed him whole. The police had told her it wasn't unusual for the river to refuse to relinquish its grasp on whatever fell into its depths.

She and Johnny had survived the devastating blow. With the loving support of Jim's family and her own strength, she'd gotten through the darkest days she thought she'd ever face.

And now she'd had the dream again. Maybe it was because of the show tonight. Maybe the prospect of showing Jim's work was what had prompted the familiar nightmare.

Still, as she watched the morning sun shyly peek over the horizon, a shiver of apprehension worked its way up her spine.

All your favorite romance writers are
coming together.

SIGNET ECLIPSE